VENUS RISING
THE UNITY SEQUENCE: BOOK TWO

DAN HARRIS

Dedication

To Isaac, and a future every bit as wondrous as this one.

Prelude

Six months ago.

The wine was cool and refreshing in the heat of the early evening. Venus took a sip and grimaced slightly. *The temperature is its only redeeming feature, though.* She gazed out over the rooftops of Parkum and the desert beyond from the balcony of the hilltop bar she had come to frequent since her arrival on Karak and in the capital of its Ruhim territory a week before. In the east, the sun was just beginning to set, bloated and red and casting the flat yellow-white landscape with a bloody glow.

The chirruping crickets in the trees nearby fell silent at a gentle cough from the doorway behind her. Venus turned and smiled at the young waiter carrying the food she had ordered. He blushed and looked down at the tray of dishes as he approached.

He expertly arranged the plates on her table. 'Your meal, mistress,' he said in a near-whisper.

In a mood to tease, Venus flicked her long black hair away from her face, catching his eye, then flashed him another smile. Her cocoa-coloured skin could pass as local, she knew, but her blue eyes wouldn't—and the poor boy looked positively smitten by the exotic creature that had appeared in his bar a few nights earlier. 'Thank you, Habib.'

'My pleasure, mistress. May I refill your glass?'

Oh, if you must. She held out her glass, and he hurriedly topped it off with the mildly fizzing, grass-scented vintage that passed for sparkling wine on the planet. Replacing the glass on the table, she idly asked, 'Could you bring me some bloodsalt, please, Habib?'

The boy nodded, clearly pleased. 'Of course, mistress. It is gratifying that you have taken such a taste to it. Most, uh, visitors such as yourself find the flavour too strong.'

'Well, I think it's just wonderful,' she replied. 'I've never tasted anything quite like it.' *And I need to know for sure that it does what it seems to.*

A minute later, Habib returned with a small pot, piled high with a finely ground red powder the same blood colour as the sinking sun. With a murmur of thanks as the waiter withdrew, Venus measured out a small spoonful and scattered it over her dish of curried goat.

She ate unhurriedly, genuinely enjoying the meal—the mild coconut-blended spice of the curry, the tangy kick of the bloodsalt. Halfway through the dish, she began to feel the same effects she had experienced the past few nights: a warmth spreading through her limbs, an increase in her heart rate, a slight blurring then sharpening of her vision.

Venus finished eating and placed her fork on the table as she looked out once more across the desert to the sunset. She shivered a little, not from any evening chill, and heard the sound of Habib's footsteps behind her as he lit the lamps that lined the balcony to dispel the falling gloom.

Time for my experiment. 'Oh, Habib?' she called quietly.

He was at her side in seconds. 'Yes, mistress?'

Venus looked up at him. He was handsome, in a boyish way, with curls of floppy brown hair framing his face. His eyes were dark brown, almost black in the dusk. She stared into those eyes, meeting his intent gaze, and felt his regard almost like a physical force. The evening sounds—the fresh chirps of the crickets, the occasional screech of night birds waking from their daytime slumbers—seemed to fade as she held the young man's attention.

Then held it *tight*.

His face slackened a little, his mouth dropping open, as she found that hidden channel and followed it, sliding through it like a snake through a culvert and into the pool of his mind beyond. *'Would you do something for me, Habib?'*

'Of course, mistress.' He answered aloud, showing no surprise at hearing her words without them being spoken.

'That's a good boy. Climb up onto the parapet for me.'

'Yes, mistress.' With no uncertainty, the young man stepped away from her and up onto the waist-high wall that ringed the balcony. He turned to Venus, away from the city rooftops, unconcerned by the hundred-foot drop at his back.

'That's a beautiful pair of wings you have, Habib. Aren't they lovely?'

'Yes, mistress. I have beautiful wings.' He looked over his right shoulder and smiled at nothing.

He sees them. *'If I asked you to fly down into the city and fetch something for me, would you do that, Habib?'*

'Of course, mistress! Anything for you. With my wings I can be there and back in a moment! What would you like me to get for you?' His feet started to move, scraping against the stone as if he were keen to fulfil the unasked request.

Venus watched, rapt. She had to be sure. He was almost at the tipping point, inching closer and— *'Stop, Habib. Come to me.'*

The young man jerked forward, leaping down from the parapet in his eagerness to comply. He came close and gazed down at her, entranced. Satisfied, Venus pulled back, releasing his mind from her grasp. Habib blinked once, twice, shook his head. She smiled up at him.

'That was all, Habib. Thank you.' With a nod and a confused look, the young man left her.

Mind racing, Venus reached for her wine glass and took a drink. She barely noticed the unrefined flavour.

It works. So smoothly, so easily. She sighed.

And so it begins.

* * *

Two months ago.

Dust. This whole damn planet is nothing but dust.

Caleb Hesch squinted, shielding his eyes from the midday sun. He peered north into the distance toward the skyline of what was apparently the city of Parkum. Behind him, the service bots were completing their checks on his ship, scanning for any leaks or potential malfunctions that might lead to an explosion and a blasted crater in the middle of the region's primary spaceport. *As if anyone would notice.*

A burbling series of beeps from one of the bots grabbed Hesch's attention, and he turned to see a green 'OK' displayed on the machine's chest. With a nod, he hefted his bag higher on his shoulder and headed for the exit. After a few minutes, he found a driver, standing proudly next to an ancient silver-coloured groundcar. The man—young, sweaty, with a wispy moustache that did nothing to make him look more mature—seemed nervous at being approached by a tall, heavily muscled foreigner with a shaven head and spiral-tattooed cheek. *Probably shouldn't mention I'm a Titan, then.* People tended to react unpredictably when they came face-to-face with someone they thought of as a genetically engineered killer. Hesch snorted to himself. *I can't imagine why.*

The sight of a large wad of Commonwealth dollars seemed to calm the driver's nerves, though. *Glad to see the money's good. On these Independent worlds, you never know until you get there.* Hesch settled into the back seat of the surprisingly well-maintained groundcar as it moved off into the light traffic along the road to Parkum. He stared out of the dark-tinted window at the desert. Flat, cracked sand stretched in all directions; the only landmark breaking the monotony was a mountain range barely visible in the far distance to the east.

It was pure chance that had pointed him in the direction of Karak—an overheard conversation in a seedy bar on Witcher, two drunken former soldiers from some war or other jawing about a commission that had sprung up on the mercenary grapevine. High level, high paying. Command. Combat. *Conquest.* That had been enough to pique Hesch's interest and send him over to the ageing mercs' table with a pitcher of beer and a made-up backstory.

He'd been looking for some interesting, paying work to while away another few months before returning to Mission, the Titan homeworld. That was still a little too hot to hold him, since he'd repaid an early release to a lifelong prison sentence by disappearing, instead of performing the assassination he'd been sent to carry out. And although the power shift still playing out at the top of the Titan hierarchy—and the Titan rebellion soon to explode into a full-blown civil war, if the rumours were to be believed—might end up working in his favour, Hesch thought it prudent to give the new leader, Luc Corralin, a little while to settle before testing his mercy.

He'd been in prison for negligence resulting in Corralin's father's death, after all. That Corralin was whom he'd chosen not to assassinate probably didn't even those scales..

A few months in this dustbowl will do just fine. He knew nothing specific about the job—it was on Karak, in the Ruhim territory, and it was military command. That was enough. A few careful questions in Parkum, maybe a small bribe or two, and he'd find his way. People were the same everywhere. He watched a dust devil spring into life and race alongside the road for a few hundred yards. *Spinning clockwise. Good luck.* The mini twister swayed in a sudden wind and veered off into the desert to the west. Hesch leaned back in the seat and closed his eyes.

Just fine.

1. Assignment

The headquarters of the Commonwealth Senate's Department of Security Operations on Nexus Prime was bland, to the point of being completely unmemorable. Across Central—the planet's bustling, sprawling capital, *de facto* centre of the galaxy and home to most of Nexus Prime's eighteen billion inhabitants—a million other office blocks fit the description of a twenty-storey slab of concrete and plasteel. A hundred of those blocks could be found within walking distance in Midtown Two alone. Newly recruited operatives in their first week on the job had been known to walk or drive straight past it, as if looking for a more imposing edifice, or at least one with a little more style. The reflective viewports dotted across the façade at regular intervals somehow failed to break the monotony, instead blending in with their own kind of greyness. All DSO employees referred to their HQ as 'The Block.'

Four and a half years I've worked here, and I'm still not sure I could pick the place out of a line-up. Dante Zo pressed his palm against the scanner to the right of the main entrance and listened for the heavy *thunk* of the electronic locks disengaging. The doorfield slid apart, and he stepped into the cool of the reception lobby and strode towards the body scanner that blocked the route to the elevators at the rear of the lobby. *But then again, it's not like I'm here most weeks anyway. I barely need an office.*

One of the smartly suited men standing nearby—former Peacetroopers, all of them—called out as Dante approached. 'Morning, Zo. How goes it today?'

'Not bad, Karl, not bad. Can't complain. How's Lisse?' Dante tossed his bag onto a belt that ran through a smaller machine to one side as he unclipped his old sidearm from his belt—the same old-fashioned metal slug launcher he'd had since joining the Space Corps ten years before—then laid it atop the bag. As he passed through the porous field and into the body scanner, Dante shivered a little, as always. *Ticklish.*

'She's getting pretty damn tired of being pregnant,' Karl replied. 'There's only a month left now—she's bigger than me, almost.'

Dante snorted as the scanner hummed to life for a moment, then fell silent with a click. 'I'd keep that little observation to yourself, if I were you.' He stepped through the rear field and retrieved his bag.

'Don't I know it. I tell her she's beautiful every day, and half the time she throws something at me.' Karl shook his head wearily.

'It gets better once they're born, I promise. See you later.' With a wave, Dante headed for the elevator.

'Have a good day, Zo.'

The elevator ride to the seventeenth floor only took nine seconds, but it was long enough for Dante to catch sight of himself in the mirrored safety field. *Damn, I'm getting pale. I could do with some sunshine.* He'd been born and raised on Kingston, a hot planet known mainly for its fishing, diamonds, and organised crime. Summer there lasted most of the year, and that sun-kissed childhood and the genes from his dark-skinned father meant Dante's skin was always at least a milky coffee brown. But after a few months on assignment in cold or cloudy environments, the tan faded and his Asian ancestry through his mother's side started to show. *Having grey eyes doesn't help, either — I look washed out, like I've just been ill or I'm about to be. Unhealthy.* He stroked his neatly trimmed beard. *At least this looks good.*

A junior operative, Helga, was speeding past down the hallway as Dante stepped out onto seventeen. She spun toward him without stopping and called out, impressively maintaining her pace while walking backwards. 'The director wants you, Zo.'

'When?' he asked.

'Twenty minutes ago.' The smile she flashed as she spun back around looked ever-so-slightly malicious to Dante.

Great. Dropping his bag just inside his own office, he went to see LeClerq.

* * *

The only obvious difference between the office of DSO Director Marie LeClerq and those of the rank-and-file operatives was that it was double the size. But that extra space was filled by a conference table that seated sixteen, making the bigger room feel more cramped than the smaller ones. Dante, as always, carefully checked behind him as he took one of the seats at LeClerq's desk, to make sure he wasn't going to bump the table. A colleague had done just that a couple of years before, scratching both chair and table. The director hadn't been impressed.

'There's coffee in the corner if you want it.' LeClerq's pale blue eyes peered at him over the top of a scrolltab. 'I'll just be a minute.'

'No, thank you.' Dante clasped his hands in his lap and looked about the room. He spotted a new painting among the selection on the wall opposite him, directly behind LeClerq's chair — a tumultuous seascape, all white foam and dark grey clouds. His gaze drifted down to the director. Her elegantly cropped hair was a slightly different colour than when he'd last seen her. *Reddish tint. Looks good.*

After a few moments, LeClerq clicked the scrolltab off and dropped it to the desk, looking at Dante. 'That's a problem for another day. Here's today's.' She picked up a second tab and handed it across the table. Dante activated it, and a young man's face appeared. Brown skin, brown eyes, military haircut. *Jalen Kane. Why does that name sound familiar? And he looks like... someone.* He looked up at the director, lips pursed.

'Jalen Kane,' LeClerq said. 'The younger brother of the senator for Vish-Kataa, Neela Kane. She's been in the news a few times for various things. There's a strong resemblance.'

Dante nodded. 'That's it. I remember seeing her on one of the news holos a few months ago. A speech to one of the big trade organisations.' He wagged the scrolltab. 'How did the brother end up on your desk? Has he been a naughty boy?'

LeClerq leaned back in her seat and steepled her fingers. 'It's possible. That's what we need to establish. He's a Peacetrooper, a highly decorated one, with an exemplary record. Fifty-three days ago, he was released from his unit—on fifty days' leave.'

'Let me guess—he was a no-show?' Dante asked.

'Correct. Lieutenant Kane is AWOL, as of seventy-five hours ago.'

Dante flicked through the information on the scrolltab. 'Okay, but I don't see how this is a problem. It wouldn't be the first time a soldier's taken a few days' unofficial leave at the end of a stretch at home. I did it once myself when I was first in the Corps. You get screamed at, go to boot camp for a few days' punishment, and that's it. Why—' His finger stopped moving. 'Oh, I see. The fiancée.'

'Indeed,' said LeClerq. 'Sara Jordaan, an archaeologist who has been based for the last year on one of the Independent worlds, Karak. It's a small, primarily desert world two-thirds of the way to the Rim. All but a handful of the populace—just eleven million or so—live crammed into a few large cities and in a smattering of decent-sized towns.'

'And the other handful?' Dante asked.

'Nomads,' the director replied, 'who have the ninety per cent of the world that's just desert all to themselves, save for scattered mining operations. Anyway, according to some colleagues of hers, Jordaan was scheduled to join Kane here on Nexus Prime twelve days ago. She never showed up.'

'And we think Kane's gone looking for her?' Dante asked.

'Naturally,' LeClerq replied. 'Except now he's ended up missing, too.'

Dante nodded. 'Fine. I still don't understand how this came to us, though. DSO has no jurisdiction over a military absence, and as for the girl—'

'It's a favour, Zo,' the director cut in. 'The request came in from Senator Kane last night—she's very concerned.'

This drew a raised eyebrow from Dante. 'And she's the kind of person we do favours for? Interesting.' *And lends weight to some of those rumours about who's actually pulling the strings in the Senate.*

LeClerq's lips narrowed. 'You needn't concern yourself about that. It has no bearing on the mission, which is simple. We believe Jalen Kane has gone to Karak to find his fiancée. To complicate matters, there are rumours of some kind of inter-tribal conflict underway, which Kane may have got caught up in. We have no firm intel. Regardless, you're to find him, in the best case. And in the worst case—'

'Find out what happened to him,' Dante finished, clicking the briefing tab off. He stood and turned for the door. 'I'll call in once I get to Karak.'

'Be sure you do. I'd like your best effort on this, Zo,' LeClerq added.

'Always, Director.'

Dante was five metres down the corridor before it struck him. *Desert world. Huh. Well, at least I'll get that sunshine.*

* * *

A fine drizzle was just beginning to fall as the transpod turned left up the road that led to Dante's apartment building. It was one of twelve in the gated community in Midtown Four that they had moved to three years earlier, when Violet was nine months old. Dante had tried to protest that their old place in Downtown Six was a perfectly suitable place to raise a child, but Phoebe had put her foot down. So they had lost the vibrant bustle of the local markets where there seemed to be a festival every other weekend, and traded it in for the bland, homogeneous safety of the residential estate, where the lawns were always trimmed and the children swam in the communal pool under the unblinking eye of the guard bot. *Not that I'm bitter.*

The field to the parking garage under the building slid open at the transpod's request, and the pod slipped through and neatly into the Zos' parking dock. Dante climbed out—with a quick glance to check for the green light to show the pod was charging—then headed for the elevator.

'Phoebe?' he called out as he entered the apartment, dropping his shoulder bag on the hallway floor. No response. *Is she in the clinic today? It's fifthday... Does she work those?* Dante couldn't remember. He was sure she'd told him, but it had slipped his mind. The purple blink of the commdeck notification light drew him to it. He tapped the play button, and his wife's face appeared in the holodisplay.

'Hi. You left early this morning; I didn't get a chance to tell you—we're going to Nadine's this evening for dinner. I'll pick Violet up from pre-school and go straight there. We'll eat at about twenty hundred—call if you can come by then, but I assume you'll be working.' Phoebe stepped away for a second, called out something that the recorder hadn't picked up, then reappeared. 'We need to leave, or we'll be late for school, and I need to be in the clinic by ten.' She paused for a moment, as if contemplating saying something. 'Okay, then. See you later.'

The recording finished with a muted beep. Dante trudged up the stairs. *Why did she leave a message for me at home? Why not send it to my terminal?* He shook his head with the same confused exasperation that he'd been feeling more and more, the last few months. On autopilot, he began neatly packing a bag for the trip to Karak, mind elsewhere and wondering when, exactly, his wife had started to drift away from him.

Dante knew they'd been happy, before. He remembered vacations: Summer with Phoebe's parents at the lake. Glacier skiing on Solokov II, before the baby was born. Violet's first trip in the low-orbit shuttle from the civilian spaceport in Uptown Two when she was almost two years old, crying all the way up but then stopping, spellbound, when Phoebe had shown her Nexus Prime. Dante had watched his child, then looked down at the planet, hanging in space and glistening silver and blue with all of its imperfections smoothed away by the distance, and seen it for just a few moments with the same wonder that was in Violet's rapt and awestruck gaze.

But then his workload at the DSO had gone up, with a promotion and extra responsibilities, and somehow... Dante sighed. *Maybe I did the drifting.* Three weeks on assignment out of every four, thirty days out of forty spent away from home for the last four and a half years. After Violet was born, they'd fought about it, a lot—but never to any conclusion. Just a recurring flashpoint smoothed over with ten days of relative domestic bliss, before he left again. But the fighting had tailed off, then stopped completely, in the last half a year. Not because anything had changed, more like...

Like she'd just given up. And I let her, because I was happy to have the peace. The bag was packed. Dante thumbed the biolock and the closetabs snapped shut. He was struck by a wave of déjà vu. How many trips? How many bags packed? Hefting the bag up from the bed, he left the room and went downstairs.

When he reached the commdeck, intending to call Phoebe, he felt reluctant. As if... *I don't know. Maybe as if I'm proving her point, and losing some battle we're fighting. Silently.* Dante shook off the feeling, flicked through the call log and tapped the link for her station at the clinic. The calling tone burbled for a few seconds, then cut off as she appeared. Phoebe looked distracted, busy.

'Hey,' he said. 'It's me.'

She gave a thin smile. 'I see that. Why are you at home?'

'I had to come back.' He forced a laugh. 'It's a good thing I did, or I wouldn't have got your message.'

'What? Oh. Sorry, I was in a rush. Violet was being a pain this morning.' Phoebe looked away briefly, held one finger up to someone to her left. 'I need to go; I've got a patient. What is it?'

'I'm just calling to say... They've given me a job. Starting today. I need to be at the port in two hours.' Dante licked his lips. 'That's why I had to come home.'

Phoebe just nodded, still looking slightly off to one side of the recorder. 'Okay.'

'So I'll see you when I get back.'

She glanced away again. 'Yeah. Look, I need to—'

'Sure, you should go. I'll call in soon. If I can... You know.'

'Okay. Bye.' Phoebe reached towards the screen, and she disappeared.

For a few more seconds, Dante stared at the space where she had been, then he reached down to retrieve his bags. The rain had strengthened, and it thumped heavily into the hallway viewport. He stepped up to it and looked out; the sky was dark grey and getting darker by the minute. As he palmed the lock on the apartment door and headed back to the elevator, a premonition struck Dante that when he returned, the place would again be empty.

But for good.

* * *

Two hours later and nine hundred kilometres away, the rain had stopped and the skies cleared somewhat as Dante climbed out of the transpod once more. His destination was on a grim, dead-end street in Downtown Five: the entrance gate of the DSO spaceport that was officially the property of WeissChem—a pharmaceutical corp that had not, to Dante's knowledge, ever produced a single drug. The transpod pulled away, *en route* back to the apartment building. He could take the masstrans back home when he returned from Karak.

Karak. On the way over, he'd read the briefing package the

DSO researchers had pulled together. There didn't seem to be much of interest about the planet at first glance. Sparsely populated, mostly desert, it had been colonised by the occupants of a single seedship eight hundred years ago, who had quickly split into eight distinct tribal groups as soon as they landed. Minor conflicts had come and gone, but the status quo had been largely undisturbed, including the Karaki's fierce desire to remain Independent from the Commonwealth.

Dante stepped up to a deceptively scuffed and battered-looking identification terminal to one side of the gate and heard the click of the security scan commencing. *What else is there... Oh, just that salt.* Apparently Karak was notable, if not interesting, for being the only known source in the galaxy of a deposit known as bloodsalt. *A bitter-tasting condiment. Hardly a major tourist attraction.* Throw in a few ruins, which excited some archaeologists—Kane's fiancée included, it seemed—and that was Karak.

And a lot of sand. Sun and sand. The scan completed, and the gate slid open just wide enough to admit one person. Dante stepped through, already looking forward to topping up his tan.

As he strode across the corner of the landing field toward the hangar where his DSO-issue microcorvette was docked, he spotted a familiar face and called out, 'Mack—you keeping well?'

The burly, shaven-headed technician stood from the engine he was tinkering with and offered his hand with a satisfied smile. 'Hello, Zo. All well, all well. There are engines to fix, that pissing rain has stopped at last, and it's nearly lunchtime. What more could a man want?'

Dante laughed. 'Simple pleasures, as always. What about that other pleasure you were talking about a few weeks back? What was his name—Felix?'

'Close. Fenux,' Mack replied. 'He's very well. A bit young, a bit enthusiastic, but what can you do?'

Dante shrugged, smiling. 'Oh, I don't know—find someone your own age and settle down?' He clapped Mack on the shoulder as he stepped past and headed for the hangar. 'Those youngsters will be the death of you.'

The tech's gruff voice came back to him. 'Worse ways to go, though, aren't there?'

The microcorvette, which Dante had nicknamed *Betsy*, looked in excellent shape, as expected. The DSO spent a significant chunk of its budget on keeping their operatives' equipment and technology cutting-edge and in perfect condition. *A budget that would make the more libertarian Commonwealth citizen either weep or write to their senator, if it were ever made public.* His flight plan had been filed hours earlier, so all Dante had to do was stow his gear underneath the bunk, slip into the cockpit's single seat and tap their course into *Betsy's* semi-sentient computer.

'Course confirmed,' said the computer's feminine yet subtly mechanical voice as the ship lifted off the hangar floor and nosed out onto the landing field. The thrum of the engine rose into a dull roar as it accelerated and angled up into the sky. Nexus had broken free of the persistent clouds and bathed the cockpit in a warm glow. Dante closed his eyes, pushing thoughts of Phoebe and domestic strife to the back of his mind.

Sun and sand.

2. Retrieval

Halfway across the galaxy, far from the frenetic industry of the Core planets, the sleepy provincial world of Corinth shivered under a blizzard. Winter was at its height, with the planet at the most distant point of its orbit around the star that shared its name. In Corinth City, the unimaginatively named planetary capital, Quinn was walking to work. *Snow be damned; I need the exercise.*

The grey stone pavements bore a few inches of crisp, crunchy snow after the overnight fall, and Quinn trod carefully as he approached the street that housed the Seryn Agency building. He was just a few yards from the corner when one of the uncommon abilities that had brought him to the Seryns' attention flared a warning. A figure, likely male by his size, was approaching the corner along the adjoining street, moving quickly. Quinn stopped and waited. *He's coming dangerously quickly, in this weath —*

The man skidded across his path and off the edge of the pavement, his yelped oath quickly muffled as he thumped into a pile of recently ploughed snow. *Lucky. There could have been a truck there instead.* Quinn walked over and helped the young man to his feet. 'Maybe take it a little slower, yeah?' The man nodded, grinned a little madly, and set off at a jog. Quinn shook his head as he watched him go. 'One born every minute,' he muttered.

A minute later, he stepped through the old-fashioned rotating door of the Agency, peeled off his thick woollen coat and shook the snow from it onto the lobby floor, earning a tut and a shake of the head from the receptionist sitting behind the ornate wooden desk to his right.

Brushing the last snowflakes from his mop of fiery red hair, Quinn turned to the petite brunette and flashed her a grin. 'Sorry, Darla. Better here than upstairs, though, right?'

'For me personally? No,' she replied. 'Upstairs would be better, because I never go upstairs. I just sit here all day and pretend to be the receptionist for a financial consultancy.'

Coat free of snow and only slightly damp, Quinn shrugged. 'It could be worse. You could actually be the receptionist for a financial consultancy.'

'Instead of the glamorous and exciting Agency, velvet-gloved fist of the mysterious Seryn?' Darla eyes widened in mock excitement.

'Exactly.'

'Hardly,' she sighed. 'The most exciting thing that's happened since I started working here is when that hovertruck ploughed into the bank across the street.'

On his way to the stairs, Quinn called back over his shoulder. 'I'll put a word in for you, see if I can't get you something more interesting.'

Her weary voice came back, 'That's what you said last month.'

As he climbed the stairs—wooden, purple carpeted, flawless reproductions of those in the hotel that had stood on the lot before burning down fifty years earlier—Quinn felt a buzz from the terminal at his wrist, and tapped the holodisplay into life. *'Roof. As soon as you arrive. Sebastien.'* Reaching the second floor, Quinn groaned at the senior agent's instructions, turned the corner, and started on the next flight of stairs instead of continuing down the corridor to the canteen. *In this weather, he picks the roof. Contrary bastard.*

Five minutes later, wrapped once more in the still-damp coat, Quinn stepped out onto the roof terrace. He had to admit, the view over the centre of Corinth City was quite spectacular in the snow. The civic buildings, solid and magisterial in grey stone, hunched under a thick layer of white. *I'd rather be seeing it through a window, though.*

'Ah, there you are. You got my message, then.' Sebastian stepped out from a sheltered corner by one of the large red-brick chimneys. As always he looked unaffected by the cold—his pale skin was no paler than usual. His icy blue eyes seemed even lighter in this weather, in sharp contrast to his coiffured black hair, flecked at the temples with grey. A child of winter, Quinn's partner Odette called him. *She's not wrong.*

Quinn extended his hand, and they shook. 'What message? No, I always come up here first thing in the morning in the middle of winter, before I've had any coffee. It really sets you up nicely for being bloody freezing all day.'

The senior agent's thin smile was barely there. 'Very good.' He pulled his leather gloves on more tightly, then tucked his hands into his pockets as he turned to look out towards the local Senate house, sprawled along the shore of frozen Lake Bear. 'I've got a job for you, Quinn. A… special job, you might say. A personal one, and one we need done quietly.'

That statement merited a raise of the eyebrows. 'And the specialness is why we're on the roof, I take it, instead of in your office.'

'Quite,' Sebastien replied. 'This is staying off the books. No trail.'

That was a surprise. It wouldn't be the first such job that

Quinn had worked, but they weren't common. *In fact, I can count the others on two fingers.* 'Intriguing. Let me have it, then.'

'It's simple.' Sebastien turned back and looked the younger man in the eye. 'She's surfaced.'

Quinn frowned. 'Who's surfa—' He stopped, stared. 'Venus.'

Sebastien nodded. 'In the flesh and raising hell.'

Venus. The woman who had recruited him into the agency. Who had taken him into her home... and her bed. Who had then vanished in a storm of fire, blood, and recrimination as her last job went spectacularly, fatally wrong. She'd reappeared for an instant a mere handful of times over the last three years, on worlds scattered across the galaxy—unsubstantiated sightings reported alongside the deaths of kings, a suicide by a prominent senator, the sudden collapse of a trillion-dollar merger. Her presence was felt but never proved. Her Agency file had been classified, locked, and stamped *Rogue* in metaphorical red ink.

Sebastien reached into an inside pocket and retrieved a small data stick. 'Here is everything we have. You can absorb it on the trip—it's a few jumps away.'

'What is?' He took the proffered stick.

'Karak,' Sebastien replied. 'A dusty, Independent world. In a nutshell, there's a civil war brewing, and our long-lost sister seems to be at the heart of it. We need to bring her in.'

Tucking the stick into his coat, Quinn looked hard at Sebastien. 'Just *in*? Or do you mean *down*, as well?'

Sebastien's face expressed distaste. *As if he'd never ordered anyone removed before.* 'Do what you need to do to remove the threat. That's all.'

'Why now?' Quinn asked.

'Why has she surfaced, you mean?' The older man sighed. 'We don't know. Perhaps you'll get the chance to ask.'

Quinn nodded as he headed back to the door. A low chuckle from Sebastien made him turn back. 'What is it?'

'Oh, nothing much.' Sebastien's lip curled. 'Just make sure you dress appropriately. I'm almost certain that it isn't snowing where you're going.'

Small mercies. Quinn patted the data stick, barely able to feel its slim form beneath his thick coat. *Venus. I always knew she'd show up someday.*

But now that day's here... Damn, I wish she hadn't.

* * *

An hour later, Quinn was back at home, a cavernous studio apartment above an old-fashioned live-action theatre in Navidad, the district of Corinth City more commonly known as the Artist's Quarter. He stood in the doorway and watched Odette as she swayed beneath the skylight. The small cylinder of her soundscaper, on the floor at her feet, rose to waist height, fanning out like a flower, with a complex pattern of coloured dots and lines projected in the space above it. A range of melodic tones hung in the air, and every so often, Odette reached down into the machine and plucked at one of the tightly packed tendril fields that were strung across the opening, adding another note to the array, more depth and texture to the sound.

After a few minutes and ten or more added notes, Odette tapped a panel at the edge of the soundscaper's lip and set the composition in motion. Music replaced the pleasant but monotonous layering of sounds—but something more than music. Quinn watched, as dazzled the two hundredth time he had witnessed his lover's gift as he had been the first. The meaningless—to a layman—pattern of dots and lines vanished, and scenes appeared, visceral suggestions hinted at and tugged from the viewer's own memories.

Pushing forward from black through red to white, the sound was the thrum of a heartbeat, quicker and quicker, then gave a rising wail. *Birth. Darkness into light.* Swaying blue and white, yellow above and below, susurration broken by occasional cries. *Summers on the beach. Gulls wheeling overhead, hunting for bits of unwatched food to pilfer.*

Shaking his head to clear his mind before he was lost in nostalgia for an hour, Quinn walked up behind the still-swaying Odette and gently tapped her on the shoulder. She tensed and spun, eyes wide, then smacked him on the shoulder as she saw his grin. 'Don't do that! You know I can't hear a thing when I'm sculpting.' She tapped the machine once more—it fell silent—then frowned. 'Did you forget something?'

Quinn shook his head. 'No, I just need to grab some things. Something's come up at short notice, and I need to go away for a few days. A week at most.'

Odette pouted prettily. 'Boo. That's not great—we've got Amelie's recital on eighthday evening.'

'I know, hon. Sorry.' Quinn leaned in and kissed her. 'But it's part of the job.' He moved over toward the storage units that lined one wall and began shoving clothes into a bag.

Odette sighed. 'It's such a boring job, though. Are you really sure this is what you want to be doing? Finance? Moving other people's money around. I can't think of anything worse.'

'Then, you should stick to sculpting, dear. And until you're famous, I'll keep doing the boring job and paying the boring bills.' Looking over his shoulder, he poked his tongue out at her.

'That's not fair!' she retorted. 'I'm just a student. It'll be at least two years before I can set up my own studio, and then—'

Packing complete, Quinn had returned to her side and cut her off with a finger on her lips. 'Hush. You keep doing exactly what you're doing. It was a joke—except for the being famous part. I'm confident that's going to happen. And in the meantime, I love what you do. Like I love you.' Another kiss. 'So I'll see you in a little while.' Toting his bag on his shoulder, Quinn headed for the door.

'Call!' she shouted from behind him.

'I'll call. I always do, don't I?' He spun, gave her a wink and a wave, and left.

* * *

The bar owned and managed by his friend Max was handily placed on the edge of Corinth City's small industrial district, close to the spaceport, and squashed between a textile factory and a company that made farming equipment. It was too early for the place to be open, so Quinn rapped on the thick wooden front door and waited.

Heavy footsteps approached. 'We're closed, and we don't need anything,' came Max's gruff voice even as the bolts were pulled back and the door swung open to reveal the stocky, balding proprietor. Scruffy grey workout clothes covered the thickset frame he'd got from years of shifting ale barrels. A pleasantly surprised smile replaced a scowl as he recognised his visitor.

'What are you doing here?' Max checked his watch. 'It's barely ten in the morning, which is early even for you. Did you get fired at last? Boss caught you slacking off or harassing the women?'

Quinn rolled his eyes. 'Dick. No, I just came to say goodbye. I'm shipping out for a little bit.'

Max whistled, mock-impressed. 'Ooh, the exciting secret agent departs on another daring mission. Yawn. Do you want a beer or not, then?' He turned to head back into the bar. 'And shut that door after you; it's bloody freezing.'

Quinn complied. 'I thought you said it was too early? And keep it down about the agent thing, will you? I know no one's likely to be listening, but I don't want to have to... you know. *Handle* someone.'

Behind the dark wooden bar, stained beyond all memory of its original colour, Max pulled two bottled ales from a chest refrigerator the size of a small car. 'Oh, for Pete's sake, you're never going to let that go, are you? How was I supposed to know that little shit was a journalist? He looked like any of the other mopes that come in here looking for lonely women and end up just getting pissed instead.'

Quinn accepted the proffered beer. 'The point is, you're supposed to just not mention it. To anyone. I don't like having to fiddle with people's brains. You'd understand if you hadn't—'

Max interrupted with the weary practice of long repetition. 'If I hadn't turned my back on the wonderful Seryn, and a glorious life of dicking about, moving boxes with my mind.' He took a swig. 'I've heard this one before, Q. I'm done; I'm out. End of.'

'Fine,' Quinn replied. 'But just remember that I'm in, still. This is what I want to do, and I don't need my best friend making a tit of himself every time he has a few beers.'

Max raised his eyebrows.

'Okay, twelve beers and half a bottle of… What was it?'

He snorted. 'You're asking me?'

Quinn groaned. 'Well. Whatever. Anyway, I didn't come over to have a go. I came to tell you that… well. This job.'

Half his beer gone, Max frowned. 'What's up?'

'It's a bit…' Quinn found he didn't know how to phrase it. 'Special, I suppose. As in, it's the one I've been waiting for, for a while. And now it's come.'

'What? Which…' He dropped his beer arm to his side. 'Shit. She's back, isn't she?'

Quinn nodded.

'Crafty bitch,' Max muttered. 'I never liked her, not even before she was a psychopath.'

A wry smile from Quinn. 'Yeah, you might have mentioned it once or twice.'

Max held up his hands. 'Don't get me wrong: hot as hell. Can't fault you for that, but still…' He shivered slightly, shook his head. 'Crafty. What's she done now?'

'Raising hell on some world in the back end of nowhere. Causing trouble for the locals and the Agency.' Quinn took a deep breath, let it out. 'She needs to be stopped.'

Max pursed his lips. '"Stopped" as in "permanently stopped," you mean. Doesn't surprise me. I'm sure you've only told me a little of what she's been up to the last few years, and even that…' He shook his head again. 'Doesn't surprise me.'

Quinn curled his lip. 'Not the sage advice I hoped for.'

'Shit, you're after advice? Bloody hell, if it's come to that, then you're screwed.' Max finished his beer, and tossed the bottle back over the bar and into a big plasmetal bin. The clang reverberated for seconds in the emptiness of the room. The big man scratched his belly, his expression thoughtful. 'Actually, I do have some.'

'Oh yeah? What might that be?' Quinn asked.

Max cocked a finger at Quinn to emphasise his point. 'Don't let her get in your head. Not for a minute, not for a second. Because if you do—' He clapped his hands. 'Then you're *really* screwed, my friend.'

Quinn nodded. *Probably the best—scratch that, only—advice I can hope for.* He polished off his beer and placed the bottle on the bar.

Max spread his arms. 'Bring it in here.'

They hugged, his friend's broad hands slapping into his back. 'Come home safe, yeah?'

Quinn chuckled as he stepped back. 'Oh, Max, I didn't know you cared.'

'Care?' Max exclaimed. 'Of course I bloody care. If you snuff it, that's twenty per cent of my regular income gone. I can't afford that. Not with—'

'Not with the number of ex-wives you've got,' Quinn finished it for him. 'I know.' He smiled. 'Later, Max.'

'See you soon.'

As he headed for the door, and stepped outside, Quinn flipped up his collar against the winter chill. *I hope you do, Max. I really hope you do.* With Venus as the objective, there was no guarantee he'd make it back from this trip.

* * *

On the edge of the Yemenis system, Quinn scanned the final page of the briefing package as his ship, one of the small pool of vessels that the Agency kept on standby for emergency transportation, ran through its pre-jump diagnostic checks before the final hop, which would take them to Karak. A day had passed since he'd left Corinth—a frustrating, uneventful day as he read, slept fitfully, and realised the paucity of the information he had to work with.

He had discovered that Karak was roughly the same size as Corinth, with a comparable population. *Replace the deserts with farmland, drop the temperature by twenty degrees and scatter snow everywhere, and it could be the same place.* But that was about all the concrete information he had.

The situation, it seemed, was this: A tribal conflict of some kind had started, unexpectedly and violently. Allegedly at the centre of it was a woman, an offworlder, whose name might be Venus. *Or possibly Vera, Serena, or Valeria.* That was all he had to go on. Not enough to drop everything and shoot halfway across the galaxy, one would think.

And yet.

Quinn sighed. *The trouble with Venus.* He'd heard that phrase said in several meetings over the few years since she'd vanished, every time accompanied by a sigh or a shake of the head. *Why couldn't she just have been a telekinetic? Or even a telepath? But oh no, that would be far too simple.*

There was no indication that the locals knew that Venus—if it were Venus—was one of the Seryn. Although the public revelation a year earlier—that the Seryn still existed as a group— had apparently reached Karak, it wasn't clear what anyone on the planet thought of it, or if they cared at all. Three decades had passed since the Seryn's famous disappearance from Serynev IV, mere weeks before it was struck by an asteroid that plunged the planet into a nuclear winter and killed millions. *Maybe the Karaki had other things to worry about thirty years ago and weren't following the news. Though they'd probably start caring pretty quickly if they realised it was one of us stirring up this shitstorm.*

He unplugged the data stick from the ship's display, and the infoholo winked out. Tapping the stick on his thigh, Quinn gazed out of the cockpit viewport at the starfield and wondered—not for the first time since he'd left—why Sebastien had chosen to send him. Sure, his particular talents stacked up well against Venus's, but why not send one of the more... offensively minded agents? There were three or four he could think of off the top of his head who would relish the opportunity to jet off across the galaxy and take a shot at bringing down the famous rogue.

A reason struck him. *Because they don't really want her brought down. Sebastien left it on the table, but he knows... that I wouldn't do it. Couldn't do it. Could I?*

His mind drifted back four years—*four and a half?*—to their first vacation together. A week in a cabin in the hills near Jasper Falls, a little town on the other side of Corinth. Quinn smiled at the memory. They'd skied, drunk too much wine, attempted to make fondue and somehow burnt it. *And talked. About what we wanted to do. For the Seryn, for the galaxy.* His smile faded.

'Jump preparation complete. Ready?' asked the ship's computer, startling Quinn slightly. He pressed a flashing panel on the dash and listened to the engine spin up. Five seconds later, the discombobulating combination of thrust and dropshift in the starfield announced they had moved into subspace. Quinn still stared out of the viewport, gaze fixed on nothing, mind elsewhere. Rolling the question over and over in his mind.

Could I kill Venus?

3. Unleashed

The old Karaki training golem was steam-powered, a relic from back when Tasha's great-great-grandfather Aziz had been part of the Hereb tribe's Sessiz Bichak. Four generations and a hundred years later, Tasha stood at the edge of the training square that filled most of this training centre, one of twelve in the Hereb capital Thrace, and faced the golem for the thousandth time. Maybe the two thousandth. After seven years of initiate training, she was eighteen years old. And she was ready.

At least, that's what they tell me.

It was a week since her induction into the Sessiz Bichak—it meant *Silent Blade* when translated into Standard—which meant that her first job would be mere days away. It was customary to give newly inducted blades something to do as soon as possible, to prevent them from going crazy imagining what it would be like. Better to get that first job done and out of the way. Settle them down. *That's the theory.*

Tasha gazed into the golem's lifeless glass eyes. Studded into a spherical head of varnished wood, they would stare back blindly until a trainee threw a switch, the gears fired up, and the golem came to life. Then those eyes would light up with a fierce green glow; the golem's four arms would rise, triple-jointed and grasping; and the golem would slide its nine-foot tall body around the training square among the twenty-five station points with uncanny intelligence. The trainee had to dodge those arms and the solid wooden hands at their ends, and—using blades or staves, usually; hands and feet for the skilled or over-confident—attempt to score points by striking the pressure points dotted over the golem's body. The session would end—and the golem stop—when the tally reached a pre-set limit. *Or when unconsciousness or a broken bone ends it.*

Tasha tied back her wavy dark brown hair into a tight ponytail and patted herself, checking for any loose clothing. Both shirt and trous were strapped down tight, black linen bound with leather straps the colour of charcoal. She looked back up at the golem.

She carried no weapons. Her hands were bare, her feet strapped with tape against the occasional splinter on the floor of the training building. Without looking down, she swung her right foot and kicked the switch to the *on* position, then stepped forward onto the square.

A rumbling groan announced the firing of the golem's engines. Those inhuman eyes blazed emerald green, and it came for her.

The machine covered the ten feet between the central station and the edge where Tasha stood in just under two seconds. Its two upper arms swung together with a thunderous clap as the two lower hands chopped diagonally. By then Tasha had dived forward and between the arms on the right side, tucking into a twisting roll as she landed, then pushing forward off her back foot to jab the stiffened fingers of her right hand into the palm-sized pressure pad at the golem's left kidney position. A man would have crumpled to the ground, incapacitated by the blow. The golem was unmoved, though a flash of light behind the pad and a brief chime confirmed the hit.

Two points.

The golem spun to face her as it rolled back one station towards the centre, its lower right arm swinging inches from the floor in an attempt to sweep her ankles, the upper dropping vertically in a hammer blow that could crack her skull. Tasha hopped to her left, her right foot sliding over the wooden floor. She waited for the golem's downward strike to miss, then flicked her right leg up and out, her toes pointed, and lashed a kick into the smaller pad in the centre of the golem's broad chest.

Light, chime. Five points makes seven.

Facing her again, the golem powered forwards, unleashing a barrage of swift punches with all its arms. Tasha executed a back handspring, which took her to the corner of the training square, then an immediate one-handed cartwheel to her right—*flashier than necessary, but there's no one watching to complain*—which took her out of the golem's range once again. Pushing and spinning off her left foot, she bounced back towards the machine and snapped out a kick that hammered into the same pad she'd struck first.

Nine points.

She could feel the sweat beading her brow as she used the golem's body to push herself off and towards the centre of the floor, just out of range of a crushing double backhand swing. Tasha landed softly, arms wide, and waited for the machine's next move.

Relentless, unemotional, showing no sign that it either knew or cared that it was losing the fight, the golem slid towards her, eyes bright—

Then dead. The rumble of the engines dropped in pitch and volume then died away. Baffled, Tasha spun to face the entrance… and the second power switch.

His hand mid-dropping from the lever at one side of the door, her cousin Duru offered her a sheepish grin. 'Sorry, Tash.

They told me to bring you immediately; no waiting.' His voice was soft.

'By who—' *Oh.* 'The Council?'

Duru nodded, the smile gone. 'It's time, Tasha. Are you ready?'

She glanced back at the golem, silent and quiet until the next time.

That's what they tell me.

* * *

Duru led Tasha from the training centre to the Meklis—the Hereb council building—by the shortest route, a winding walk through Thrace's foundry district. Thousands of entrepreneurs smelted metals of wildly varying quality from the ores that rolled through the Hereb capital's gates as soon as they opened every morning, some having travelled several thousand miles from the mines at the furthest reaches of the territory. The foundries ranged from tiny clay-built hovels, crammed cheek-by-jowl into alleys barely wide enough for a man to pass down, to the brand-new behemoths built by the cooperatives that had started to emerge in the last ten years. *Progress,* Tasha's father, Taj, would have said, shaking his head in bemused bafflement.

The stench of sulphur dioxide hung heavy in the air, irritating Tasha's nose and throat as she followed Duru down yet another back alley, past another row of tiny backyard foundries. She coughed and spat. The acrid taste remained. It occurred to Tasha that she hadn't asked after her aunt Sofia—her mother's sister—and uncle Bor.

'How are your parents doing?' she asked, ducking under a wire inexplicably draped with damp clothes. *Who's doing their laundry in the foundry district?*

Duru shrugged. 'Okay. Not great. The restaurant isn't doing so well, so they had to lay off two of the servers. I hardly see them most days; they spend so much time at work.' He glanced at her with a slight smile. 'But the Bichak keeps me busy enough myself, so...' He shrugged again. 'It is what it is.'

Tasha nodded. *It is what it is.* A common saying all over

Karak. Whatever people did for a living, whichever industry or business they worked in, it always seemed that life was just... *Hard.* Her father had told her that sometimes he thought the planet itself was to blame. *'It's like Karak doesn't want people here, Tash. Just dust and sand and the wild goats. It would scour us all away, if it could. And it tries.'*

She knew that she was protected from the realities of everyday life, by virtue of the family she had been born into and of the path she had started on at such a young age. Her only experiences of a normal childhood had been holidays spent with family on her mother's side, at her uncle and aunt's farm outside Thrace. Tasha would spend a week there twice a year, feeding the livestock and playing with her cousins Bunji and Ches, and return home wondering what it would be like to live that life every day. What her future would have been, if she had just been someone else's daughter, just... normal. She'd never wished for it—she was perfectly happy—but that never stopped her from wondering.

Bells pealed in a temple nearby to announce the midday hour, which snapped Tasha out of her reverie. 'Who's there today, Duru?'

He half-turned. 'At the Meklis? Everyone.' He turned away again and stepped over a pile of discarded impure malachite. 'There's a full house.'

Everyone? Tasha's nervousness grew. She'd been expecting the call to the council's presence for days, and the prospect of her first real job for the Bichak didn't faze her. But she'd expected to meet three or four of the councillors at most. Why would all thirteen need to be there, just to tell her she needed to eliminate some corrupt businessman or gang leader?

The answer struck her. *Because the job isn't going to be like that.* She almost tripped over a feral dog dozing in her path, righting herself just in time but still stepping on the animal's tail hard enough to elicit an outraged yelp.

Ten minutes' more walking took them out of the foundry district, through the narrowest corner of the market district and into the civic centre. The Meklis, a wide one-storey sandstone edifice, dominated one side of Commencement Square. Tasha and Duru crossed the cobbled square in fits and starts, dodging the groundcars and motortrikes that weaved across the space in complete disregard of the faded road markings that had been laid down a century before.

After a few near misses, they reached the broad double doors, which stood open at all times and led into the Meklis's foyer. Thirty more paces took them to the door of the council chamber itself, a square slab of solid copper etched with a depiction of a Hereb victory over the Ruhim in some notable battle from two centuries earlier. Tasha studied it briefly as they approached, her eyes narrowing as she followed the story of the battle, wondering what incident had triggered that particular conflict out of the hundreds that had flared over the eight centuries since Karak had been settled. *I wager some on the council would know the answer.* Certainly Pharc, the smiling historian. Probably Bej, the solemn career politician. *He never misses a chance to sermonise on Hereb history when he's campaigning for re-election.*

Duru stopped when they reached the door. 'I'll leave you here, Tash. They said to send you in on your own.' He flashed a smile and squeezed her shoulder. 'That probably sounds worse than it is. I wouldn't worry about it.'

Tasha found a weak smile in return. 'I'm sure I'll manage, Duru. Thanks for fetching me.'

He snorted as he turned away, and he headed back out. 'Oh, of course. I had so much choice in the matter...'

Tasha watched him walk away for a few seconds, then turned back to the council chamber door. Taking a deep breath, she gently pushed it ajar. The heavy door easily and silently swung open, and she stepped into the chamber.

Thirteen gazes fixed upon her, a murmur of chatter dying instantly as she stepped over the threshold. She scanned the faces. A few councillors, she knew personally. Of those, slender Pharc offered a smile and a wink as she caught his eye. He had been an old friend of her father's. *I haven't seen him since the funeral,* she realised. She nodded slightly to him.

Around the semicircular council bench, three places to Pharc's right sat portly Halim, another contemporary of her father's. He had long sought greater transparency from the Bichak, a position that had brought him into direct conflict with Taj in his later years, after her father had left the field and moved into the strategic side of the organisation. *'I've become a manager, Tash. Can you believe it? I have a desk!'* She smiled at the memory. Halim's jowly face stayed fixed in his perpetual scowl.

The spokesman, Alu-Jak, she only knew by reputation. He sat at the centre of the bench, directly opposite the door. His expression was closed and inscrutable as he watched her enter, one hand rising to smooth his oiled black beard. Tasha stepped to the centre point of the room, atop the golden six-pointed star etched into the flagstone floor of the high-ceilinged chamber. She clasped her hands behind her back, fixed her gaze on Alu-Jak, and waited.

Beard apparently sufficiently smoothed, Alu-Jak clasped his hands together on the mahogany table that fronted the council bench. His voice was sonorous, filling the room. 'Welcome, Tasha bint Taj.'

She gave the formal reply. 'I am at the service of the council and the Hereb. Command me.'

Alu-Jak nodded—almost absentmindedly, it seemed. 'Command you we shall, Tasha. It has been one week since your blooding, and your induction into the Sessiz Bichak could not have been more timely. There is a task of great importance, which we would have you undertake.'

Tasha kept her expression blank, but her mind raced. *If this task is so important, why me? Why an untried, untested...* Her breath caught. *Unless...*

Alu-Jak continued, his tone solemn. 'We must warn you, this mission will be extremely dangerous.'

...Unless they don't expect me to succeed. She kept her voice steady. 'I am ever yours to command, councillor.'

'You are aware, of course, of the recent encroachment of the Ruhim upon the territories of the other tribes.' He looked down at the table in front of him and shuffled some papers. 'Already the Bobun and the Mani have fallen to the sudden aggression of the Ruhim. It seems certain that other tribes will follow.' He looked up and met Tasha's gaze. 'We must attempt to prevent that, lest the Ruhim sweep across Karak and end eight centuries of balance.'

Out of the corner of her eye, Tasha saw a smirk cross Pharc's face, and she understood what he was thinking. *Balance, yes. If you ignore the interminable minor wars and the thousands killed.* 'What would you have me do, councillor?' She had no idea where his preamble would lead. How could they expect her to help end a war of conquest that spanned the whole planet?

'The Ruhim are not as they were even a year ago, Tasha. Their longstanding rulers are gone, usurped. By an offworlder, a foreigner who seeks to dominate the world. That'—Alu-Jak slammed his fist down on the table—'is what we must prevent. Ending this usurper's life before she can do more damage is what you must do.'

Tasha blinked, stunned that her first mission was to be such an important one. 'I… If I may, councillor… why me? Of all the Bichak?'

Alu-Jak had regained his composure, his hands pressed flat against the table. 'Do not be coy, Tasha. The masters have told me of your abilities. They say it seems you have inherited every ounce of experience in your father's line, that you are skilled way beyond your years.' He nodded, assured. 'You are the one we need, and Parkum is where you must go. The masters will give you the rest of the information.'

Tasha understood she had been dismissed. Straightening further, she bowed deeply, turned and headed for the exit. As she neared the copper door once more, her gaze caught on an image on one small panel: a soldier carrying the Hereb banner, run through by the curved sabre of an attacker behind him. Tasha shivered.

I hope that's not an omen.

* * *

She stepped back out into Commencement Square, blinking against the daylight after the gloom of the Meklis lobby.

'Tash!' The shout from her right startled her. She turned and smiled at the approaching figure when she recognised her brother.

'Ruben, what are you doing here?' Tasha wrapped him in a quick hug. *Thank you for being here.*

'Waiting for you, obviously.' He smiled, teeth flashing.

'You've had your hair cropped again.' The same slightly wavy dark brown hair as Tasha, but reduced to a no-fuss crew cut.

'Yeah.' Ruben scratched his head, ruefully. 'The commander said it was getting too long again.'

'There's still someone in the Demir Yumruk who outranks you, then.' Tasha punched him gently on the arm, then frowned. 'But why are you here? You should be out on manoeuvres, shouldn't you?'

'I'm heading out tonight. The unit can live without me for half a day. Even with everything that's going on. And I wanted to be here; I heard they'—he nodded towards the Meklis—'were calling you in.' His expression went serious. 'How did it go?'

Tasha blew out her cheeks. 'I don't know if… fine, I suppose. I just can't believe what they told me. Do you know what they—what my—'

Ruben nodded. 'I heard rumours.'

'Isn't it insane? Me. I haven't done anything, haven't proved myself in any way, and they think I can—' She dropped her voice. 'From what I've heard, what this woman, this offworlder, is supposed to be…'

'Some kind of witch, you mean,' Ruben finished.

Tasha sighed. *Damn. I hoped he wouldn't confirm that.* 'I know it's probably just exaggeration and myth, but if even a small part of it is true… What chance do I have?'

Ruben shook his head. 'As good a chance as anyone, Tash.

I've seen what you can do. In friendly situations, yes, but I've no doubts you're as qualified as anyone.' He looked away. 'And I don't want to put any more pressure on you, but you might even be the best chance we've got, if the Ruhim set their sights on Thrace.'

'How come?' Tasha asked.

'If the intelligence we've gathered about their conflicts with the Bobun and the Mani are true, then the whole Yumruk might not be enough to stop them. They've been pacifying cities within hours—a fierce initial clash, then the defenders just capitulate in waves. Whole units laying down their weapons and giving in.' He shook his head, clearly worried. 'It makes no sense.'

Tasha smiled weakly. 'Aren't you supposed to be reassuring me, Rube?

He snorted. 'Sorry. Getting caught up in my own problems. I just wanted to catch you before you go and do... whatever it is you're going to do. We're probably not going to see each other for a while; we'll be deploying to the border immediately after the manoeuvres.

'What I wanted to say, was just... trust yourself. Trust your training. If there's one thing I've learned since I joined up, it's that when you don't know what to do—and there'll be plenty of times when you don't—you can always fall back on your training. That'll get you through.' Ruben reached out and squeezed Tasha's shoulder. 'You'll be fine.'

Tasha nodded. 'Okay. Thanks.' *You're a lot more confident than I am, Rube.*

'Go and see Mama first before you see the masters; they'll probably want to send you straight out.'

'I will.' She opened her arms and he wrapped her in another hug.

'Baba would be proud,' said Ruben. 'He always was.'

She smiled up at her brother. 'Of both of us. I'll see you soon, Rube. Keep safe.'

He smiled again. 'Oh, you know me. Luck of the demon and everything.' As one, they gestured the ancient ward against evil, then laughed.

'Take your demon with you and go,' said Tasha. 'Your men are waiting.'

Ruben turned away with a wave, and she watched him start across the square toward the adjacent block where a sand-coloured heavy vehicle was parked, its treads gleaming with oil. A trio of Yumruk commandos standing around it with studied nonchalance.

Tasha snorted. *Soldiers. No subtlety.* Feeling somewhat better, she went to find her mother.

* * *

Scratch the head, flick the ear, stroke the jaw.

Tasha didn't recognise the guard who, in response to the seemingly casual three-gesture signal, nodded her through the entrance to the Bichak's headquarters, a nondescript two-storey building near Thrace's east gate. That unfamiliarity wasn't surprising: the blades rotated into and out from guard duty regularly. The masters were careful to not let anyone's reflexes grow dulled by too long spent away from the front line.

Front line. I've never understood why we call it that. That line was more of a tangled web, crisscrossing all of the territories on Karak, and ensuring the masters had all the information they needed to ensure the safety and security of the Hereb people. *'And through the masters, the council learns just enough to be able to function without causing too much trouble.'* Tasha smiled, remembering her father's words.

An hour earlier, her mother had been resolute and stoic at the revelation that Tasha would be leaving immediately on her first mission. Tasha had wondered how many times before her father—or Ruben—had told her mother similar news. *Twenty-five years of Baba in the field, six years of Ruben in the Yumruk... It must be hundreds.* But her mother had been born into a military family, too, and greeted such things with smiling resignation. She had even been generous enough to laugh at Tasha's obvious enthusiasm. *I hope she doesn't worry too much.*

Tasha walked down the hallway, passing classrooms on both

sides. Inside, small groups of initiates would be learning the varied theories of their profession: administering poisons, reading body language, learning pressure points of the body, dressing to blend unnoticed into a crowd. *It seems like just yesterday that I began my training, but... it's been seven years.*

Ahead of her, behind the broad desk that blocked the staircase up to the masters' rooms, sat Kaya. He was crippled from the waist down from a mission that had gone awry two decades earlier, but Tasha knew for a fact that he had a brace of throwing knives within reach, with which he could discourage any unwelcome visitor. *And a far less subtle scattergun for anyone truly determined.*

A smile split the veteran's craggy face as she approached the desk. 'Hello, Tasha. How was your meeting this morning?'

Is there anyone who doesn't know my whereabouts? 'It went well, Kaya.' She frowned as a thought occurred to her. 'Though I don't know why the council needed to give me the news. Surely I could have just been briefed here?'

Kaya chuckled. 'I'm sure Sessin had his reasons. We don't want them to feel left out of events.' He shrugged. 'Politics.'

Sessin? Tasha gulped. 'Is... Is he the one I'm here to meet?'

'Aye, child. He's upstairs in the meeting room. You don't want to keep the First Master waiting, do you?' Kaya waggled his bushy eyebrows and grinned. Tasha heard him chuckle again as she scurried past him and up the stairs.

She entered the long meeting room that spanned the whole back wall of the building, and she found Sessin leaning over a map that covered half of the oval wooden table in the centre of the room. She coughed to announce her entrance.

The master spoke in his famous lazy drawl. 'Yes, Tasha. I heard you come in. I heard Kaya laughing at your discomfort, too.' He looked up, his eyes—brown irises so dark that they appeared black—twinkling.

Tasha had always found the First Master intimidating. Not just because of his position, but his appearance. *The eyes; the shaven, oiled head; that thin beard. 'Malevolent, he looks,'* her mother would say. But she never once questioned his decisions. *And nor did Baba.*

'You have a job for me, master?' The rote, ritual words slipped easily from Tasha's lips.

Their incongruity to the gravity of the situation wasn't lost on Sessin. He snorted. 'I have a job for you indeed, Tasha. As you know.' He reached down and picked up a slim beige folder, tossed it across the table towards her. 'You know the goal already. Elimination, pure and simple. We may not understand how this witch can do what she does, but we know she needs to be stopped. The details are in that folder. Film, maps, contacts—everything. You leave for Parkum tonight.' His gaze narrowed on Tasha.

She returned his silent regard.

A slight smile curved Sessin's lips. 'This is the point where you ask questions, girl.'

Tasha flicked her gaze to the folder in front of her. 'I have none. I trust you have given me all the information I need.'

That drew a guffaw from the First Master. 'Quite. That's what I deserved for treating Taj bin Doah's daughter like any other new blade.' He nodded to her. 'I have faith in you, Tasha. We all do—all the masters. Make us proud. Make us safe.'

Emotion welling up in her, she could only nod.

Sessin waved to the door. 'You have a rendezvous to make.'

With a stiff bow, Tasha turned and left, her brother's earlier words echoing in her mind.

'Baba would be proud. He always was.'

* * *

The first name in the contact list contained in the file Sessin had given Tasha was Oruk, a young man a few years ahead of her in the Bichak. They knew each other only vaguely, from some inter-year training exercises. He waited for her just outside Thrace's east gate, leaning against a bland-looking sandspeeder, which he had parked away from the road and out of the way of the light but regular traffic. The long, sleek two-person speeder looked unassuming, with none of the flashy extras or decals that adorned the vehicles of the rich youths who spent their nights racing laps around Thrace's walls. But Tasha knew the seemingly sedate beige machine before her could leave any of those racers choking on sand, if there were a need. *The Bichak take no chances.*

Oruk pushed himself upright and waved as she approached. *'Selam,* Tasha.' They shook hands. Oruk was a head taller than her, slim and wiry. He had an easy smile, which she didn't remember seeing much of during their training exercises.

'How are you, Oruk?' she asked as he turned back to the speeder and yanked open the storage trunk at the rear.

'Good. Very good. Nice to have something interesting to do, even if it is only chauffeuring you across the desert.' He flashed that smile again as he took from her the bag Kaya had handed to her on her way back out from headquarters.

'Changes of clothes, all the standard field gear. Do you have any personal items you want to pick up?' he had asked. She hadn't.

Tasha climbed into the passenger seat behind the driver's as Oruk slammed the trunk lid back down. 'Do you know where we're going?'

'Of course. A straight shot across the desert, stopping five klicks out of Parkum.' Nimbly he hopped into the driver's seat. 'It'll take six hours, more or less, so you might as well get some rest.'

I'm so wired, I doubt I'll be able to sleep, she thought as the speeder engine roared to life and the machine rose two feet off the ground, bobbing gently on the air cushion below it.

'Ready?' Oruk called over his shoulder.

'Let's go!' Tasha shouted back. With a nod, Oruk gunned the throttle, and the speeder shot forward over the sand.

Some time later, she awoke to see the first moon low in the night sky, which was that dark-bright blue that told her the sun had set not too long before. She didn't remember falling asleep; Tasha had watched the desert speeding past below them for... well, she had no idea how long. She tapped Oruk on the shoulder.

He half-turned to her. 'You're awake! Good. I hope you had a decent rest; we're coming up to the drop-off point soon.' He pointed forward to the horizon. 'You can just make out the lights in the distance. That's Parkum. Well, it had better be, or I'm in trouble!' He laughed.

Tasha smiled. *Whether he's deliberately trying to make me relax or not, the humour is appreciated.* She took a deep breath, and mentally reviewed the details she had read in the file. She was to avoid the main thoroughfares that led into the city, as those were dotted with guarded checkpoints at all hours of the day. Identification checks were common, and it had grown uncomfortable for non-Ruhim travellers.

Instead, Tasha was to enter Parkum via a small, pedestrian-only gate in the city's north wall. Apparently it was only used by local residents who kept small herds of livestock on the scrubby grasslands north of the city. The likelihood of anyone accosting her was minimal.

The city skyline grew larger and brighter on the horizon. Just as Tasha considered tapping Oruk on the shoulder to ask him if was time for them to stop, he killed the engine and let the speeder cruise to a halt.

He pulled his driving goggles up to his forehead and turned around. 'This is where we part, for now.'

Tasha nodded silently, all of a sudden unenthusiastic about the prospect of leaving familiar company behind and heading out alone.

Oruk seemed to sense this, as he reached out and clasped her wrist. 'You're going to do fine, Tasha. I know this.' He grinned. 'More than once, you got the better of me in our little skirmishes—those Ruhim don't stand a chance!'

She laughed a little as she climbed out of the speeder. 'Oh, so you think you're so much better than the Ruhim, now? From what I remember, you were not so tough an opponent.'

Oruk's eyes widened in mock horror. 'You cut me deep, Tasha! So cruel. Not one day into your first mission, and already your pride is showing.'

She pulled her bag from the trunk and slipped the straps over her shoulders, then stepped up to Oruk and clasped his hand. 'Thank you, Oruk. Have a safe journey home.'

He nodded, solemn-faced for once. 'And you, Tasha—once your work is done. Come back to us, and I will show you how tough I really am.' He winked.

Tasha shook her head. *Always a joker.* 'I look forward to it.' She waved as she turned away and started towards the city. Ahead of her, barely visible in the dimming light, was a narrow and hopefully unguarded gate. The low roar of the restarted engine rose in volume behind her, then faded into silence. Soon the only sound Tasha could hear was her own footsteps, a gentle crunch against the hard-packed desert sand.

Just me, now.

4. Probing

Dante stepped down from *Betsy* onto the dusty tarmac of the spaceport landing field, a hundred miles from the Ruhim capital, Parkum. The ship had entered the atmosphere over the ocean at the planet's northern pole, then cruised down over mile after mile of completely empty sand, broken up only by the occasional ravine or squat, craggy mountain range, until Parkum had appeared on the horizon — the first sign that the planet was populated at all. Karak seemed to be the perfect antithesis to Nexus Prime, where all but a tiny fraction of the surface was covered by the urban sprawl of interlocking conurbations, where every empty square metre was potential space for business or living, with astronomical value and infinite demand. Dante had stared down at Karak's empty, tranquil desert, compared it to the swarming people and vehicles, the noise and lights and bustle of the Commonwealth's capital world, and briefly wondered which was the more desirable.

Squinting in the sunlight, Dante pulled a pair of tinted glasses from his breast pocket and slipped them on. It was early morning in the Ruhim territory, but the glare from Carsus II was almost dazzling even through the shaded lenses. *Not a cloud in the sky, and white-gold dust in every direction. The locals must have permanent headaches.* Nodding at the service bots as they rolled towards the microcorvette, Dante headed for the long, low building on the far side of the spaceport.

The automatic door beneath the sign marked 'Arrivals' in four languages slid open jerkily as he approached, and Dante entered a lobby that was barely cooler than the outside. A chiller unit high up on the wall wheezed tiredly, emitting more noise than cold air, the sound vying with a telenovella playing on a flickering screen hanging in the corner above the entrance.

Of the two occupants of the room, one sat snoring open-mouthed in a corner chair, dressed in dusty, oil-stained overalls; the other had balanced his obese form precariously on a high stool behind what had to be a reception desk. He watched Dante with an expression of complete disinterest, sweat glistening on his bald scalp.

As Dante approached, removing his glasses, the man spoke in heavily accented Standard, at the same time proffering a tablet that looked a hundred years old. 'You fill in detail here. Name, ship registration, where you come from, any cargoes.' He tapped the edge of the tablet with a pudgy finger. 'Is self-explaining.' Duty fulfilled, the official sighed deeply and turned his gaze to the telenovella on the screen.

Nothing like a man who loves his job. Repressing a smile, Dante began tapping his information—Dante Cole, the usual commodities trader role he used for light-cover assignments—into the form.

Hardly needing to concentrate as he entered the familiar details, Dante casually broached the subject of real interest. 'Oh, while I'm here, perhaps you can help me. An acquaintance of mine told me he might be coming to Parkum this month, but I haven't heard from him in a while. He probably would have landed here, I think.'

The fat man shrugged, gaze still fixed on the telenovella that struggled to make itself heard over the chiller unit. 'Okay. So.'

'He's an offworlder, like me. From the Core.' *Who hopefully didn't enter under a fake name like I am.* 'The name's Kane. Jalen Kane.'

Dante looked up from the paperwork to see the man's beady gaze slide to meet his. 'You know Kane? He friend?'

Huh. Easier than expected. 'Well, as I said, more of an acquaintance.'

'He land here. Eleven days now. His ship still out there.' The official wagged one finger towards the landing field. 'He only pay ten days. You find him, you tell him. One more day, I have ship moved. Will cost him to get it back.'

His entry form completed, Dante slid the tab across the desk to the official. 'Of course. I'll be sure to do that if I catch up with him. Thank you.'

The man nodded wearily. 'Good. Can't have ship taking up room, not paying. I run spaceport here, not...' He frowned, gaze dropping to the desk. Then shook his head. Whatever he wasn't running would remain a mystery.

Patting the desk, Dante took a step away and smiled. 'Well, I'll be back within ten days, don't you worry.'

The pleasantry was lost on the man, who turned back to the screen with a grunt. Dante turned to leave. The other occupant had remained stolidly asleep throughout the exchange. His snores, Dante noticed, were synchronised with the groans of the chiller unit above him. Shaking his head, Dante stepped out into the morning heat.

He'd confirmed that Kane had come to Karak. That was the first, and most important, hurdle. It had been a fair bet that Karak was where the missing man had gone, and an equally decent guess that this spaceport would have been his arrival point, but neither had been a certainty. *Always nice to get two out of two straight off.* Restoring his glasses, Dante headed back to *Betsy* to retrieve his holdall and check that the service bots had finished their checks.

Fifteen minutes later, he sat in the driver's seat of an old but serviceable groundcar that he had rented from a rake-thin man who seemed just as tired and bored as his counterpart on the arrivals desk. Dante had bartered his way down to a daily rate that would cover the purchase price of the vehicle in a hundred days, instead of in fifty. His bag on the passenger seat at his side, he steered the vehicle out of the lot onto the highway that led to Parkum. The city skyline ahead sat low on the horizon, with just a few gleaming towers breaking the otherwise featureless monotony. *I hope you're still here, Kane.* Cranking up the air-cooling system to a dull roar, Dante settled back for the drive.

Here, and still breathing.

* * *

Two hours later, Dante walked up to another reception desk. A public information kiosk had provided directions to a reputable hostelry in a quiet residential district near the centre of Parkum, and he'd checked into a small but clean room overlooking the front courtyard and facing street. A short conversation with the elderly proprietress yielded the location of Parkum's two universities. The smaller of the two apparently specialised in engineering disciplines, so Dante had set out for the larger one on the far side of the city.

He'd quickly found the humanities department and been grateful to step out of the fierce midday heat into the cool of the flagstone-floored lobby. The smart-looking young woman behind the desk stopped tapping into her notepad and looked up, closing the thick, old-style paper book she had been referring to.

Dante smiled as he reached the desk and pointed at the book. 'I haven't seen one of those in a while.'

The woman patted the book gently. 'You must not spend much time in universities, then.' Her Standard had the barest hint of an accent.

He shook his head. 'No, not for quite a few years, I'm afraid.' Dante placed his hands on the desk, and gave her the friendly look of easy-going intent that he adopted in this sort of situation. 'I'm hoping you can point me towards the archaeology department.'

'Of course. Follow this corridor,'—she pointed to her left—'all the way to the end. Then go through the double doors, cross the courtyard to the building on the opposite corner, and archaeology is on the second floor.' She smiled, frowning slightly. 'Though I must say, I wouldn't have guessed you were an archaeologist.'

Dante laughed easily. 'And you'd be right, too. I'm just visiting a friend. Well, a friend of a friend.' He moved off with a wave. 'Thanks for the directions.'

Five minutes' walk brought him to the archaeology floor. Cabinets lined the long corridor that ran the length of the building, filling the walls from floor to ceiling and stuffed with an array of bones, fossils, potsherds, and metal fragments, each carefully tagged with a label giving a short description and the location of the find. Dante leaned in to peer at a large skull, the double rows of sharply pointed teeth indicating a fierce predator. *'Skull of desert wolf (colde kurt), adult male. Extinct. Found Hereb terr., ca. 720 (Karak), 3120 (Comm.)'. Mean-looking bastard.*

He walked along the corridor, peering into the rooms he passed. He passed seven that were empty or locked before he found another soul. The man bent over a wide wooden table, thick spectacles pushed back into a mop of curly grey hair, and peered through a magnifying lens at a shard of metal, which lay with several others like it on a piece of white cloth. Dante tapped the doorframe, and the man jumped, his head snapping up, blinking rapidly in surprise.

'Apologies. I didn't mean to startle you.' Dante took a step into the room as the man stood and, after a couple of failed attempts, located the glasses atop his head.

'No, no—no need to apologise.' The archaeologist smiled a little sheepishly. 'I'm lost to the world whilst I am studying a piece, especially these.' He gestured to the pieces of metal before him. 'Centuries old, but no sign of corrosion! Amazing. You could have walked up and tapped me on the shoulder, and I wouldn't have heard you.'

Well, nor would most people if I didn't want them to, but anyway... 'I'm sorry to bother you, Doctor...'

'Altan. Elmas Altan.' The man reached out a hand, and they shook.

Dante gave his cover name out of habit. 'Dante Cole.'

'How can I help you, Mister Cole?'

'I'm looking for the fiancée of a friend. Her name's Sara Jordaan; she's from...' Dante tailed off at the sudden change in Doctor Altan's expression on hearing the name. 'I'm sorry; is something wrong?'

'No, I am the one who is sorry.' Altan sighed deeply, shaking his head. 'Miss Jordaan has not been seen for some time—twenty days, now. Her team was working at a site in one of the deep valleys—a hundred, hundred and twenty miles north of Parkum. The site is inside the perimeter of one of the bloodsalt mining operations in that area, but it was fine; they had a concession from the authorities, all the required documentation. But that was from before the trouble started.'

Dante raised his eyebrows. 'The trouble?'

Altan nodded. 'The old Efendi taking up with that offworlder, that woman. Marrying her—*marrying* her! After just weeks. And then the old man dies, all of a sudden.' Altan tapped his own chest with one fist. 'His heart goes boom, and the offworlder is in charge. The next thing anyone knows, we are at war. The army is going out, raiding and conquering... the Bobun, then the Mani. In one month! And we Ruhim, we don't know why. No one says anything.' He shook his head again.

There's more to this inter-tribal conflict LeClerq mentioned than we knew. Dante frowned. *Something smells bad about this.* 'How did this affect the archaeology team, though?'

'That's another thing that makes no sense. Suddenly,'—he clicked his fingers—'they don't have clearance any more. No one is allowed within the area of the mining operation. Months it's not a problem, and then it is. Most of the team, they just do what they're told; they pack up, they go elsewhere. But the offworlder—I beg your pardon, Miss Jordaan—she doesn't listen. She leaves, but then she goes back.

'Twice they catch her, the authorities; the second time she comes back here with a black eye. One of the militia hit her with a truncheon. Said it was an accident. Animals.' Altan shook his head sadly. 'Yet Sara goes back again. And this time, she doesn't come back.' He looked up at Dante, genuine sadness in his eyes. 'Twenty days ago, and we have no idea where she is.'

Frowning, Dante looked down at the metal shards. They gleamed as if freshly oiled even in the dim light.

It's not going easier than expected any more.

* * *

Dante felt a little dispirited as he returned to where he'd left the groundcar just outside the university complex. A couple of quick questions had determined that if Jalen Kane had also visited the department looking for his fiancée, Doctor Altan hadn't seen him. *Another dead end.* He slipped into the driver's seat and shut the door. *I'll just have to do this the old-fashioned, tedious way.*

It seemed clear that Jordaan's disappearance, and Kane's, were directly linked to the emergence of the mysterious foreign woman who had come from nowhere to rule Karak's largest tribe in such a short time. If Dante could understand what was behind that meteoric rise, there was a good chance he might stumble across Kane along the way. But he needed more information.

Dante spent the afternoon crisscrossing Parkum. He wandered through markets that sold meat, fruits, cloth, and bootleg technology. He stopped into cafes and bars, and had a hundred seemingly idle conversations, which he steered towards one topic: the new ruler of the Ruhim, the exotically named Venus. Almost everywhere he found citizens willing or even delighted to discuss the mystery woman who had appeared out of nowhere to cause such upheaval.

One particular opinion was surprisingly prevalent, given how ridiculous it seemed to Dante—though he hid his scepticism, of course. More than half of the people he spoke to believed that Venus—also known variously as the offworlder, the foreigner, or 'that witch'—had somehow bewitched the old Efendi. She had definitely tricked him into marrying her—'and him not a day under seventy years old!'—and then had him killed. Some even muttered that she may have killed him herself, using 'dark arts.'

Among the few nuggets of hard information that Dante unearthed was the revelation that the Efendi's palace, home to Venus, was not merely a palace. It was a fortress, built above several subterranean levels dug out centuries earlier—levels that served as Parkum's jail. *How convenient for the ruler who needs to house, say, an illegally detained archaeologist.*

The second detail that piqued Dante's interest fell into his lap in a cafe down the street from a militia barracks. An elderly gentlemen, of great age but still sharp-eyed and upright, preferred to discuss the military aspect of the current tumult. He'd served in the militia as a young man, and two of his grandsons did now: those young men had told him stories of the *other* offworlder who had arrived on Karak some time after Venus, and quickly positioned himself at her right hand.

'My boys tell me he is her adviser. Not only that, but he has complete command of the militia. A foreigner.' The elderly gent's voice was strong and clear. He shook his head in disgust. 'They say he trains them like a demon. Drills, exercises, day after day. New tactics, foreign ones: moving quickly in small squads, breaking resistance, taking and holding buildings with just a few men. Killing with and without weapons.'

The description stirred a glimmer of recognition in Dante's mind as he listened to the old man, sipping coffee the strength and consistency of petrol. *Small squads, unarmed combat…*

'And they say the man himself is not quite human. More than a man. Seven feet tall, the strength of three men. Fast, like a striking cobra.' The old man shook his head wearily as if he didn't believe any of this. 'But young men have too much imagination. They create heroes and monsters too easily.'

Dante smiled and nodded, but his mind raced. That spark of recognition had caught, and burned with a fierce certainty.

A foreign woman arrives on Karak, inveigles herself into the ruling family of the largest tribe, then takes over. Before anyone can blink, she moves against two neighbouring tribes, rumour has it with a view to conquering the planet entirely. But not alone, it seems. Which begs the question…

The old man continued. '… This man who is more than a man. He calls himself Hesch…'

What is a Titan doing leading a war of conquest on Karak?

* * *

The sun had set on a day that had yielded more questions than answers. Dante had been taken aback by the sudden shift in the nature of his investigation. *Like stepping into a puddle only to find out it's a lake, and you can't see the bottom.* He had left the groundcar at the hostel and started walking south. Apparently there was a famous bar, popular with foreigners, beneath a clock tower in one of the large squares in that direction. After ten hours immersed in local life, Dante felt he could do with being around some people with a more detached perspective.

As he walked, he turned over in his mind the little information he had. But after a few minutes, Dante gave up. *I just don't know enough yet. And I'm hardly going to storm a fortress prison single-handedly, looking for a woman who might not be there. I need more information, then a plan.* He came to the edge of a broad square, and looked up to see a clock tower, the copper hands of the dial showing twenty minutes past ten o'clock. Below it hung the sign of the bar he was looking for: The Sickle Moon. *But before either of those, I need a drink.*

Five minutes later, he sat at one end of the bar, his back to the corner and a tall glass of the local ale in front of him. The place was filling up; in one corner, a group of young men were playing a noisy game of holohockey on an old machine like the kind Dante had played on in his uncle's bar as a child, growing up in Port St. Louis on Kingston. He smiled as he watched the men batting frantically at the glowing puck that whizzed between them. A cacophonous mix of the scoring team's cheers and their opponents' remonstrations met every goal. *Those were the days.* He took a sip of his beer, then frowned, his smile vanishing. *Actually, no. Come to think of it, they weren't.*

In the corner of the bar across from Dante sat an attractive woman, dressed in a figure-hugging lime-green pant suit, which looked better than he would have expected, when wrapped around her dark brown skin. She had been checking him out with not much in the way of subtlety ever since he'd walked in, but Dante resolutely ignored her gaze. *Not what I'm here for.* He could have slipped into the seat beside her and struck up a conversation easily enough, and maybe even gathered some useful information, but he just didn't have the energy to play the seduction game. With that realisation, Dante snorted. *I must be getting old.*

His gaze roved constantly across the entrance and back, looking for... something, he didn't know what. As a result, Dante saw the newcomer as soon as he came in. Obviously an offworlder, with red hair, green eyes, and the kind of pale skin that didn't belong in Karak's unforgiving heat. Taking a sip of his beer, Dante watched over the rim of his glass as the man approached the bar. His controlled movement, the way he casually scanned the faces of the clientele, the way his gaze flicked to the emergency exit on the back wall; after years in the field, Dante recognised the pattern.

He's a spook. As surely as... well, I am.

The man reached the bar and pulled out a stool three spots down. He waved to the bartender and called out for a draft beer. After a few seconds, as if sensing he was being observed, the newcomer glanced to his right and caught Dante's gaze. Eyes narrowing slightly, he nodded. 'Good evening.'

Dante returned the nod. 'Evening.' *So what are you doing here?*

5. Observation

Earlier the same day.

'There's a civil war brewing, and our long-lost sister seems to be at the heart of it.' Typical understatement, Sebastien. She's not at the heart of it; she's the whole bloody reason.

Quinn lowered the binoculars, then slapped the back of his neck. The local biting insects seemed to have a taste for the sunblock formula he'd sprayed on every morning since arriving on Karak. His arms and neck were dotted with angry red spots, and he was irritable. *She couldn't have shown up on a nice cold world, one where the local fauna doesn't try to eat you a tiny bit at a time. Oh no. That would be far too convenient.* Quinn sighed.

He stood at the window of a tenement block across the street from the rear of the Ruhim palace in Parkum, a grey-slab monstrosity with zero aesthetic appeal. For a building in such a... tactical location, there had been nothing in the way of security to stop Quinn from entering the tenement—smiling as he held the door behind the old lady who had opened it on her way out—and climbing to the top floor. A moment's concentration had roughly located the consciousnesses in the surrounding apartments, and a minute more had been plenty to identify and break into an empty one.

Quinn had arrived on Karak a day earlier, and checked into a cheap motel in downtown Parkum. He'd wandered out to find a drink, and ended up with something even better; the gossipy waitress in the bar down the street from the hotel had proved a font of useful information, once he filtered out the torrent of inane and wildly inaccurate speculation about the Ruhim's new ruler and her even more mysterious associate. A key detail had been the fact that it was possible to sneak a peek down onto the balcony of the palace's master apartments, if you could get high enough up on the north side. *High enough, and with a decent pair of binoculars.*

Quinn was ninety per cent sure he didn't need to be here, that there was no need to confirm it was indeed Venus who had so swiftly altered the balance of power on the planet. Every piece of information he'd teased from the locals added weight and colour to the meagre details in the Agency briefing. He knew in his gut that it was her. And yet…

For some reason, I need to see her with my own eyes. Just for… Just to be sure.

And so he'd spent the last few hours standing in the semi-darkness of a stranger's apartment, staring out of a half-shuttered window down and across the street to a balcony that a completely unreliable source had told him was connected to Venus's rooms. A beggar with legs cut off below the knees had told Quinn on his way past that the Mistress—as some called her—was indeed in residence today. A couple of Commonwealth dollars had drawn a gap-toothed grin from the invalid, and a cheery nod as he'd dragged himself away on a wheeled board. *I wonder what he spent those two dollars on. Nothing healthy, probably.*

Movement caught Quinn's gaze and dragged him out of the

distracted reverie he had drifted into after so long spent waiting. Two figures had emerged onto the twenty-foot square balcony that had stood empty for three hours. He brought the binoculars up and focused in.

The first of the newcomers was a man. Tall, Caucasian, and heavily muscled, with close-cropped hair. He wore nondescript, unmarked clothes that somehow still screamed 'military.' Zooming in as close as the binoculars would allow, Quinn noted a black spiral-pattern tattoo on the man's right cheek. That marking reminded Quinn of something, but he couldn't remember what.

A few steps behind the man came a slim, cocoa-skinned woman, dressed in a white blouse and matching loose-fitting trous. Quinn's breath caught. Even if he'd only been able to see her silhouette, the way she moved would have been confirmation enough.

Hello, Venus. Nice to see you again.

He watched the two converse. The man stood at the corner of the balcony, his gaze scanning the street below, while Venus leaned against the balustrade, face turned up towards the afternoon sun. *She did always love the sun.* After several minutes, the conversation seemed to grow heated: Venus stiffened and crossed her arms. The man stopped watching the street and turned to stare at her with a motionless intensity that Quinn could feel even from this distance. A few more words were exchanged, and then Venus threw up her arms in what looked like exasperation before stomping back indoors. After one more scan of the street below, the man followed. Quinn lowered the binoculars once again, and made ready to leave. *Hmm. Interesting.*

Trouble in paradise, my dear?

* * *

Hesch stepped back into Venus's apartment and slid the balcony door closed behind him, shutting out the blazing late-afternoon heat.

Venus stood at the waist-high, marble-topped bar that lined

part of the far wall, pouring a pale liquor into a chunky crystal tumbler. After a second's pause, she called out without turning. 'Do you want one?'

We're still being civil, then. 'Yes, thank you.' He moved further into the room, hands clasped behind his back as he wandered towards a faded painting on his left. It always caught his eye, whenever he met his employer in her apartments. While far from being an expert on any kind of art, Hesch had enough of an eye to know that the piece was objectively hideous. *The colours clash, the perspective is off on several of the figures, and yet...* Something about it drew his attention. The scene was of a gathering of people, a horde clustered around a small hill, atop which stood a speaker, arms spread. Hesch had no idea what event in local history the scene depicted, or if it was even supposed to be Karak. But regardless, the artist had managed to capture something in the speaker's expression, some... passion. Fervour. It struck Hesch that the man wasn't just speaking to the crowd. *He's prophesying.*

'Here.' He turned to see Venus holding out a glass. Hesch took it with a nod, sipped the lightly scented brandy. *Pleasant enough.* Venus looked at him intently. He met her gaze, waited.

After a moment, she sighed. 'I know how much this irritates you. You've mentioned it often enough.' She sipped her own drink. 'But you need to defer to my judgement on this issue.'

Hesch raised one eyebrow. 'Regardless of the fact that you hired me in part for my strategic counsel?'

Venus cocked her head. 'I did, and I value that counsel. When it comes to strategy in the field, you have complete command. But the timetable of the overall plan is mine to decide.' She turned and took a seat in an overstuffed chair.

'It would assuage some of my concerns if you were to explain why, exactly, we need to move so quickly against the next target. Pacifying two tribes out of seven in less than two months seems progress enough—why rush the third?' Hesch sat down opposite her. 'We no longer have any element of surprise; our spies report that all of the other tribes have ramped up their military preparedness. Consolidation of our own forces would seem prudent.'

Venus shook her head slowly. 'I'm sorry, Caleb. I know how much it pains you, but I can't share everything with you. You'll just have to trust me when I tell you that we're pushing up against a deadline. I don't know exactly when it will come, but I know we're racing against time. Hence...'

Hesch sighed. 'Hence, the Ghelt. Tomorrow.'

She nodded. 'Tomorrow.'

He placed his glass on a side table, stood. 'If I can't dissuade you, fine. You'll ride with me in the vanguard as before?'

'Naturally,' she replied. 'There's nowhere I'd rather be.'

'And we can rely on your... talent, being as effective as it was against the Bobun and the Mani?' Hesch thought for a moment that he saw a flash of red in his employer's blue eyes.

Venus smiled prettily. 'Of course. Even more effective, I'd imagine.'

Hesch repressed a faint shudder. *Damned Seryn. One day, Corralin's going to wipe you from the face of the galaxy, witch. And I'll be far, far away. Not shedding a single tear.*

Venus downed the last of her drink. 'You have preparations to make, I assume. Don't let me keep you.'

With another nod, he turned and headed for the door. Hesch could feel the weight of her regard on his back as he left the room.

Not a single tear.

* * *

Ten minutes had passed since the woman and her male associate had disappeared back inside. *It doesn't seem like they're coming back out.* Tasha collapsed her ultralight field telescope, and frowned.

She lay on her front at the rooftop edge of an apartment block that overlooked the back of the Ruhim's hideous fortress, only her eyes and the top of her head visible to anyone looking up, had anyone bothered. No one had in the four hours since she'd scaled the block's opposite side, using drainpipes, window ledges and washing lines to propel herself up the twelve storeys: The porter in the front lobby had prevented her from just using the stairs. It had been the middle of the day, with most residents presumably out at work or school; as a result no one had spotted her on her way up, though she and a scrawny black cat on the second floor had startled each other.

The effort of climbing had been worthwhile. Tasha had only seen her target for a few minutes, but that had been plenty of time to take several clear images of her using the camera built into the telescope. *She doesn't look like a witch, though she has beauty enough to glamour people the old-fashioned way. Glamour men, at least.*

She'd taken a few good shots of the man too. He looked intense, hard, and... *scary. Not a nice man, I think. Hopefully I won't need to go past him to get to her.* Though somehow Tasha sensed that was a forlorn hope.

She shuffled carefully back from the roof's edge before climbing to her feet. Tucking the telescope into the pouch strapped to her waist, Tasha headed for the opposite side of the roof to begin her descent.

Gripping the top of a drainage pipe firmly with one hand, she swung her legs over the edge. The light adhesive in the palms and fingers of her thin gloves gave her a solid purchase, as did her rubber-soled pumps, and she descended quickly. As she climbed down, half-consciously selecting the next foothold or handhold—*left foot on that ledge, right hand on this one, swing to the left, right foot on the pipe*—Tasha thought about the other person of interest who she had snapped with her telescope camera: a man, obviously foreign with his pale skin and red hair, who had strolled with apparent casualness into the street about an hour after she had taken up position.

He had chatted briefly to an indigent, then walked to another apartment block below Tasha and to her left. The man had waited for a few minutes, aimlessly loitering it would seem, until a woman had exited that building, at which point he'd slipped inside. *Which was quite smoothly done, if you weren't expecting it.* Tasha had obviously lost sight of him, then, until five minutes or so later when her peripheral vision had caught some motion: a shutter being slid half-closed in an apartment on the block's top floor. Partly hidden behind that shutter was her mystery man, who was also interested in the occupants of the ugly grey palace across the street.

Tasha sighed as she dropped the last six feet to the ground and slipped off her gloves. *Other parties involved means complications. I'll need to keep an eye out for that mystery man.* The gloves followed the telescope into her waist pouch as she nonchalantly walked back towards the road.

That, and kill the witch quickly.

* * *

The sun had almost set by the time Quinn had returned to his hotel room. The orange light through the half-closed blinds painted the black-and-white bedspread in tiger stripes as Quinn pulled a slim, rectangular case from beneath the bed and placed it on top. Gently he gripped the front corners of the case with the thumb and forefinger on each hand, and closed his eyes. Quinn waited through the brainwave and fingerprint scans, then a faint vibration in his fingertips told him he had passed the identity check. *And if I hadn't, the results would have been messy.* He flipped up the front clasp, and the case swung open.

Inside was a portable subspace wave communicator, roughly a foot square and powered by a nuclear microcell. Quinn checked the charge strip that ran along one edge. *Four bars out of five. Plenty of juice.* He could always return to his ship to recharge it, if the need arose.

Quinn tapped the screen that filled most of the communicator's top. It lit up with a quiet beep, and displayed the top ten entries in the list of known transceivers. Every member of the Agency, every friendly contact, every key location—coordinates for all of those were stored in the memory of the small grey box. He quickly filtered the list to Agency, then Corinth, and tapped Sebastien's entry.

He watched 'LOCATING...' flash on the screen for half a

minute, then disappear with a click as 'CONNECTED' appeared.

Sebastien's voice came through crisp and clear. 'Quinn—hello. Sorry for the delay in my answer. I had to relocate to somewhere more private.'

Quinn sat down on the bed next to the communicator. 'Are you still at the office? I assumed you'd be home. It's late evening where you are, isn't it?'

'Indeed it is, and I am, but we have some people over. Elise made one of her feasts.' Sebastien chuckled dryly. 'You've saved me from a boring conversation with a particularly tedious friend of hers. But I digress. Your report.'

'I arrived in Parkum yesterday, settled in.' Quinn rubbed his jaw. *I should shave before I go out.* 'A few hours ago I confirmed her presence—not that there was much doubt.'

'Quite. We may not have had a lot of intel, but it was good. And it was unmistakably Venus.'

Quinn grunted. 'It was unmistakably her this afternoon, too. Coming out of the master suite of the Ruhim palace.'

A few seconds of silence followed, then Sebastien released a long sigh. 'That's unfortunate. Do you believe she's taken control?'

'Completely. A few months ago, from what I've gathered. She's also the one who instigated the inter-tribal conflict.'

Sebastien snorted. 'Well, it follows, doesn't it? You don't take over the largest population group on a planet and then *not* use their military.'

The sun had set completely, and Quinn stood and walked to the window to close the blinds. 'Speaking of military,' he called back over his shoulder, 'Venus isn't alone. I saw her with a very serious-looking individual. Tall, heavily muscled... familiar somehow, too. Had a black spiral tattoo on his right cheek.'

'Are you certain?' Sebastien's tone had changed from languid to sharp in an instant.

Quinn turned back to the bed, frowning. 'Yes. What is it?'

'It's a tattoo that's forced on convicted felons, to mark them out to the general populace as such.' Sebastien sighed again. 'On

Mission.'

Mission... Wait. What? 'Mission? As in the Titan homeworld? *That* Mission?!' Quinn barked.

'The one and only, thankfully,' Sebastien replied.

Quinn dropped back onto the bed. *Shit.* 'That wasn't in the briefing. Makes this considerably more complicated.' He thought furiously. 'Is there any chance we want to bring them in?'

'The Titans? Good lord, no. It doesn't matter that young Ariadne is our most mercurial new agent after her exploits beyond the Rim, or that Corralin is her dear friend. Or that we're savouring our first ever détente with the Titans. None of those make them our allies.' Sebastien snorted again. 'And their methods are hardly suited to a delicate situation such as this. No, we'll continue as planned.'

Translation: You're still on your own. 'Understood, Sebastien. I'll check in again when I have news.'

'I look forward to it, Quinn. Keep well.' The communicator connection cut off with a beep.

Quinn sat in silence on the bed for a few more moments. *Damn Sebastien and his obstinacy. A few squads of Titan shock troops could end this in a few days, but oh, no — I have to do it the hard way.* He sighed. *I need a drink.*

Ten minutes' walk took him to a wide open space nearby. Old-fashioned electric lamps dotted around the area, casting it in a welcoming glow. On one side stood an imposing clock tower, and directly beneath it hung a metal sign that was just starting to rust. *The Sickle Moon. If that's not a bar, I've never been in one.* A noisy group of youths spilt out of the door as Quinn approached, releasing a cacophony of voices behind them. He pushed the door open again and stepped into the noise and smoke.

Quinn scanned the room as he headed towards the bar and took one of the open stools. After ordering a beer, he glanced over and caught the eye of the fellow who'd watched him enter. *And if you're not from Nexus Prime, I wasn't born there.* He nodded. 'Good evening.'

The man placed his beer on the bar and returned the nod. 'Evening.'

6. Meeting

Quinn shook his head. 'No, that'll be all, thank you.' The barman headed for the kitchen with his order, and Quinn turned back to his new acquaintance. 'Sorry, I missed that.'

The man—Dante Cole, he'd said—smiled slightly. 'Don't worry, it's not terribly interesting. I was just saying that I'm a commodities trader.'

Quinn nodded. 'Ah. Buying or selling?'

'Buying, mainly.' Cole sipped his drink, and wiped a speck of foam from his mouth. 'I hop about the galaxy, and when I find an interesting product at a reasonable price, I make a deal. The operations folks back home on Nexus Prime sort out the shipping.' He shrugged, self-deprecating. 'It's a job.'

Quinn smiled. *He's a very good liar, this one.* 'And what kinds of products are you finding here on Karak?'

'Some surprisingly good liquor, which I didn't expect. But the main item is the bloodsalt. Have you had any yet?' Cole reached for the bowl of nuts in front of him and took a handful.

Quinn shook his head. 'I take it it's something you eat, then?'

'That's right. I've no doubt you'll get a bowl with your meal when it arrives.' Cole gestured towards the barman, who approached carrying a tray. 'Ha, good timing. It's just a condiment. It has an interesting taste, sure, but the only reason I care is that it's unique to this planet. That doesn't happen very often.'

Quinn looked down at the tray the bartender had placed in front of him. Sure enough, alongside the plate of lamb and vegetable stew sat a small bowl filled with a red powdered substance. He looked up at Cole with a smile. 'Safe to eat, is it?'

Cole laughed. 'Oh, absolutely. It's not to everyone's taste, so I can't promise you'll actually enjoy it.' He drained his glass. 'Buy you another beer?'

Why not? May as well get a free drink while I work out why you're telling fibs. 'Sure, thanks. I'll get the next one.' As Cole waved over the barman, Quinn dipped his little finger into the bloodsalt, and popped it in his mouth. *Tangy. That's not bad.* He scattered a spoonful over his dish.

'Like it, then?' Cole asked, eyebrows raised.

Quinn chuckled. 'Aye, it's got an interesting taste. I can see why you think you could sell it offworld.' *Or realistically pretend you were going to sell it offworld, rather.*

The barman arrived with two more beers. Cole took a swig of his before turning back to Quinn. 'So what brings you to Karak, then?'

Quinn swallowed a mouthful of saucy lamb, and licked his lips. 'I work for a university on Capricorn II. We're trying to set up an archaeological exchange program with one or two universities here. Karak has some amazing history, if you can dig it out of the desert.'

Cole smiled—a little oddly, though Quinn couldn't place why. 'I've heard that's true. I actually walked past the university here in Parkum earlier today.'

'Oh, really?' *Bullshit.* 'What a coincidence.'

Quinn and Cole continued to chat about trivial things—places they'd visited, Commonwealth politics, the jetball championship—while he consumed his meal. Quinn had almost finished eating when he started to feel hot; his hands and face began to sweat. *That's odd. There was no spice in that dish.*

'All right, there? You've gone a little bit red.' Cole looked at him with a slight frown.

'I'm fine, sure. Just a bit hot, is all.' Quinn took a big gulp of his beer. *Just a bit hot. But now I'm getting a headache. A bad headache. A really bad shit hellfire holy fuck—.* He squeezed his eyes closed as pain shot from his temples to his sinuses. His eyes began to water. Cole was a blurred double vision, gesturing towards him and saying... something, but Quinn couldn't hear. There was a pounding in his ears, a roaring noise that filled his mind and was only getting louder.

He gripped the bar, barely conscious of his surroundings, as the pressure built in his head, built and built, until—

It released.

Quinn screamed in pain as a shockwave of mental energy burst out of him, the agony yanking him up straight in his seat, then toppling him backwards onto the floor. He passed out.

And awoke some time later. *Seconds? Minutes?* The pressure had gone, along with the pain and the acute fever.

Groggily, Quinn pushed himself up into a sitting position, and looked about.

'Oh, shit.'

Every other person in the bar was unconscious. He stared about for a few more seconds, looking from face to face. *Out cold, all of them. What the hell just happened?*

A groan from behind him spurred Quinn to his feet. *Probably best not to hang around here. I'm pretty sure there'd be questions.* As he turned to the door he spared a glance for his new acquaintance Cole, who was face down in a puddle of spilled beer. *Sorry, fella.*

Stepping over an unconscious girl who was sprawled across the doorway, Quinn made his exit.

* * *

'Urrrrrrrgh.' Dante gingerly lifted his head from the bar, grimacing as his right cheek came away with a wet slap. He smelt stale beer and vomit, the latter somewhere nearby but thankfully not too close. Wincing at even the dim light inside the bar, he opened his eyes. In all corners of the place slumped and lay the patrons. *All unconscious, it looks like. And one of them lost his dinner.*

'What the hell was that?' he muttered under his breath, as he shakily climbed back off the bar stool. He remembered talking to that spook, Quentin—*as if that's his name*—while the man ate his food, and then... what? He'd complained about being hot, and then had some kind of fit or seizure. *Like ten migraines all at once, it looked like. Then... he screamed.* Dante couldn't remember anything after that.

He weaved his way around the bodies of groaning or unconscious patrons to the exit and shoved open the door. The night air was blessedly cool, and Dante gulped down lungfuls of it. His headache slowly started to clear. *Except now I've got another mystery to get to the bottom of. Marvellous.* Shaking his head in despair, then wincing as pain lanced through his temples, Dante stumbled in what he was fairly confident was the direction of his hotel.

Forty minutes, one morphine tab, and a shower later, he felt halfway back to normal, if exhausted. Dante lay back on his hotel bed and closed his eyes, rolling the events of the day around his mind. The question of what exactly had happened in that bar seemed more immediately answerable than how he was supposed to extract Sara Jordaan and find Jalen Kane. *I just need to find a pale, redheaded man named Quentin. How hard could it be? Even if his name isn't Quentin.*

As he dozed off, Dante kept seeing the man's anguished face in his mind. But it couldn't keep him from sleep.

The next morning, Dante awoke feeling surprisingly refreshed. He breakfasted quickly, and then quizzed the proprietress on the location of other hotels in the city. After five minutes of reassurance that he wasn't thinking of checking out early, the elderly lady grudgingly printed a list from a clicking, wheezing terminal that looked even older than she was, and gave it to Dante. Armed with some possible locations for his quarry, Dante headed out.

It was tiring, old-fashioned legwork. Trudging from hotel to hotel under the baking morning sun reminded Dante of a few tours he'd taken during his few years in the Space Corps. *Of course, back then I had a pulse rifle slung over my shoulder. Though I don't think having one now would make anyone more talkative.*

After four hours, he'd visited seventeen hotels and was almost halfway through his list. At every place, his pitch was the same: *'I'm here to visit a friend, tall fellow, pale, red hair... No one like that here? Oh, I must have the wrong hotel. Sorry!'* Simple, believable, inoffensive.

Number eighteen was a cheap-looking motel in the downtown area, and there Dante got lucky. The wizened Asian man at the desk—*Is anyone in the hotel business on this planet under a hundred years old?*—told him that 'Mr. Quentin not here. Gone out.' Dante had thanked the man kindly, told him he'd come back later, and left. Though he didn't go far—just over to the handily positioned cafe across the street.

Another two hours later—and after four cups of jet-fuel coffee; he would need to pee soon—Dante's wait came to an end. A familiar mop of red hair bobbed down the street, atop a tall, pale figure who looked a little sunburned. *Somehow I'm not sympathetic. Maybe it's because I've still got a faint ringing in my ears and the smell of beer in my hair.* With a wave to the proprietor, Dante rose out of his seat and tossed a few dollars on the table, then slipped out of the cafe.

His mark was almost at the door of the motel and was reaching into his pocket, presumably for a key. Dante called out, 'Quentin, isn't it?'

The man turned sharply, eyes wide. Dante kept his arms down, clear of his body, palms out.

After a few seconds, the man managed a small, slightly

sheepish smile. 'Cole. What a coincidence. How are you?'

Dante kept his gaze on Quentin's face but watched the hand in his pocket. 'Better than I was at about eleven last night. As are you, it looks like.'

The man nodded, his eyes narrowing, but said nothing.

Dante pressed on. 'I think it might benefit both of us if we had a short chat.' He glanced up and down the street, then back to Quentin. 'Somewhere more private, though. What do you say?'

A few seconds passed, then Quentin pulled his hand from his pocket. Dante tensed, then relaxed as he recognised it as a keycard. The other man slipped it into the lock by the front door, which slid open with a clank as he turned back to Dante with a cheery grin and waved him in. 'After you.'

With a nod and a smile, Dante stepped past him and into the motel.

* * *

Quinn had spent the day traipsing around Parkum, talking to anyone and everyone, searching for any information that would give him a clue to Venus's life—her routine, her actions day to day, anything that might suggest an opportunity, however slight, for him to make a move. What he'd discovered had been disheartening. *She spends all day, every day, inside that fortress. With one exception: When she leads the army in one of their raids on another tribe... and is surrounded by several thousand armed men and a bloody Titan. Great opportunity, that.*

One rumour had been persistent enough for Quinn to believe it was true. It seemed that Venus wasn't satisfied with just the recent conquests of the Bobun and the Mani. Allegedly the Ghelt were the next on her list and would be crossed off it soon. *Very soon. Tomorrow.* Quinn had been racking his brain, trying to come up with a plan to take advantage of that detail as he returned to his hotel.

Until the man who called himself Cole had shown up.

Now they stood in Quinn's small hotel room, Cole by the window and Quinn on the opposite wall. He watched Cole peer out through the blinds into the street. 'I've a bottle of whisky, if you fancy a drink?'

Cole turned. 'Sure, thanks.' He smiled. 'You never did get me a drink back, in the end.'

Quinn retrieved the bottle from a compartment in the wall next to the bed. 'Sorry about that. I had other things on my mind.'

'I noticed.' Cole wandered over to the chair at the foot of the bed and sat. 'Everyone in the bar noticed. You might say it was the main event of the evening. Care to enlighten me as to what exactly that was?'

I have my suspicions. But first... He poured two measures and walked over to Cole, who took the glass with a nod. Quinn sat on the foot of the bed and looked at his guest. 'I think we need to put our cards on the table first. Don't you?'

Cole sipped the whisky, nodded appreciatively. 'Certainly. By which you mean we should tell each other what we think the other's holding, and see how close we are?'

Quinn smiled slightly. 'You've played before, then?'

'Once or twice.'

'All right.' Quinn took a drink. 'I'll go first. You're from Nexus Prime, as you said. I believe that. I was born there myself, so I know the style. You're not hiding it.'

Cole smirked.

Quinn continued, 'You're name's not Dante Cole, but you gave the first name more smoothly than the last, so it's Dante something.'

'Zo. But you can call me Dante, if you prefer the first-name-only thing.'

'What do you know? It even rhymes.' Quinn smiled. 'So we've established you're from the heart of the Commonwealth, and you're here on Karak using a fake name at what's about to be the most turbulent period in this planet's settled history. Throw in the fact that you tracked me down in half a day, and I'm going to guess... DSO.'

Dante placed his glass on the arm of the chair and applauded gently. 'Very good. I'm impressed. Though I must be honest, finding you wasn't actually that difficult. You don't exactly... blend in with the locals.'

Damned complexion. Quinn took another drink. 'I'm more of a snowy climate sort of fella.'

'I guessed.' Dante's eyes narrowed on Quinn. 'My turn, then. Your name's not what you're using, either. I don't believe Quentin for a second—mainly because I don't want to believe anyone's parents would be that cruel.'

Quinn laughed. 'Harsh. I've a good friend back home called Quentin. But it's not my name, you're right. It's Quinn.'

'Quinn...' Dante raised his eyebrows.

'Just Quinn.'

'Ahhhh.' Dante leaned back in his seat, smiling contentedly. *What's he so pleased about?* 'Just Quinn, you say? No last name? Interesting.' He watched Quinn intently. 'Like the way some people are called just... Ariadne. Or Venus.'

Quinn stopped breathing for a second, then relaxed. He'd been planning to share that information anyway, as he had a strong gut instinct that it would be worth it further down the line. But Dante seemed to already know quite a lot. 'You're pretty well informed.'

'I pay attention,' Dante replied. 'After that business at the edge of the galaxy a year ago, and you and your compatriots coming out from hiding, we all got a little more familiar with the Seryn. In my line of work... Well, we did some extra digging. Just out of interest, you understand.'

Quinn nodded. 'Oh, of course. Due diligence, and all that.'

'Quite. So I arrived on Karak acquainted with some of the more well-known Seryn... characteristics, shall we say. But not thinking they'd be relevant to what I was trying to do.' Dante took a swig of his drink, then waggled the glass at Quinn. 'This is very good.'

'It's from Yemenis.'

'Ah, that'd be why, then. Anyway,' Dante continued, 'I land on this dustball and find it's being taken over by an evil witch with magical powers and one name. That's almost a direct quote from someone I spoke to, by the way.'

Quinn smiled. 'I've heard much the same today.'

'I'll bet. So there I am, not knowing what's going on, but with thoughts of the Seryn a little closer to the top of my mind than they were before... when I run into you. Who promptly short-circuits the minds of everyone within forty feet without apparent cause. Except...' Dante pointed a finger at Quinn. 'I think there is a cause. Maybe the same cause that's behind what your girl Venus is doing.' He took another sip, cocked one eyebrow. 'And I think you have an idea what it is.'

He's sharp. Sharp enough to be useful, if we're on the same side. And if not... then he's not going to leave this room. 'Venus isn't our girl any more; that's the problem. She went rogue years ago. She's unstable.' Quinn sighed. 'And I'm not absolutely certain of the cause. But I think it's the salt.'

Dante frowned, then his expression cleared. 'The bloodsalt.'

Quinn nodded. 'You know enough about me, about us, to know we have... gifts. Abilities. From what I experienced, the salt amplifies those abilities. Dramatically. When you factor that in to the current situation, and the fact that it's unique to this planet—'

'—You get the reason why Venus would be here, and not anywhere else in the galaxy,' Dante finished.

'Exactly.'

Dante frowned again. 'I don't understand how it would help her, though. I thought you people were all about telekinesis, telepathy. Are you saying you can control people's minds?'

Quinn shrugged. 'Not really. Most Seryn can influence an individual to some extent. It's a facet of telepathy, which is inherent to most of us. But it's not a big deal: I could make you think it was a good idea to scratch your head, that sort of level. Some others who are better at it could make you bark like a dog, or give them all of your money, then ten minutes later you'd have forgotten it ever happened.'

Dante nodded. 'Fine. Disturbing as hell, but fine. And

nothing that would help someone take the kind of control Venus has.'

'No. Venus's gift is... rare. To the extent that she's as unique as the bloodsalt. And for that we can all be very, very thankful.' Quinn sighed, then downed his drink. 'Venus is memetic.'

A few seconds passed in silence.

Dante looked blank. 'I'll be honest. I have no idea what that means.'

Quinn smiled weakly. 'It means she's able to implant ideas in people's minds. But not just to temporarily influence them—for her, it's permanent. Not only that, but the first person becomes a carrier, a host, of the idea, which she can trigger to replicate itself organically in the minds of people near the host. I've seen her do it.' He shivered. 'It's... unnerving.'

Dante stared into space. His voice, when he spoke, was low and quiet. 'And what would you do if you were a mentally unstable individual with memetic powers, a planet full of a spice that boosts those powers... and nothing holding you back?' He turned to Quinn, the fear in his gaze unmistakable.

Quinn nodded once. 'You'd take over the world.'

* * *

Dante and Quinn sat in silence for half a minute. The Seryn— *First one I've ever met; how about that?*—stared at a blank spot on the wall, thinking who knew what. Dante's mind was a whirl as he tried to absorb the information he'd been given, and extrapolate from it to... the natural conclusion.

'It's not just the world, though. This world. That's the larger problem, isn't it?'

Quinn turned to him, face pale. 'It's not just a problem. It's potentially cataclysmic. Think about it.' He stood from the bed, shook himself. 'She wouldn't need an invasion fleet. No warships, no battles. There's nothing your Space Corps could do—or the Titans, either. She could just send one person to every planet in the Core, in single person microcorvettes or on passenger liners—they'd be just another traveller.'

'They step out into a city, head to the largest population

centre… and it would just be a matter of time.'

'While Venus just sits back and waits.'

Dante frowned. 'Until what, though? What's her endgame, here—what message, or idea, would she send out into the galaxy?'

'Amongst Venus's many and varied psychological traits is a tendency towards megalomania. Though so far, given what some people think of her, she doesn't seem to have bothered spreading her influence into the general Ruhim population, the army is hers. Body and soul, to a man. I spoke to three different soldiers today, under the guise of a lost tourist, and asked a few questions.'

Dante raised his eyebrows. 'And?'

Quinn sighed. 'One of those soldiers, I think he was a… colonel, or their equivalent. You know the type: immaculate uniform, nearing middle age, so his hair's going grey, but he's still in better shape than I am. Probably got three kids and eight grandkids at home. A proud man. Honourable man, who's spent his life defending his people.' He shook his head, scowling. 'And then you hear the way he talks about her, as if the sun literally shines out of her arse. She's turned him into a puppet. He and the whole bloody army—they worship her. It's complete and utter devotion, with a fervour that's practically—'

Shit. Dante cut him off. 'Religious. She's setting herself up to be… a god.'

Quinn nodded. 'Incarnate. The theology of Karak's tribes is a confusing amalgam of polytheism and hero-worship, but I'm sure there's a role for a living goddess that Venus can step into when the time comes.'

Dante snorted. 'And if not, she can just create one.' He thought for a moment. 'Someone needs to bring her down, that's obvious. I'll call it in to my superior tomorrow, and see if she has any bright ideas.'

Quinn frowned. 'Tomorrow? Why not today?'

'Because I want to have some firm news for her on the mission that brought me here in the first place.' Dante stood and retrieved the whisky bottle. 'Long story short, I'm looking for a senator's brother who went missing on Karak while looking for his own missing fiancée. All signs point to her getting caught up with the wrong people—guess who, it's our megalomaniac friend—and my best bet is that she's locked up in the basement of that big ugly block they call a palace.' He handed Quinn a fresh drink.

'Thanks.' Quinn took a sip. 'You're assuming she—and the brother, by extension—are prisoners and not buried in a shallow hole in the desert somewhere.'

Dante shook his head. 'Not at all; I'm almost certain one or both of them has been killed.' He shrugged. 'I need to prove it one way or the other.' *Somehow.*

Quinn looked thoughtful. 'How would you feel if I offered you a little help?'

'Really? What's the angle?'

'How cynical you are.' Quinn smirked. 'The angle is that the sooner you're done with your trivial missing persons job, the sooner you can help me clean up my mess and save us all from becoming members of the pan-galactic cult of Venus. What do you say?'

'I'd say it sounds like a plan. But I'd also wonder why you'd trust me not to skip out as soon as my mission's complete and leave you holding the bag.' Dante smiled. 'Not that I would, of course.'

'I'm a pretty good judge of character,' Quinn replied.

'And I strike you as trustworthy? That'd be a first.'

Quinn laughed. 'Good one. No. But you strike me as smart enough to realise that if you don't help me, and Venus gets her way, you're just as buggered as the rest of us.'

'Ah, that's more like it. Partners, then?' Dante held out his glass.

'Partners,' Quinn replied. They clinked.

'Grand. So, phase one: We just need to get into the most heavily guarded building in the city. How difficult could that be?'

Quinn smiled. 'Funny you should ask. I just happen to know that it's going to be considerably less guarded than normal from tomorrow morning—as soon as the Ruhim army rolls out of town to spread the gospel of Venus to the unlucky Ghelt.'

Dante shivered a little. *The thought of someone messing with your mind... It's just unnatural.* He glanced at Quinn. *Even if it is pretty common to some people.* 'Okay, so that's the plan. We go in tomorrow, and see what we can find.'

Quinn nodded. 'Grand. And after that,'—he grinned—'we save the world.'

7. Infiltration

Venus squinted against the glare of the morning sunlight reflected from the rear of the armoured combat vehicle ahead of hers in the convoy. She pulled a pair of tinted glasses from the shoulder bag in her lap, gripping the back of the driver's seat in front of her as they bounced over another pothole. *I should have someone see to fixing these roads.* She slipped the glasses on and leaned back in her seat. *Later, maybe. If we have time.*

Her vehicle was one of twenty in the convoy, rolling through the main gate of the palace compound. From above, Venus knew, they would look like an enormous, disjointed metal snake, carving its way through Parkum to the east gate, where they would join up with the other sixty vehicles that comprised the rest of her attacking force.

They drove past shops, businesses, a school—everywhere, the citizens of Parkum turned to watch their army go past. Venus saw no elation in those faces, no patriotic fervour. Just the instinctive, reactive interest any animal would take upon seeing something unusual. *They don't understand why I do this. They don't know why their lives have changed.*

Caleb had put her in the eleventh vehicle to depart—chosen at random and identical to the other nineteen—to give any interested observer no chance of knowing which she rode in. *Poor Caleb. He does worry about me.*

The old-fashioned shortwave radio in her bag burbled and vibrated. Venus smiled. *Speak of the devil.* She pulled the radio out and flicked the talk switch. 'Hello, Caleb. Did you miss me already?'

'It'll take us fifteen minutes to get to the rendezvous point, then it's five hours across the desert to the first of the Ghelt settlements.' He ignored her flirtatious tone, his voice the same as ever, cool and detached.

Yet I never stop teasing him. One day, I'm going to get a reaction. 'Thank you, Caleb, but you've told me this already.'

'Just confirming,' he replied. 'Our advance scouts have reported in; there's limited resistance at the outlying towns and villages. The Ghelt forces appear to be concentrated around the capital. They seem to think they have a chance of holding it.'

'Now now, let's not get too confident. Didn't you tell me that?'

Caleb snorted. 'Confidence is perfectly fine when it's justified. It's overconfidence that kills you. In this case, I'd strongly favour us even in a straight battle with the Ghelt forces. They're overmatched. Once our troops close with the opposition and your... effect, comes into play, it should be over quickly.'

How delicately he puts it. He can't hide his distaste, though. Abruptly, Venus found herself irritated by the man's condescending tone. 'Understood. We'll speak nearer the time.'

She clicked the radio off and looked out of the reinforced glass window—resistant to explosions, projectiles, even a plasma slug, she'd been assured. She pressed her palm against the window and felt a slight warmth from the sun's heat even through the thick glass. *We can build walls to protect ourselves and shield us from those who would do us harm... but something always gets through.* Venus dropped her hand to her lap.

As the Ghelt are about to discover.

* * *

'And you're absolutely sure this is safe?' Quinn didn't sound convinced, even after Dante had spent the whole hour since sunset assuring him that the plan was nothing to worry about.

Dante finished tightening the clamp to the wall of the apartment block roof and turned to his companion. 'Of course. Are you telling me you've never zip-lined across a hundred-metre gap before?' he answered with a smile.

Quinn was a little wide-eyed. 'It's not really my style, no. I'm normally more of a walk-in-the-door kind of fella.' He stepped up to the edge of the roof and looked down and across to the Ruhim palace across the street as Dante attached the harpoon rifle to the clamp. 'Pretty long way to fall.'

Dante straightened, the rifle fixed in place. 'You won't fall. I've done this...' He paused.

Quinn turned to him. 'You *have* done this, right?'

'Yes! I was just counting. Twelve times in live missions. Hundreds in training. It's simple. Here, hold this.' He tossed Quinn a lightweight pulley he'd retrieved from his backpack.

Quinn caught it and inspected it briefly. 'Finger holes. Clever.'

'Yep. Makes it that much easier to not fall off and die.' Dante grinned as his partner flashed him a dark look.

'Funny.'

'Now, let's get our cable deployed.' Dante knelt down behind the harpoon rifle and assumed the firing position. Peering through the telescopic sight, he scanned the rooftop of the palace. *There.* 'I've got a high stone wall above a doorway. No movement nearby — there don't seem to be any guards on the roof.' He gripped a lever on the clamp and pulled it down, locking the rifle into position with a loud click.

Quinn snorted. 'Why would they? Only an idiot would try to break in via the roof.'

No surprise that these Seryn agents are more about the mental than the physical. Dante took a deep breath, released it, and slid his finger over the rifle trigger.

Shhhuunk. The ultra-light, ultra-strong cable shot out of the rifle behind the thumb-sized harpoon and covered the hundred metres in less than a second.

Dante kept his eye pressed to the scope until he'd confirmed the harpoon had solidly embedded itself in the target wall, then stood. 'We're set. You first.'

Quinn spread his arms. 'Why me?'

Dante paused for a moment. 'Would you rather go second?'

That shut him up. It took Quinn thirty seconds of overly cautious wriggling until he had perched atop the wall next to the clamp, his hands securely gripping the pulley, and ready to go.

Dante patted him on the shoulder. 'Good. Now just swing your legs over, and let gravity do the rest.'

Quinn's voice was low and unenthused. 'It's gravity I'm worried about.' But he conquered his fear before Dante could say another word, throwing his legs sideways and off the wall with an ungainly jerk that set his body swinging wildly side-to-side as he accelerated across the chasm.

Attaboy. Dante waited until his partner had safely touched down on the other side, then took his own pulley from the bag and smoothly attached it to the cable. With a smile, he launched himself forward.

* * *

That was unpleasant. Quinn stood leaning over, hands gripping his knees, and gulped down deep breaths. A gradually loudening buzz announced Dante's approach, shortly followed by the click-thump of him smoothly detaching his pulley and dropping to his feet on the rooftop.

Quinn turned to him. 'You didn't tell me I was supposed to do that.'

His partner winced. 'Yeah, sorry about that. It slipped my mind, and then I saw you, kind of…'

'Hit the wall.'

'Hit the wall, yeah.' Dante nodded. 'You look okay, though. A bit pale, maybe.'

Dick. I'll get you back for that. Quinn stood, slightly less nauseated. 'Let's get inside; we don't have all night.' He slipped his hand into the pack at his belt and pulled out a small package he'd brought, which he unwrapped to reveal a soft putty-like ball that he held up to his partner.

Dante grinned. 'Thermite, nice. I brought a few nitroglycerin patches too, but we can do it the old-fashioned way.'

The door into the palace was a solid slab of metal, likely steel. The lock was large and imposing, but mechanical. If it had been an electronic lock, with the typical multi-deadbolt mechanism, getting in would have been harder.

Quinn went to work. He rolled the thermite into the shape of a fat worm and carefully kneaded it into place all around the edge of the lock. Once it was in place, he reached into his pouch once more and pulled out a small pipette.

'Glycerol?' Dante asked.

'That's the one. You should step back a bit; it's going to get hot pretty quickly.' As Quinn reached out and squeezed a few drops of the chemical onto the thermite-permanganate putty, he heard Dante shuffle back a few feet—then he himself turned and scuttled several yards away from the door.

It didn't take long for the reaction to start: wisps of smoke appeared, quickly followed by the first sparks. Seconds later, the whole area flared into light, blazing fiercely for ten seconds or so with a heat that Quinn could feel even from his safe distance.

Then it was over.

What once was lock, now is hole. He turned to Dante and waved toward the door. 'After you. Let's find a way down to that prison level.'

Three short flights of stairs brought them to another door, that one happily unlocked. Dante edged it slightly open and listened for a few seconds, before peering out at the corridor beyond. He ducked back into the stairwell. 'All clear.'

I could have told you that. Might as well share, I suppose. As they began walking down the corridor, Quinn spoke quietly. 'It occurs to me I've never told you about my particular... skill set.'

Dante glanced at him. 'No, you haven't.'

'It doesn't really have a name. It's not telekinesis, or telepathy, or teleportation—'

That got a sharp look from Dante. 'You have people who can teleport?'

'Just other objects. Not themselves. That'd be ridiculous,' Quinn admitted, then continued, 'No, my ability is basically a... sensitivity, to mental activity.'

'Which means what, exactly?'

Quinn smiled. 'It means I know there isn't anyone within a hundred feet of us in any direction, for a start. So there's no need to spend ages peering around doorways.'

Dante emitted a low whistle. 'That's pretty nifty. We could use you in the DSO.'

Quinn snorted. 'Thanks, but I have a job.'

'What else can you do? You said "for a start."'

'Oh.' Quinn ran his hand through his hair as they turned a corner and started down another short flight of stairs. 'You've seen that one in action.'

Dante stopped. 'You're telling me you can do that on purpose? Knock people out?'

'Not to that extent, no; I can't normally shut down a whole room full of people like that. But I can send three or four at a time to sleep, sure. Leave them out cold for half an hour, or an hour.'

His partner nodded. 'And what can you do to just one person on his own?'

Quinn turned to Dante, who looked him in the eye. *Not many folks would think to ask that.* He nodded. 'I can put him down for good.'

Dante looked away, his expression carefully blank. 'Let's hope it doesn't come to that.'

They turned another corner and stepped through a doorway, into a corridor that looked as though it stretched the whole length of the palace. A dark red carpet lined the floor as far as Quinn could see, and signs dotted along the walls and hanging from the ceiling at regular intervals.

Dante pointed them out. 'Good. That means we must be on one of the upper administration levels, below the apartments. If we're lucky, one of them will point us in the direction of an elevator to take us down.'

Quinn turned to his partner. 'And do you know what the Karaki word for *elevator* is?'

Dante rolled his eyes. 'Not yet, no—but give me a second.' He pulled a small terminal from his trouser pocket and spoke into it. 'Visual translation, Standard to Karaki. Word: *elevator*.'

Two seconds later, the translation appeared on the screen: *Asansör*.

'Nifty,' Quinn said. They started down the silent and empty corridor, looking up at the signs. Fifty feet later, they struck it lucky. Quinn pointed up at the sign ahead of them. 'There. *Asansörs*.'

It was a five-minute walk to reach the elevator. Three times *en route*, Quinn sensed people approaching, and they slipped into the nearest empty room to avoid detection. They made it to the elevator without incident and stepped inside.

Dante pushed the button for the lowest floor. 'I very much doubt this is going to come out in the prison itself. We'll probably need to switch to another one, or take the stairs.'

The elevator accelerated downwards, and Quinn was only half listening.

Dante frowned. 'Did you hear me?'

'I heard you, but I'm also sensing someone almost directly below us. Just in front, as if—'

'They're standing outside the elevator door.' Dante reached into the holster under his left arm and pulled out a chunky sidearm.

Quinn raised his eyebrows. 'A gun? Really? I think we can do better than that.' He turned to face the door and waited for the lift to come to a stop.

Ding.

The doors slid open, and Quinn glimpsed a young, surprised face before he focused a concentrated burst of power into the man's mind. The guard—*unless their admin staff wear fatigues and carry weapons, as well*—slumped to the ground. Dante stepped past Quinn and tugged the insensate man into the elevator, then looked at Quinn with a smile. 'That's nifty, too. When it's not happening to you, that is.'

They stepped out of the elevator into an empty hallway.

On the adjacent wall was a staircase, leading down. Quinn frowned, pointing it out to Dante. 'Huh. That was... surprisingly easy.'

Dante groaned as they started towards the stairs that would hopefully take them down to the prison. 'Oh, do I wish you hadn't said that.'

* * *

The stairs were cut from the same grey flagstone blocks as the palace itself, and they spiralled downwards for far longer than Dante had expected. *Two storeys, at least. They built this prison deep.* Finally the staircase ended at a door, which Quinn opened without hesitating. *No one's nearby, then.* They stepped through.

To the right was another unmarked door. Quinn gave the handle an experimental twist, then shook his head. To their left and into the distance ran a corridor, as long as the one they had travelled at the top of the palace. *Almost identical. Just replace the plush red carpet with bare, damp stone, and the helpful signs with flickering halogen striplights.*

Quinn nodded towards the corridor, and they started down it. He spoke in a low voice. 'I'm assuming you know what the soldier and his girl look like? This is going to take a lot longer if we have to ask people's names.'

Dante pulled out his pocket terminal and tapped a few times, then held it up to Quinn. Two images appeared on the screen, side by side. Kane's latest Peacetrooper mugshot was on the left, him unsmiling with a close-cropped military haircut. On the right was Jordaan, smiling in the sunlight in a photo she had sent to some friends on Nexus Prime.

Quinn peered at the photos, then nodded. 'Pretty girl. Fella looks kind of serious, though.'

Dante snorted. 'Not a military man, are you?'

That drew a smile from his partner. 'What would we need a military for?'

They started down the corridor. Based on the doors at regular intervals, with signage suggesting names and titles, this area seemed to be for administration and staff. They arrived at the door of what looked like a guard post. Dante peered through the small window in the door to see three men sitting around a table, playing a game that involved dice, plastic discs of various colours, and cash. He stepped back and held up three fingers, then realised Quinn doubtless already knew their number.

Quinn nodded, smiling ever-so-slightly, and took the position at the window. For a few seconds he was still, then he nodded. 'They're out for the next thirty minutes. Hopefully that's enough time.'

'There's likely another sentry on patrol,' said Dante. 'Keep your... mind peeled, I guess.'

Quinn laughed. 'Haven't heard that one before. Like it.'

The next door along from the guard post was windowless, with a serious-looking electronic lock below the handle. A small sign at eye level read *Müdür*. Dante snapped an image with his terminal and activated the translation.

Quinn peered over his shoulder. '*Warden*. Bingo. Have you got anything in your bag of tricks for that lock?'

But of course. It took Dante less than ten seconds to attach and prime the magnetic lock scrambler he'd pulled from his pack. Another five, and the scrambler announced its success with a quiet beep—the *thunk* of the retracting bolts confirmed the door was unlocked. Dante turned to Quinn and grinned. 'A little more subtle than thermite.'

Quinn rolled his eyes. 'Come on. Let's find out if our missing lovebirds are anywhere in this dump.' He stepped past Dante and slipped into the warden's office.

Another happy occurrence greeted them; the warden, presumably comfortable with the security afforded by the lock on his office door and the sentries just down the hall, had neglected to shut down the terminal on his desk before leaving for the day. Quinn leaned over the station and began tapping into the old-fashioned mechanical keyboard. He called out without looking up. 'Whoever coded their system did it in Standard, thankfully. I wouldn't fancy doing this in Karaki, no matter how good that little gadget of yours is.'

Dante stepped up and peered over Quinn's shoulder as he navigated to the inmate records database. 'Filter by arrival date: Jordaan's been missing for twenty-two days, so we can ignore any entries before that.'

Quinn's fingertips flew over the keyboard. The terminal chugged for a few seconds, then the records appeared. There were only three. 'Two men, both in their fifties, one booked in for assault, one for public drunkenness. Neither a good match for our missing trooper,' said Quinn.

Dante skimmed the details of the third. 'Female, name not given, twenty-nine years old—estimated—and arrived here... twenty-two days ago.'

'Block M, cell seventeen,' finished Quinn, straightening from the desk. 'Sounds like our girl.'

Dante nodded. 'Let's hope so—and that she knows what happened to Kane.'

As they were leaving the office, Quinn paused to look at a narrow rack hanging on the wall next to the door. 'Wait a minute. These look like keycards.' He riffled through them. 'They're marked with letters. Skeleton keycards for the blocks, maybe?'

'Is there an M?' Dante asked.

Quinn extracted and flourished a card emblazoned with that letter. 'That there is. Let's see if we've got lucky.'

They left the office and continued down the corridor. After ten metres, the cells began; long corridors bisected their path, spanning the width of the jail, each lined with two rows of facing cell doors. Dante and Quinn crossed twelve such corridors, the corresponding block designation carved into the floor at each crossroads, before reaching block M.

Dante led the way past eight pairs of cells, odd numbers on the left, even on the right, then stopped before cell seventeen. *Now where have they put...* 'There.' He pointed at a narrow slot at waist level on the right-hand side of the cell door.

'Got it.' Quinn squeezed past and slipped the card into the lock. Nothing happened. He turned to Dante. 'Shit. Well, that's that plan down the drain. What's the fallback?'

Dante looked at him for a few seconds in silence. *You're kidding me.* 'Trying the card the other way around.'

Quinn frowned, then brightened. 'Ha. Good idea.' He reversed the card and slipped it back into the slot. They were reward with another *thunk*, and the cell door swung open.

The flickering halogen lights in the corridor did little to illuminate the unlit cell, but Dante could just make out a form sitting on a cot against the rear wall. Slight movement suggested a head rising to peer out.

'Sara Jordaan?' Quinn asked, pushing the door open further. More light stole in, and Dante could just make out the features of the woman on the bed. Thinner and paler than in the image he'd shown Quinn, but she was recognisably the archaeologist.

The voice that came to them out of the darkness was hoarse from lack of water, but her words suggested she hadn't lost her spirit:

'With skin like that, I'm going to go ahead and guess you're not Karaki.'

* * *

Tasha waited until the last of the three garbage trucks was directly beneath her, then dropped from the window ledge of the office building she'd broken into after it emptied out at sunset an hour before. It was a fall of only ten feet or so, onto a layer of—thankfully dry—garbage. She threw herself flat, below the level of the walls around the flatbed, and concentrated on the turns the truck made.

She'd seen the three trucks run the same route the night before; their next stop after the junction where Tasha had waited was the palace compound. There would be plenty of garbage to pick up every night from all of the soldiers barracked in the grounds. *Not so much tonight, with most of them away, but hopefully they haven't changed the schedule.*

They hadn't.

Left, left again, right. Tasha visualised the turns; they should be on the broader avenue, which ran past the small gate in the compound's west wall. She waited for the truck to slow… *There. Now wait for the gate to open…* She heard the low rumble of metal wheels that could only be the gate sliding open.

The truck started up again, slower than before, and pulled left.

And into the compound. Slowly and carefully, Tasha raised her head above the edge of the flatbed. She had dressed in her complete stealth ensemble, with only her eyes visible through the small gap in the charcoal-coloured hooded mask. She spotted two sentries at the gate they were pulling away from, then swivelled to see one more standing at the corner of the main palace building a hundred feet away. He looked in her direction for a few moments, then hoisted his rifle and strolled away around the corner.

Now. Tasha climbed over the back edge of the still moving truck and dropped to the ground. Turning as she landed, she stayed close in the wake of the garbage convoy as it rolled up to a pair of double doors in the palace wall. The scents wafting through a nearby open window told Tasha that these doors led to the kitchens. She slid over to the wall and rose to peer through the window.

It was the kitchen, all right. Three long islands stood between her and the far wall, where two porters were grabbing garbage cans and dragging them over to the double doors to be collected. They were the only people in sight. *It seems preparation for the evening meal hasn't started yet. Lucky.*

Tasha waited until both men were in the doorway, then

smoothly pulled herself up onto the window ledge and inside. She landed noiselessly on the white tiled floor and moved quickly, staying low behind the nearest island as she crossed the kitchen to a doorway she hoped would lead into the main body of the palace, and to Venus's apartments.

It took thirty-five more minutes of slow, careful movement, breathless waiting, and an occasional crouching run, for Tasha to climb the three floors and cross to the rear of the palace where she'd seen Venus and her associate the day before. She'd avoided contact with the servants, guards, and late-working government staff who had crossed her path, but her luck ran out when she found the sentry stationed outside Venus's rooms.

Or his luck has run out, rather.

He was seated, which made her job easier. Hidden in the shadows of a recess twenty feet down the corridor, Tasha extracted a slim metal pipe from the pouch at her belt. Putting it to her lips, she held her breath for a few seconds, then blew sharply.

The guard slapped at his neck, then looked at his hand for a dead biting insect that wasn't there. It only took thirty seconds for him to start to nod, his head dropping to his chest as the tranquiliser took effect. The drug would keep him a man his size unconscious for fifteen to twenty minutes, depending on how much he'd eaten recently. *That should be plenty of time.*

Tasha waited until she heard the sentry's snores, then edged out of her hiding place and padded forward to the apartment doors. After borrowing the keycard poking out of the man's breast pocket, she deactivated the lock and slipped inside.

Wow. She stepped into the most opulent room she'd ever seen. Fur rugs lined the floor, gold leaf the walls, and a sofa the length of the entire living room at her mama's house in Thrace sat opposite a wafer-thin screen that was just as wide. It was obvious, and garish, but Tasha couldn't help but feel slightly jealous. *Perhaps I'll take something small on my way out.*

Less than a minute of searching located the bedroom, which was slightly more tasteful in its furnishings. *But still looks like the inside of a brothel, as Mama would say.* Tasha walked to the bed and stroked the silk coverlet with a brief sigh before dropping to the floor and wriggling under.

She flipped onto her back, her nose inches from the underside of the bed frame. Working by feel, she pulled another device from her pouch. This was a small plasmetal disk, small enough to fit in the palm of her hand. *And contains enough explosives to blow parts of this bed through that beautiful screen in the next room.*

The mine was weight-activated, set to go off under a set amount of pressure. Tasha had programmed it to blow at just under what she estimated to be Venus's minimum weight. She didn't want it going off early if, say, one of the servants dropped a bag on the bed.

With a thin layer of adhesive gel from a small tube she'd pulled from her surprisingly capacious pouch, Tasha stuck the mine to the bed frame. Taking a deep breath—one couldn't be too careful with explosives—she gently pressed the button in the centre of the mine.

A green light came on, and Tasha exhaled. *This is my gift to you, Venus. I hope you have time to enjoy it.*

She carefully rolled out from beneath the bed, and she headed to the apartment door to begin the long return journey out of the palace. A gleam caught her eye; a slim, white-gold bracelet, studded with a row of tiny sapphires.

Tasha paused, then reached out and picked it up. She slipped it into her pouch, smiling behind her mask.

Just something small.

8. Exfiltration

Quinn sighed. *I really should get a bit of a tan. She's been imprisoned for twenty-odd days and even she's making cracks.* 'I'm not Karaki, no. Well spotted.' He gestured at Dante. 'Neither is my associate here. My name's Quinn.'

'And I'm Dante. We're going to get you out of here—and your fiancé, if you know his whereabouts.'

Sara slowly stood from the bed, her movements stiff. She shook her head as she walked towards them. 'I don't know his whereabouts, but I don't think you're going to find him.'

Quinn studied the woman's face as she stepped into the light. Her face held no expression, her gaze cold and hard. *Blank. Like she's shut down, repressing everything. Oh, no...*

Dante began to ask the question Quinn already knew the answer to. 'Is he—'

'Dead.' Sara finished. 'I overheard a conversation between two of the guards four... five, days ago? I've lost track of the time. Either they didn't know I speak Karaki, or they didn't care. Apparently Jalen attempted to rescue me, but—' She closed her eyes, swallowed hard. 'They stopped him.'

She's going to crack at some point soon. We need to get her out of here. Quinn turned to Dante and gave him what he hoped was a meaningful glare.

His partner nodded. 'I'm very sorry for your loss, Ms. Jordaan. But we need to get moving now; we've a limited window of opportunity to exfiltrate.' Dante's tone was brisk, businesslike—harsh, even, which was probably the right approach.

But who says 'exfiltrate'? Quinn turned back to Sara.

She had stiffened at Dante's words, but she nodded. 'Okay.' She even managed a weak smile. 'I don't have anything to pack, so I'm ready to go now.'

Dante waved her forward as he turned to leave, and Sara stepped past Quinn to fall in behind the operative. Quinn swung the cell door closed behind them, and the lock reengaged with a *thunk*.

He caught up to the other two as Dante explained how they were going to make their escape. ' —reverse of how we came in. Up to the roof, then propel across a zip-line to the apartment building across the street.'

Sara didn't sound enthusiastic. 'Propel? What does that mean?'

Dante patted his backpack. 'We attach a gas canister to the pulley, and then open a valve. The gas fires out, and the pulley shoots off up the zip-line, taking the rider with it.'

'Great.' Sara sounded even less thrilled. 'Fantastic.'

Quinn gently patted her shoulder. 'Don't worry. It's perfectly safe.' He offered her a smile. 'Dante's done this hundreds of times.'

They turned the corner into the main corridor and headed for the stairs.

Hundreds of times. Perfectly safe. Sure.

* * *

Let's hope the path is as clear on the way back up. Dante turned to Quinn and waved him forward. 'You take point, same as before.'

His partner nodded and slipped past to take the lead. The trio walked quickly but quietly back along the corridor. Quinn nodded in the direction of the guard post as they passed. 'They're still unconscious.'

Sara touched Dante's arm. 'What did you do to them?'

'That's... not an easy question to answer,' he replied. 'But don't worry about it. They're unharmed... Not that I would expect you to be bothered, if I'm honest.'

She shrugged slightly. 'I don't know. Who exactly killed Jalen, or why, or... anything. It's all unreal. I feel like if I think about it too much I might—' She shook her head. 'I just don't know what's happening.'

They didn't speak further as Quinn led them up the staircase to the ground floor and back to the elevator. The unconscious guard was where Dante had left him, propped up against the wall. Sara started slightly as she saw the body, then entered the elevator.

'He's alive, too,' Dante said. She smiled weakly, looking pale in the brightly lit elevator. *Looks like a delayed reaction to the stress. We need to get out before she has a breakdown.*

The ride up passed in silence, and they exited on the same floor they had traversed on the inbound journey.

Quinn spoke over his shoulder as he hurried them along. 'There was a lot of movement on the ground floor just as we got in the elevator. Could be a shift change, or the evening meal. Doesn't seem to be much activity up here yet.'

We might just get away with this. Sara moved a little sluggishly, Dante noticed; he touched the small of her back and nudged her forward gently. She mumbled a 'sorry' and picked up her pace.

They covered the length of the corridor at a fast walk, their footsteps muffled by the plush carpet. Dante could see the doorway at the end of the hall that led to the roof access stairs, and was about to point it out when Quinn raised his fist and came to a sudden halt.

'Movement, on the left—just one body. Below us, but climbing. There must be a service staircase of some kind that runs up this side of the building.'

Dante quickly stepped over to the nearest doorway on the left and tried the handle. *Locked. Damn it.* 'Sara, get behind me, as close to the wall as possible and crouch down. Now.'

She complied, fear writ large on her face in her wide eyes and deathly pallor. *Keep it together, please. Just for a few more minutes.* Dante took a deep breath and pulled out his sidearm, training it in along the left wall and ready to drop any hostile that appeared.

Ahead and to his right, Quinn stood, relaxed and motionless; his head was cocked at a slight angle, as if he were listening hard.

Gaze and concentration fixed on the far end of the corridor, Dante just made out Quinn's words as he muttered to himself. 'Why… why are you moving so slowly? If you were a guard…'

Half a minute more passed before Quinn straightened sharply. A second later, a head appeared, wrapped in black, peering out from the furthest doorway—and freezing as it caught sight of them. Five seconds passed. No one moved. Five more seconds. *Who is this?* Dante could feel his heart thumping in his chest as he slid his finger to the trigger of his weapon.

Quinn lifted a hand and waved.

'I hope he knows what he's doing,' Dante muttered.

It seemed to work—the body below the head appeared as the figure stepped through the doorway, tense as if ready to spring back at any moment. It was a woman, Dante realised, short and slim, and dressed for stealth.

Pitching his voice low and quiet, he called out to Quinn. 'Something tells me she isn't supposed to be here either.'

'I'd got that impression myself, aye.' Holding both hands up, palms open, Quinn slowly walked towards the stranger.

As he approached, she reached up to her neck and pushed back the mask that had covered her face. Huge brown eyes shone out of a dusky-skinned face. *Looks like a local.* Dante watched, weapon still raised, as Quinn and the stranger exchanged a few quiet words for half a minute that seemed an eternity to Dante.

Finally Quinn turned back. 'We've agreed not to kill each other, which is a good start. And we've agreed that we should have this conversation upstairs.' He waved them forward.

Dante holstered his sidearm and slipped his other hand under Sara's arm, helping her to her feet.

The archaeologist had settled a little. 'She's not one of the bad guys, then?'

'Not for us, no.' They started forward after Quinn. 'But I have a feeling the Ruhim might disagree.'

* * *

Tasha left her mask pulled back as she led the way up the access staircase to the rooftop. Her mind buzzed with a hundred questions. *Foreigners. Speaking Standard with strange accents. From the Core worlds? The Commonwealth, probably. Why are they here?*

She'd immediately recognised the red-headed pale one as the man from the street next to the palace. *Somehow I knew we would meet sooner or later.* Tasha glanced surreptitiously at him. He looked capable. Unafraid. *Why would he stand in plain sight, unarmed? What is he hiding?* The other man had looked equally tough as he held his weapon trained on her position. He hadn't moved an inch.

But the woman... She clearly wasn't the same as the men. Foreign, but not so tough. They had made her crouch down, to protect her from danger. *Who is she?* Tasha frowned as she rounded the corner and started up the second flight of stairs. *Complications.*

A minute later all four of them were on the roof. Both moons were out, and it was a clear, cloudless night with plenty of light to see by. The dark-haired man, his weapon now holstered, swung the access door closed.

Tasha noticed the hole burnt through the lock and nodded. *Capable.*

The red-headed one spoke first. 'So. Who's going to start?' He flashed her a smile, which faded as Tasha maintained her silence and kept her expression blank. 'Okay, well—there are more of us than you, so we'll go first. My partner and I'—he gestured at the dark-haired man—'are here to retrieve our new friend here.' He pointed to the woman. 'She was being held in the prison down below.'

'Why were they holding you?' Tasha asked the woman.

'Hmm?' She didn't look fully coherent. 'Oh. I'm a—an archaeologist. My team were doing some work, over…' She waved vaguely to the northeast. 'We were trespassing, they said. My team quit, but I went back to the site. Twice. The second time the army caught me, they brought me here.'

Tasha nodded. 'What was the site?'

'Nothing special—some ruined foundations, some potsherds, the usual things. It was in the middle of a large mining outpost; that was the only unusual element.'

Tasha turned back to the redhead. 'And what is she to you?'

But the other man answered, 'She's a Commonwealth citizen.' He said it in a way that suggested that was reason enough to break into a heavily guarded compound.

Tasha nodded slowly. 'You take good care of your citizens, then.'

That earned her a slight smile. 'We do our best.'

'What about you?' asked the redhead. 'What's your reason for creeping around the palace in the night? I hate to tell you this, but if you were rescuing someone too, then you've left them somewhere.'

She had to smile. 'No. No rescue.'

The dark-haired one cocked his head. 'So…?'

Tasha thought quickly. *These are no friends of the Ruhim, it seems. There is probably no harm.* 'I left a gift for the witch. A deadly one.'

'Venus?' The redhead's eyebrows shot up. He looked impressed.

Tasha nodded. 'When she returns after the current battle in

her needless war, she will die. And Karak will be free again.'

There was silence for a few seconds, then the dark-haired man started chuckling.

Tasha glowered at him. 'Do you think I am joking?'

He raised his hands in a placatory gesture. 'No, not at all. I don't know you, but I can believe you're capable of such a thing. It's just—' He turned to the redhead. 'That would save us the trouble of doing it ourselves.'

Themselves? 'You? Why would foreigners care about what happens on Karak?'

The redhead coughed. 'No offence, but—well, we don't. It's Venus we care about. And I'm pretty sure we know a lot more about her than you do. Let's just say there's a good reason why she needs to be stopped, and if what you've done tonight makes that happen... great.' He smiled—somewhat wistfully, Tasha thought.

The dark-haired man started pulling items from his backpack. Two looked like pulleys of some kind, the other four were cylinders that Tasha couldn't identify. The redhead turned to Tasha with a frown. 'I just realised we haven't introduced ourselves. I'm Quinn, that's Dante and Sara.'

'Tasha.' She pointed at the cylinders. 'What are they?'

The dark-haired one—*Dante, such a strange name*—picked one up, along with the second pulley. 'Canisters of highly compressed gas. Fires the pulley and the rider up the cable.' He attached it to the pulley with a click, then reached up and hung it over a dark cable that Tasha hadn't noticed until then. It disappeared into the night, but it was presumably attached to a building across the street.

Dante continued, 'You first, Quinn, then Sara, then...' He turned to Tasha. 'I was going to say Tasha, but I suppose you have your own plan for getting off this roof?'

She reached into her own pouch and pulled out her prize possession: a crossbow with a small grappling hook on a line attached to a motorised winch. She held it up to Dante, who seemed to understand immediately.

He grinned. 'Very nice. So...' He turned to look out across over the compound to the street beyond. 'Fire at one of those rooftops, jump off, and winch yourself in just enough to clear the compound wall?'

Tasha smiled. 'That was the plan. But if you wouldn't mind... You seem to have a spare canister.'

Dante's smile faded. Quinn coughed and turned away. *What did I say?* 'We do. You're welcome to it. Come on, Quinn. Let's get moving.'

The redhead sighed and reached up to grip the pulley. 'This is going to be even worse than the way down. I can tell.'

Dante patted him on the back. 'The canister trigger's by your left thumb. Just remember to dial it back before you hit the wall, yeah? And to send the pulley back down.'

'Dick.' Quinn took a deep breath, puffed it out—and flicked the trigger. He yelped as he shot forward and off the roof. Tasha watched him speed across the chasm, and could just still make him out as he reached the roof of an apartment block.

The woman, Sara, stepped forward. 'This is a little bit surreal.'

Dante smiled. 'Don't worry. It'll be fine.' The pulley reappeared a few seconds later. Dante detached the spent canister and attached a fresh one, and soon enough Sara shot across the void to join Quinn.

Dante turned to her. 'Ready?'

'Of course. This is easy compared to what I was going to do.'

That drew a laugh from him. 'You're not wrong. I'd like a look at that grappling crossbow of yours, later. If you don't mind.'

She nodded. 'Of course.' *Professionals. We are not so different in some ways, I think.* A faint thrum announced the pulley's return. Tasha smiled.

My turn.

* * *

Once they had all crossed the gap, the going was easy. Quinn had fully recovered from the exhilarating terror of the reverse zip-line by the time Dante landed and set about disassembling the harpoon rifle mount.

Quinn also had an idea. 'Tasha, can we borrow your hood? For Sara, that is. We don't want to take any chances when we're moving through the streets.'

The Karaki didn't look immediately convinced. 'That... would be fine, I think. I will need it back, though.'

'Oh, of course.' Another idea struck Quinn. *I'm on a roll.* 'I'm going to go out on a limb here and guess that you're not from Parkum. Do you have anywhere to stay?'

'I'll find somewhere safe. It's easy to hide in a city.'

Quinn held up his hands. 'Oh, I've no doubt. But I was thinking, why don't you stay with us for a day or two instead? And if your plan doesn't quite work out when Venus returns... maybe we could pool our resources.'

Tasha frowned. 'Pool our... Sorry, my Standard isn't perfect.'

She understands 'out on a limb,' but not that. Baffling. 'Team up. Join forces. Three being better than two, or one.'

Quinn sensed he might have slightly offended the young woman by suggesting her plan might not work flawlessly, but he was happy to see her nod after a few moments. 'It makes sense. I agree. But I must warn you,' —she looked from Quinn to Dante and back—'if either of you betray me, I will kill you.'

Dante snorted. 'Seems reasonable.'

With a sharp nod, Tasha slipped off her hood and handed it to Sara, who inspected it briefly before pulling it on and turning to Quinn. 'Does it suit me? I'm not sure it goes with what I'm wearing.'

Quinn smiled. *She's going to be all right, this one.* 'It's perfect. Everyone's wearing a hood with stained prison-wear this season.' He was delighted to see her smile in response, then coughed and looked away. *Easy, tiger. Odette wouldn't appreciate my flirting, and Sara's got enough to worry about.*

Dante had finished disassembling the harpoon rifle and stuffing the parts into his backpack. He slipped it onto his shoulders and turned to them. 'Are we ready? Back to mine, I assume. It's a little bigger than yours, Quinn.'

Show-off. 'Fine. Let's just make sure we don't attract any attention.'

They slipped out of the apartment block without incident, and the thirty-minute walk to Dante's hotel was largely drama-free. Twice they saw army patrols coming towards them on the street, but both times they had enough notice to allow them to switch routes and avoid risking conflict.

The ancient-looking lady on reception at the hotel—*She looks almost as old as the fella at my place*—didn't blink as her tenant arrived with three companions in tow. *Two guys and two girls? Must look pretty dodgy, but she's probably seen it all by now. Twice.*

They crowded into the hotel room. Dante gently guided Sara to the bed, and the archaeologist slipped between the sheets. She fell asleep almost immediately, snoring gently as Quinn and Tasha took the chairs in the room. Dante leaned against the wall by the window, occasionally peering through the blinds at the street, but without much dedication. He knew as well as Quinn that if they'd been followed, they wouldn't have gotten this far.

After a minute, Dante gave up completely and sat on the floor leaned against the wall. 'There are some extra blankets under the bed. Pillows, too. It won't be the most comfortable night you've ever had, but it shouldn't be the worst.'

Quinn turned to Tasha. 'So, did you prepare any backup plans in case your first attempt on Venus doesn't cut it?'

'Not really. I mean, I can always just shoot her from a distance, but it doesn't send the same message.' The young woman blinked, seemingly unbothered by the dispassionate ruthlessness she'd just expressed.

Jeez. She is... cold. At, what—seventeen? Eighteen? They start them young here.

Dante sounded tired. 'We'll think of something if Tasha's plan doesn't come off. There's plenty of time, and there are three of us now. Between us we should be able to think of something.'

'Do you want to set a watch?' Quinn asked.

Dante snorted. 'Hardly. The lady at the front desk is a

dragon in disguise. I don't see her letting anyone past. She's probably got a scattergun stashed under that desk.'

'All right.' Quinn sighed. *Not much to do but wait, and sleep, and see what tomorrow brings. So...* 'Have you got any whisky?'

Dante brightened, looking more awake all of a sudden.

We make a good team.

9. Adjustment

A day and a half passed before the Ruhim army returned to Parkum.

Dante had spent the first day at the hotel, communicating with various contacts to arrange passage for Sara offworld. The archaeologist herself had only slept, waking just for a few minutes in the middle of the day to eat something before passing out again. Dante had seen the like before, in both soldiers in the Corps and operatives—a delayed reaction to shock or trauma, resulting in the body just shutting itself down for a while. *She can sleep for a day; it'll be good for her. But tomorrow she needs to get off this rock.*

While Dante worked his subspace wave communicator, Quinn and Tasha had taken turns venturing out into the streets for a short time to ask the locals if their soldiers had rolled back into town. Quinn returned from his final excursion at sunset, just as Dante had finished arranging the last few details of Sara's departure plan. Quinn had just shaken his head and poured himself a drink.

The second day had dawned cool and misty. 'There's a storm coming,' Tasha had said, looking none too happy at the prospect.

'You have rain here?' Dante quipped.

'Sometimes. Four, five times a year. When it rains, it rains heavily.' Tasha had nodded towards Sara, who dozed again on the bed. 'You should hope it is not so heavy that the ship coming for her cannot land. Twice in the last few years, the storms have shut down the spaceports. Flooded them.'

That had been three hours earlier, and sure enough, the mist had given way to dark grey thunderheads and torrential rain. Dante was back in the rental groundcar, speeding along the highway back to the spaceport. The road was covered by a five-centimetre depth of water, and the groundcar skidded a little every few minutes.

Sara was in the passenger seat, awake but quiet. She had a small bag packed with some basic travelling supplies that Tasha had bought from a local market. Dante glanced over. *Might as well try to bring her out of herself a bit.* 'So… the ship we're meeting is the *Jackrabbit*. It's run by a woman called Mags. She's a trader, freelance. Does some low-level jobs for us now and again.'

Sara just nodded slowly.

'She'll take you as far as Gonzaga—that's the nearest Commonwealth world—and put you on a liner that'll take you back to Nexus P. It may not be the fastest trip you've ever had—might take a week or ten days—but you'll get there.'

'Okay.' Her voice was quiet, her mind far away.

At least she said something.

Despite Tasha's warning and Dante's fear, there was no trouble at the spaceport in the end. They met Mags without incident; apparently the port controller had warned her about the rain, then finished with: 'Is your ship. You want to land, land. Don't crash.' *Sounds familiar. I wonder if he's moved from that stool.*

It was time to depart. Sara offered Dante a weak smile, and a few words of thanks, then slipped into the *Jackrabbit*'s cabin. Mags watched Sara enter, then turned to Dante. They were both drenched, and Mags's shaved scalp gleamed from the water. 'She's not the chattiest girl I've ever met.'

'Go easy on her,' Dante replied. 'She's had a rough time.'

'Yeah, you told me the sad story. Don't get me wrong—I'm glad of the work. Just would have been nice if the cargo was more talkative.' They shook hands. 'Right. I'm getting out of here before the rain starts messing with *Rabbit*'s electrics. See you, Zo.'

By the time Dante got back to the hotel, the rain had become a true storm. Thunder boomed every half-minute, accompanied by rippling flashes of sheet lightning along the now-black cloud banks. He opened the hotel room door to find Tasha pacing and Quinn slumped in a chair.

'Did she get away all right?' Quinn asked.

Dante nodded. 'What's the news?'

Tasha paused. 'The army has returned.'

'Okay. And…?'

Quinn sighed. 'Returned *without* its new leaders. Neither Venus nor Hesch came back.'

'Shit.' Dante plonked heavily down on the bed. 'They must have realised they're targets now. Retreated to somewhere more secure. Do we have any leads?'

'None.' Tasha looked furious. *Annoyed that Venus won't get her surprise.* 'We need to find them. Soon.'

Quinn stood and stretched, then clapped his hands. 'Let's make a plan, then. Play to our strengths.' He pointed at Dante. 'You and me, we stay here in Parkum. Keep pumping the natives for information on our friends' whereabouts, and failing that, try to think of a way to draw them out.'

Dante nodded. 'Fine. Tasha, you know Karak far better than we ever will. If you were trying to hide, where would you do it? And who would know, anyway?'

Tasha frowned, pacing again. 'In the desert. Outside the

towns, maybe a village. Or an old outpost. There are abandoned fortresses all over Karak—they could hide in any one of them.' She stopped, turned to Dante with a smile. 'But the nomads would always know. They use those outposts on their migration routes; a lot of them are built on natural springs and have room to shelter a herd of goats or llama.'

Quinn grinned. 'Now we're talking. So what do you think— can you find us a nomad?'

She nodded. 'Of course. I'll leave immediately for the Ghelt territory. Try to pick up their trail.'

'Good. And in the meantime...' Dante grimaced. 'I really should call my boss.'

* * *

Quinn watched Tasha head off up the street, the rain obscuring her before she'd gone thirty yards, then closed the hotel's front door. She had promised to call in when she had any information. *Something tells me she's going to get it.*

He returned to the room to find Dante tapping into his subspace wave communicator, which he had set up on a table by the window. The operative turned as Quinn entered and held up a finger to his lips. Quinn nodded and slipped into a chair. The call connected quickly, and a woman's voice filled the room.

'Zo, this is LeClerq. Good of you to call. How are you finding Karak?' She sounded mature, perhaps nearing middle age, with the assured tone of someone who wasn't new to command.

'Surprisingly rainy, Director,' Dante replied. 'How are things with you?'

The director chuckled dryly. 'As interesting as ever. The sooner you can wrap up your current business, the better. There are a few other items that could do with your expert attention— but I digress. Give me your status report.'

Dante paced slowly in front of the communicator. 'The headline is that this business is going to take longer than expected. The parameters of the situation have expanded.'

Quinn rolled his eyes. *Why do these folks insist on talking like that?*

'Oh? How so?' Quinn could imagine LeClerq's eyebrows raised in surprise.

It took less than two minutes for Dante to brief his boss. He described his meeting Quinn and their joining forces, the new political situation on Karak vis-à-vis Venus and Hesch, their rescue of Sara, and the revelation of Jalen Kane's demise.

That last drew a low curse from the director. 'The senator will be devastated. You're certain?'

Dante nodded to nobody. 'As sure as I can be. The alternative is that Jordaan's captors were misleading her, but I can't imagine a credible reason why they would bother.'

'Hmm.' LeClerq paused. 'No, I agree.' She sighed. 'Okay, carry on.'

Dante circled back to Venus and revealed what Quinn had told him, dispassionately laying out the threat that faced them.

There was silence for half a minute when he finished.

'That's... hard to believe.' The director sounded stunned. 'Even with what we've discovered during the past year, with the Seryn sharing information. This seems... unreal. Is he there with you? The Seryn, Quinn?'

Dante turned to him and gestured to the communicator. Quinn stood and walked over. 'He's here, Director.'

'Ah, good. Quinn: First, thank you for your assistance in the attempted rescue of Jalen Kane. It's much appreciated.'

Nice of her to say. 'You're welcome, Director. I'll be honest, my motives weren't completely pure. I'm banking on having Dante's help in return, with my Venus problem.'

'From what Zo has said, we all have a Venus problem.' LeClerq sighed. 'Assuming his briefing was accurate, which I do—how good is your intelligence here? Are we certain her capabilities are as fearsome as that?'

'I'm afraid so. My intelligence is...' Quinn paused. 'Well, it's first-hand. I've seen up close what she's capable of. And I've experienced the effects of the bloodsalt, myself. Put those two together, and it's exactly as bad as Dante described.'

'Fine.' A faint tapping came over the communicator. Quinn

could picture her drumming her fingernails on a desktop. 'Okay. Zo, you'll remain in place. I need to brief Senator Kane on her brother's death, and on the new situation. Let us hope the former doesn't overwhelm her ability to process the latter.'

'Understood,' Dante replied. 'When can I expect your contact?'

'I don't know exactly when, but as soon as possible. It might be within a few hours, definitely within a day. Can you patch your communicator through to your personal terminal, in case you're away when I call?'

Dante frowned. 'Hmm… probably. Karak's satgrid coverage is a little patchy, but it should be just about good enough. I'll do my best.'

'As always, Zo.' Some of the warmth had returned to her voice. Quinn smiled wryly as he turned away. *She got over the shock quickly.* 'I'll be in touch. LeClerq out.'

The call ended with a beep. Dante folded the communicator closed and slid it into a shock-resistant case, then shoved it to the back of one of the wall cupboards. He turned to Quinn. 'Right. Time for us to make a plan. There's no guarantee Tasha's going to find them, so we need a way to draw them out.'

Quinn nodded. 'Yep. You know, I always do my best planning after a couple of beers.'

Dante snorted. 'You and me both. Where shall we go?'

'There's this great little bar nearby called The Sickle Moon. Have you heard of it?' He grinned.

Grabbing a jacket, Dante shook his head. 'Anywhere else, I think. We can check, but I'm pretty sure you're not welcome there any more.'

* * *

'I've got to say, this is much more pleasant than the last place we went to.' Dante sipped his whisky and looked out over Parkum's skyline. It was late. The sun had gone down hours before, and he and Quinn were the last customers at Alta Vista, a tiny hilltop bar with a stunning view that explained the name of the place. Though the name wasn't in Karaki or Standard, which was odd.

I wonder where the owner's from, Dante mused.

Quinn hiccoughed. 'What place?'

'Hmm?' Dante murmured.

'Nicer than what place?' They were both quite drunk.

'Oh.' Dante frowned. 'The Sickle Moon. Place where you mind-blasted me and thirty locals into oblivion because you couldn't hold your condiments.' He snorted.

'Ahhhh.' Quinn nodded. 'Aye, it is nicer.' He slapped at his neck. 'Shame about the bloody insects.'

That's what you get for having skin that pale, brother. Biters can't resist. Dante was about to share that pearl of wisdom with his partner when a burbling chime interrupted his train of thought.

Quinn turned to him, took a drink, then composed himself. 'Whassat?'

Dante rummaged through the various pockets that lined his combat trousers. 'Personal terminal. Probably LeClerq.' He retrieved the slim, palm-sized device and pointed it at Quinn. 'You shut up. Let me talk.' He took a deep breath, then tapped the answer panel.

'Good evening, Zo.' LeClerq's voice came through crisp and clear in the night air. *Huh. It seems the satgrid's better than I thought.*

'Evening, Director.' Dante kept his voice steady. It wasn't the first time he'd been briefed while inebriated. 'You have news? I didn't expect your call until tomorrow. Experience suggests this is either a good thing or a very bad thing.'

LeClerq exhaled sharply. 'It's not a good thing, Zo. It's not a bloody good thing at all.' Her tone was tight and clipped. She was clearly furious. 'I briefed Kane on her brother, and the situation, as we discussed. She took the news well, which was a decent start, but after she got off the line with me she must have immediately called that bloody bastard boyfriend of hers.'

Dante frowned. 'I'm not following. Who's the—'

'Corralin,' LeClerq interrupted. 'The recently elected—crowned, whatever—Primarch of the Titan people and supreme bloody ruler of all he surveys. And despite being barely old enough to drink on a lot of planets, he's not afraid to throw his weight around. And by his weight, I mean a significant chunk of the Titan fleet. They're on their way to Karak, Zo. Right now.'

Dante felt a sudden chill ripple over his skin, and only half as drunk as he had been seconds earlier. He glanced at Quinn to see his partner's eyes were wide. 'What in the—what happened?'

He imagined LeClerq pacing her office, fists clenching. 'It's simple, Zo. Corralin quickly grasped the threat inherent to the situation on Karak, and decided that he wasn't comfortable leaving it in your capable hands. In order to prevent Venus's influence from spreading beyond the world, he's perfectly happy to wipe the entire planet clean.'

The chill spread to Dante's bones. 'You're talking about a purge.'

'Exactly. They'll leave nothing alive—it'll be Djinn-Ket all over again.' The Director sighed, sounding tired. 'The long and the short of it is you have six days to bring her in or take her down. Six days, from an hour ago. One minute more, and a Titan fast-response strike fleet lances every population centre from orbit. Then deploys shock troops to wipe out anyone and everyone who's left alive.'

Dante vaguely heard the clinking rattle of Quinn placing his glass on the table with a shaking hand. The background noise of the insects and local wildlife had fallen silent for a moment.

'Six days.' LeClerq's voice rang out, sad and desperate in the night.

* * *

Holy buggering shit on a stick. Quinn took a deep breath, then exhaled sharply. *Six days.*

'Here. Take this.' Dante held his palm out, offering a thin, paper-wrapped tablet.

Quinn raised his eyebrows. 'I don't think now's the time to be getting loaded, to be honest.'

Dante rolled his eyes. 'Ass. It's a sobermint. We need to sharpen up.'

Ah. Makes more sense. Quinn took the proffered stimulant and swallowed it down. He closed his eyes through the familiar falling-backward sensation as the chemicals screamed through his bloodstream, neutralising the alcohol, then winced as the faint semi-hangover headache kicked in. 'Well, that was a waste of four hours' perfectly good drinking.'

Dante stood and walked over to the wall lining the balcony. He leaned on it, staring into the night for a few moments, then shook his head. 'Fucking Titans,' he muttered.

Quinn got up and joined him. 'So. We need a plan, in case Tasha's game of hide-and-seek in the desert doesn't pan out.'

His partner nodded. 'A lure.'

Quinn glanced at him. 'Aye. And what does Venus want?'

'World domination, apparently. But I'm not sure how we'd gift-wrap that for her.' Dante smiled wryly.

Quinn snorted. 'Quite. But more practically... She wants bloodsalt.'

Dante turned to him. 'It's the whole reason she's here. So what would bring her out of hiding?'

Another insect nibbled Quinn's neck, and he slapped it away. He frowned. 'Who's next? On her list?'

'What do you mean?'

'Which tribe?' Quinn replied. 'She hasn't been conquering them in any order of size, or military power, I know that much. The Bobun, then the Mani, and now the Ghelt. Why that order?'

Dante pulled out his pocket terminal. 'Let's see what the ComCodex has to say.' He held up the palm-sized device. 'ComCodex lookup: Karak. Cross-reference: list tribal groups ordered by all relevant parameters.'

The terminal beeped in confirmation and went to work. Quinn cocked his head at Dante. 'How come you don't have one of those neural implant jobbies? The whole tablet in your pocket thing's pretty old-fashioned.'

'No, I do.' Dante tapped his left temple. 'One of the best. It just doesn't work on Karak. The satgrid net's not good enough. They're using technology my grandfather would have thought was old-fashioned.' He held up the pocket terminal and smiled. 'Good enough for this little guy, though.'

Another beep from the terminal signalled the search was over. Dante peered down at the device, flicking through screens with one finger. After a few moments he stopped. 'Ah.'

Quinn moved closer to look over his shoulder. 'What?'

'Look,' Dante pointed. 'Bobun, Mani, Ghelt. The only table they're one, two and three in.'

Should have guessed. 'Gross bloodsalt production.' Quinn nodded. 'Of course. And next on the list... the poor, unlucky Yalta.'

'Fine,' said Dante. 'So we can safely assume they're going to be the next target. But how do we make Venus move more quickly than she would otherwise? What's the bait?' He spoke into the terminal. 'Expand: Yalta. Key characteristics.'

Quinn watched the screen flicker, then settle. He scanned the text on screen; it didn't take long to spot the information they were looking for.

'There,' he and Dante said at exactly the same time. Quinn grinned.

Dante nodded. 'Quoma's Mouth. Deep in the heart of Yalta territory, and the biggest bloodsalt deposit on the planet. Ten per cent of the annual global bloodsalt output comes out of that mine.'

Quinn straightened, and, turning, reached for his drink. 'Perfect. Based on that, Venus wouldn't be pleased if someone were to, say —'

'Blow it up.' Dante smiled coldly.

'Aye.' Quinn nodded. 'She'd probably come running.'

10. Nomad

The storm had broken overnight, and as Tasha pulled the stolen sandspeeder up to a small farmstead, the early morning sun was burning away the last of the lingering clouds. It looked set to be a blazingly hot day.

The farm stood alone, near a village that sat atop a hill close to the edge of the Ghelt territory. Thirty miles in one direction was the border with the Ruhim; the Bobun-Ghelt border was forty miles in another. Tasha had headed for the village after bivouacking overnight in the desert, having decided a low-key incursion was called for. *Visiting the Ghelt capital will be a little too exciting for a while. Even for me.*

She killed the engine, and the speeder sank to the ground. Tasha had borrowed it from outside a noisy bar in Parkum's centre. It was a flashy thing, all chrome and unnecessary detail, so she'd assumed the owner was using it more for pleasure than work and so wouldn't miss it too badly. She'd return it when she got back. *Probably dirtier than it has ever been, but... some things can't be helped.*

As Tasha swung herself down from the speeder's driver's seat and pulled the goggles she'd found stashed in a compartment up onto her forehead, movement on the farm caught her eye. A man had emerged from the main building and started towards her, his gait — for the moment — suggesting more interest than alarm. Tasha gave him a wave to calm any hidden nervousness, and headed over to speak to him.

'That's a beautiful sandspeeder you have there, my dear.' He was old and wrinkled, and as bald as an egg, but straight-backed and wiry from a life of hard work. His grin showed a few gaps where teeth had once been. 'Which means you're either very interesting, or lost.'

Tasha smiled. 'I am not lost, *baba*, and I don't know how interesting I am, but either way, I am hoping you can help me.'

A trio of kid goats had wandered over and peered up at Tasha with their uncanny gaze. The farmer clicked his tongue at them, and they gambolled away happily enough. He turned back to Tasha. 'I will do my best, of course. What kind of help are you looking for? There is food, and water — even a spare bed if you are tired. But somehow I doubt your needs are so mundane.'

She shook her head. 'I am seeking news of the Ruhim.'

The old man's eyebrows rose, and he shook his head with a weary sigh. 'What news, exactly? How they invaded our lands, unprovoked? How it is told they have already occupied our capital, that Juba fell within two days and is held by a mere handful of Ruhim warriors?' He shook his head again and spat angrily to his side. 'Power-hungry animals, and our defenders were weak. Cowards. In my youth, we would not have fallen so easily.' His eyes blazed for a moment in his fury.

Tasha waited for the farmer's anger to subside before continuing, 'This is news I expected, *baba*, though I thank you for confirming it. But no — I am following a trail that leads from Juba, to I know not where. I am hoping that a nomad might be able to point the way.'

'A trail, eh?' The old man's gaze narrowed on her. 'Interesting, I thought; and interesting you are.' After a moment, he nodded slowly. 'There may be some who could help you. Not close, but not too far.' He pointed towards a line of low hills on the horizon. 'There is small oasis exactly due west of here. From there you will find a trail that leads towards the Domu hills in the distance. Follow that trail, and you should catch up to a pair of herders; they passed this way two days ago, but moving much slower than you. Three hundred head of goat with them.' He cackled. 'You can only go so fast with that many goats!'

Tasha smiled. 'Thank you, *baba*. That is exactly what I needed.'

The old man nodded and turned away with a wave. 'Luck to you, child. I hope you pick up your trail.'

She turned and headed back to the speeder. *Thank you, baba. If you knew what was at the end of it, you wouldn't just hope; you would pray.*

Tasha found the oasis within an hour. The trail was dotted with marker stones at quarter-mile intervals, the grey and red rocks sharply contrasting with the white-yellow sand of the desert. She kept a course fifty yards parallel to the right of the trail and let the sandspeeder eat up the miles.

It was almost midday, and the sun was high in the sky, when she spotted her quarry. At first it was just a line of brownish grey in the distance, but as she closed in, the blur resolved into a seething mass of trotting goats. Tasha gave the animals a wide berth so as to avoid spooking them, and steered the speeder around to stop a few hundred yards in front of the herd. She killed the engine, stepped off, and waited to be noticed.

The two men leading the animals didn't hurry, stop, or show even the slightest interest in her arrival.

Tasha believed that they would have ignored her and continued on past, the herd parting around her as if she were a rock in a stream, had she not called out, 'Good morning.'

The man on the left, fifteen yards away, glanced at her

briefly. The other looked up into the sky for a few moments, then at her. 'It's afternoon.'

Oy. Tasha smiled. 'My mistake, brother.'

The one who had spoken turned to his partner. 'I believe she wants us to stop, Omar.'

The man on the left sighed deeply. 'But we have such a fine rhythm today, Kali. Look how happy the goats are. Who is to say we can find this rhythm again?'

Kali cocked his head. 'Ah, but this is always the risk we take. We take it every night, when we stop to eat, and talk, and sleep. There is always another day and another rhythm.'

Omar stopped, just a few yards from Tasha and nodded. Kali halted, too. 'You are wise, Omar. Let us see what the girl wants.'

As one they turned to Tasha and fixed her with their gazes. And waited for her to speak.

Tasha felt a little nervous under the stares of the two men of the wild. She cleared her throat. 'Thank you for stopping, brothers. I am searching for someone—two someones, in fact—and I need to find their trail. I hoped two travellers such as yourselves might have heard rumours of their passing.'

Kali nodded slowly. 'Possible. Possible. Who are these travellers, and where did they come from?'

'They led the Ruhim force that invaded this territory not two days past. I had thought they would return to Parkum from whence they came, but they have disappeared. Into the desert, I believe.'

Omar whistled, and turned to his partner. 'She is looking for the witch, Kali.'

Kali nodded. 'And the other offworlder, the big one.' He cocked his head and peered at Tasha. 'Why do you seek such notorious individuals, sister? It seems to me that you would be better off not finding them.'

Tasha took a deep breath and stood tall. 'Because they need to be stopped. Driven from Karak. And I need to find them to do that.'

She waited for the men to laugh. Neither did, though Omar

pursed his lips slightly.

After a while, Kali nodded again. 'You seem certain. It is good to be certain.'

Omar gestured at the goats. 'These goats are certain. Look how happy they are. No doubts at all.'

His partner frowned slightly. 'Yes, well. We do not know where these two who you seek are hiding, sister.'

Tasha slumped. *Damn. Damn it all.*

'But we do know someone who might.' Kali smiled. 'You should go and visit Shadaman.'

Omar clapped his hands. 'A fine idea, Kali. Shadaman will know.'

'Well, he might. He is a thousand years old and completely blind, and his travelling days have been over since before my grandfather was born. But he hears all. Sees all. If anyone knows where these invaders are hidden, it is he.'

Tasha smiled, and gave a small bow. 'Thank you, brothers. It is much appreciated.'

Kali waved her thanks away. 'It is nothing. Knowledge is free, is it not? Now come, and I will draw for you a map.'

* * *

The map Omar and Kali had given Tasha led her on a winding path through the Domu hills, then north, keeping the hills to her right as she approached the small oasis on the border with Bobun lands, near which Shadaman could allegedly be found.

The mid-afternoon sun beat down with brutal intensity. Tasha's face felt damp with sweat even in the shade of her loose hood. Steering the speeder left and around a scree of fallen rocks, she took a sip from her water bottle, then shook it. *Half empty. If this oasis isn't where the map says it is... I might be in trouble.*

But sure enough, after another half hour's ride Tasha spotted her destination. A row of brilliant white triangles on the horizon gradually became tents as she neared. The flashes of reflected sunlight that dazzled her as she crested a low rise were surely from the oasis, at the centre of the camp.

She throttled the speeder down to a slow, growling crawl and angled it towards a wide gap between two large tents. Tasha was a little surprised to see two other speeders parked in the shade of one of the tents, next to the expected group of masticating camels. *Nomads on speeders?*

She pulled her speeder up alongside the other pair and brought it to a halt. As she stepped off, two of the nearest camels turned to inspect her, never pausing in their thoughtful chewing. Tasha smiled as she looked into their beautiful brown eyes, ringed with long black lashes that fluttered prettily with every lazy blink. She'd always liked camels.

'Hello, pretties. How are you today? Hot, isn't it?' She walked over and stroked one on the neck, the short hair coarse like the welcome mat on her mama's porch. The camel snorted in agreement, nostrils flaring, then closed its eyes for a nap.

Inordinately pleased to have met a friendly camel, Tasha headed further into the camp towards the oasis with a bounce in her step.

'Have you run away from home to join us, sister?' The voice came from her left, from the shadowed entrance to a wide, low tent. To each side of the entrance sat cages containing a variety of small colourful birds. Tasha squinted into the dark interior just as the owner of the voice emerged.

He looked a few years older than her, with short, curled black hair and eyes as big and brown as those of the animal she'd petted moments before. Dressed only in loose white trous, his torso was smooth, lean-muscled without being too big. Her pulse sped up a little.

'See anything you like?' Her gaze shot up to meet his as the young man grinned and wagged his eyebrows.

Tasha felt her face warm. 'No! I haven't left home. What?' She looked away, ready to hurry off.

'Sorry, sorry. Don't rush away. I was just joking.' The grin turned into an apologetic smile. 'I didn't mean to embarrass you.'

'You didn't. I'm just—' She took a breath. 'I'm looking for

someone who's supposed to live here. His name's Shadaman. Do you know him?'

The young man barked a laugh. 'I should. He's my great-great-grandfather. But that's not saying much—he's everyone's great-grandfather, almost.' He held out his hand. 'My name's Amir.'

'Tasha.' She shook his hand. Her sleeve slipped back, uncovering the bracelet that she'd taken from Venus's apartments on her wrist. The white gold and sapphires flashed in the sunlight.

'Pretty jewellery,' said Amir, pointing at it. 'Almost as pretty as you.'

Tasha rolled her eyes at that terrible line. 'So where can I find Shadaman?'

'The biggest tent, on the other side of the oasis, right on the water's edge.' Amir pointed the way. 'He should just be waking up from his afternoon nap around now.' The young man grinned again. 'The benefits of being ancient, eh?'

Tasha found herself smiling back. 'Thank you.' She turned to leave.

'Oh, and Tasha?' She looked back. 'If you ever do decide to run away from home, I've got plenty of room.' Amir winked.

Shaking her head and repressing a satisfied grin, Tasha turned away again and headed for the oasis, and a nomad older than time itself, apparently. *Who is hopefully awake from his nap.*

Fifteen minutes' walk took Tasha around the oasis to the large tent Amir had described, which stood in an astonishingly lush garden, surely the only one like it for hundreds of miles in any direction. An elderly woman sat on a stool next to the tent's entrance flap, shelling peas into a bucket and dropping the pods into the cloth covering her lap. She looked up as Tasha approached, eyes narrowing slightly. *Probably the old man's granddaughter, if the rumours of his age are anywhere near accurate.*

Tasha offered a friendly smile. 'Hello, *mama*. I hoped to speak to Shadaman—if he's awake, that is.'

The old woman eyed her in silence for some time, then went

back to shelling peas. Tasha was about to try again when the woman answered, 'Shadaman is sleeping. He isn't taking visitors.'

A voice called out from within the tent, wavering only slightly. 'Who are you talking to, Dree?'

The old woman sighed, and looked up at Tasha. 'He *was* sleeping.' She turned slightly and shouted into the tent. 'Just a girl, *baba*. From the cities.'

'What does she want?' came the voice.

'I don't know. To speak to you. She won't say what about.' The old woman turned back to Tasha and raised her eyebrows.

You never gave me a chance to say. Tasha smiled again, opened her mouth to speak to the old woman, then thought better of it and faced the tent entrance. 'I need your help, *baba*. I am searching for someone. Two someones, actually. I spoke to herders on the other side of the hills, and they told me I should come to you.'

There were a few moments of silence from within the tent. Tasha waited, ignoring the glare the old woman gave her.

Then the old man called once again, 'You should come in, my girl. I don't know why you're standing out there, shouting.'

Tasha closed her eyes briefly. *Oy, save me from the whims of the elderly.* With a curt nod to the old woman, she entered the tent.

The room was wide and dark—lit only by red lamps hanging in two of the corners. Canvas walls to her right and left separated it from the rest of the tent. There was a faint smell of spice, herbs, and something else Tasha couldn't identify.

Directly opposite the entrance sat a low square bed, and propped up against a small mountain of cushions was Shadaman. His eyes gleamed milky-white in the dim light, cataracts covering his irises. Tasha walked up to the left side of the bed and was a little unnerved by the way the old man tracked her with his sightless gaze.

He smiled through the thick white beard that hung to his chest as Tasha stopped level with his feet. 'I'm not so blind as I look, my girl. Not in this room, at least.' He leaned forward with some effort and stared up at her. After a few moments, he nodded to himself and settled back onto his cushions. 'Two someones, you said. I have an inkling who those two someones might be, but why don't you tell me.'

'Venus. And her shadow, the Titan. They have disappeared from Parkum.'

Shadaman nodded. 'Indeed they have. Into the desert they went with their small army, and then they disappeared. Or so they thought.' He smiled again. 'It's rare to have such notorious personages hiding in my desert, so they didn't remain hidden for long. But why do you want to find them, child? Danger, there.'

'They need to be stopped. Killed, if need be.' Tasha was aware of how young she sounded, and how ridiculous that statement might seem coming from her.

But the old man didn't scoff; he just nodded. 'Do you have help in this endeavour? Or are you alone?'

'There are others.' *I won't mention that they're also foreigners.*

'Good. You will need their help, I think. Now listen, and listen well.' He closed his eyes, and his voice dropped to a strange, almost chanting, monotone. 'The path as it lies from this place: Across the Domu hills. South into the Ghelt farmlands. Cross them until you reach the capital, Juba that is now lost. Strike east for fourscore miles until you reach the Ativan Basin, then skirt it to the south until you reach the Droosi border. Twenty miles south along the border is a fortress—ancient, abandoned, empty for years on years. But no longer.' Shadaman opened his eyes.

The Droosi? Tasha was surprised, somehow; the Droosi were the smallest tribe on Karak, rarely getting involved in the bickering and occasional warfare that marked the planet's history. *Actually, hiding there makes perfect sense.*

'Did you follow, child?' Shadaman asked.

'I did, *baba*. Thank you,' Tasha replied.

'Good. Now go.' He waved her away with another smile. 'Let an old man have his rest. It's time for my evening nap.'

11. Lure

Dante squinted up at the morning sun, bright even through his tinted glasses, as he guided the rented sandspeeder around a slow-moving herd of llama and back onto the highway. In the passenger seat to his left, Quinn sprayed on yet more sunblock.

'How much longer until we reach Yej?' he asked as he dropped the canister into his lap and began rubbing the lotion into his arms.

Dante checked the time displayed on the rental speeder's dash. 'Thirty minutes. Maybe a little less.' He snorted. 'It'll be nice to see some water again.'

'How so?' Quinn asked.

'Oh, sorry,' Dante replied. 'Apparently, Yej is built on an island—a big one, in the middle of a huge lake. It's supposed to be the biggest body of water on the planet, other than the oceans at the poles.'

'Huh.' Quinn had finished applying the sunblock and wiped

the residue from his hands onto his khakis. 'I think I might have flown over that on the way in.'

A few minutes passed in companionable silence, the sandspeeder smoothly covering mile after indistinguishable mile of desert road, before Quinn spoke again.

'You married, Dante?'

Where did that come from? 'Uh, yeah. I am.'

Quinn chuckled. 'You don't sound entirely sure.'

'No, no, it's—nothing,' Dante replied. 'Yeah, six years. Her name's Phoebe. We've got a four-year-old, Violet.'

'Pretty names. What do they think you do for a living?' Quinn asked.

Dante glanced at him, frowning. 'My wife knows exactly what I do. Violet doesn't care; she's too young. Why wouldn't I tell them?'

'Oh, I just assumed.' Quinn shrugged. 'My girlfriend thinks I work in finance. I thought the DSO would have the same sort of… policies, as we do, for that kind of stuff.'

Dante shook his head. 'No. It's left to the discretion of the individual. I didn't want to lie to Phoebe when I started, so I told her. Making something up and sticking to it seemed more hassle than it was worth.'

Quinn nodded. 'Good for you. Honesty's the best policy, I guess. She must be quite understanding, then. About the job, I mean.'

Not exactly. Dante hemmed. 'Sometimes. In the early days. Now… not so much.'

'Ah.' Quinn looked away. 'Sorry I brought it up.'

'Don't be. There's nothing to… It is what it is.' He sighed. *Yep. It is what it is, and 'what it is' is a damned shame.*

Another few minutes passed before Quinn pointed at the horizon ahead of them. 'Look.'

They were approaching a gentle rise over a range of low hills that broke up the monotonous flatness of the desert plain. Just visible above the hilltop were a few glistening spires and tower-tops.

'Must be Yej,' Dante said.

'Let's hope so,' Quinn responded cheerfully.

They crested the hill a minute later and came upon a stunning vista that was in sharp contrast to the surrounding desert. Still fifty kilometres or more in the distance, in the middle of a vast basin, Yej sat at the centre of a dazzling disc fringed on its inner and outer edges in verdant green. Along the horizon at its back stood a range of low mountains. Gleaming hairlike tendrils snaked down from the foothills of that range: rivers feeding the only lake on Karak worth the name.

First picturesque thing I've seen on this rock. 'The banks of the lake are the most fertile land on the whole planet, they say. It's where most of the world's fruit comes from,' Dante offered.

Quinn glanced at him. 'Thanks. If it's all the same, I can live without the local encyclopaedia. Don't want to clutter up the old brain.' He tapped his temple with a grin.

Dante snorted. 'Fine, just making conversation.' He pointed to the left of the lake. 'We'll head that way — the entrance to the nearest causeway into the city should be just a little way around that edge.'

The air became more humid as Dante steered the speeder down into the basin towards the lake. *Huh. First time in a week that my throat hasn't itched. I could get used to this.* The highway — which had devolved into a rough dirt road as they came through the hills that edged the basin — was in a better state of repair as they neared the city. Dante turned left as they reached the edge of the strip of mixed grassland and forest that lined the lake, obscuring the towers of Yej from view.

'Do you want to stop for some fruit, then?' Quinn asked.

Dante rolled his eyes. 'Maybe on the way back.'

'That's if the Yalta let us leave. I can just imagine it now. "Crazy foreigners, threatening to blow up our mine. Let's throw them in jail and lose the key."' Quinn wagged his finger at Dante in mock remonstration. 'You laugh, but it could happen.'

The relentless banter is getting a bit old. Happily for Dante, the highway curved to the right around a cluster of towering palms, and they came upon the causeway gate.

It was wide open, the two massive copper doors hanging wide from posts of white stone that must have been thirty feet high. Dante steered the speeder through the gate and onto the broad gravel causeway that would take them—*hopefully*—into the city.

'Nice of them to leave the doors open for us,' Quinn remarked.

'Hmm.' *I doubt we'll find the same at the other end.*

The causeway was wide enough for three vehicles and at least three kilometres long. Their vehicle blew up a cloud of white dust from the gravel bed beneath them as they sped down the man-made road.

They neared the city, the towers they had first spotted from a distance seeming vast and imposing up close. Dante had read that the Yalta were one of the more technologically advanced tribes on Karak, with many of the amenities that citizens of one of the Core worlds would demand and expect. He opened his mouth to share that nugget of information with Quinn, then thought better of it.

When they were mere hundreds of metres from the city wall, the far causeway gate came into view. Sure enough, that one was closed, the copper doors shut tightly. A guard post stood in front of the gate, and figures were visible in the road ahead of them.

'Right, then,' Quinn said. 'Time to put the friendly business traveller face on.'

Dante slowed as they closed the remaining distance, then stopped the speeder just short of the waiting sentries. There were two; both looked young, bored, and nervous. *Wonderful combination for getting shot in a cultural misunderstanding. I really hope Quinn doesn't—*

'Hi there!' Quinn waved with wild enthusiasm. 'We're here to visit Yej. This is Yej, isn't it? Sorry if I'm not saying it properly—we're not from Karak.' He slapped his forehead. 'Idiot. Of course you know we're not from Karak. Look at us!' He guffawed.

He's going to get us killed. He's actually going to make them shoot us in the face. Dante searched desperately for the words to calm the situation, then realised the approaching sentry wore an expression of amused bafflement.

Dante smiled slightly, finally recognising the old idiot foreigner gambit. *Good call, Quinn.*

The sentry had come up alongside Quinn. 'Your identities, please.'

Dante pulled out his Cole cover papers and handed them to Quinn, who passed them on, along with his Quentin Mallory identicard.

As the sentry began examining the documents, Quinn kept up his patter. 'I'm here to visit the university. I hear you have some wonderful archaeological sites here in Yalta. Can I say that? Yalta? Or is it Yalta territory? I'm never sure.' He scratched his head, frowning briefly.

Dante stifled a grin. *Nice touch.*

Quinn went on, undeterred. 'Anyway, very excited about seeing some of these digs. My friend Mr. Cole is a trader. He's looking to buy up every crate of liquor you've got in the place. I hope you're not thirsty!' He laughed.

Before Quinn could offer any more unasked-for information, the sentry handed back their documentation, and waved them forward. *He looks worn out already.*

The copper gates slowly swung open as Dante gunned the speeder engine to life. He kept their speed slow and steady, nodding to the second guard as they passed, then they were in. The highway ran ahead into the centre of Yej, and Dante kept them going straight.

After a few hundred metres, he was sure they were out of earshot of the gate, and turned to Quinn, who watched him with a grin.

As one, they burst out laughing.

* * *

It's quite modern-looking, this place. For Karak, anyway. Quinn took in the towering skyscrapers and immaculately kept highway and turned to Dante. 'How come the Yalta are so much more developed than the rest? Did you come across that in your research?' He grinned.

'I did actually,' Dante replied. 'But I thought you weren't cluttering up your brain with local knowledge.'

'I make an exception for things I'm actually interested in.'

'Charming.' Dante smirked. 'It's not complicated; the Yalta have huge diamond deposits on their land, a completely state-run mining industry, and a history of unusually sound financial investments.' He shrugged. 'Basically they got rich by being lucky, and richer by being smart.'

'Good for them.' Quinn nodded to himself as they sped down the arrow-straight highway towards the centre of Yej. 'It could pass for a city on any Core world, couldn't it?'

'Almost.' Dante smiled. 'We've got slightly higher standards on Nexus P. How come you left, anyway? You said you grew up there.'

'To be trained. The Seryn found me—I'm still not completely sure how—and convinced my parents that we should all relocate.'

'To Corinth, yes?' Dante asked.

Far too many people know that these days. Quinn sighed. 'Right. Though I'd appreciate you keeping that to yourself as much as possible. I know we're all friends now, but... still.'

'Don't worry. I know how to keep a secret.' Dante snorted. 'I've got a few myself.'

'So that was that—we left Nexus Prime when I was seven years old, moved to Corinth, and I got trained up. As soon as I was eligible, I applied for the Agency, and that was that.'

'Your parents are still there?' Dante asked.

'My mother is,' Quinn replied. 'My dad died, a few years back. Trex disease.'

Dante winced. 'Shit. That can't have been long before—'

'Six months before they finally worked out the cure.' Quinn shook his head. 'What can you do?' *'Nothing' is the answer. You just watch your old man waste away, then a few months later, see the cure for what killed him.*

Dante coughed. 'Let's work out where we're going, shall we? Terminal: locate Yalta Congress building, Yej, Karak.'

Quinn raised his eyebrows. 'Congress? They really are working that Commonwealth model, aren't they?'

The terminal beeped, and a bird's-eye view map of the city appeared on screen. An androgynous machine voice said, 'Left, nine hundred metres.'

Dante steered them through the busy midday traffic. Another fifteen minutes' drive brought them to their destination.

Quinn stared up at the edifice as Dante brought the speeder to a stop in an empty parking bay. 'Jeez. How big is this congress of theirs? This place must have seventy floors.'

He climbed out of the speeder and wandered over to a flashy holosign. It suited the building perfectly, but somehow it still managed to look incongruous. *Probably because however modern this place is, the desert is still only a few miles away.*

Dante finished locking up the speeder and came alongside. He scanned the sign. 'Ah. This isn't just the congress, then. Looks like the entire government and half of their big businesses are here.'

'Makes sense,' Quinn replied. 'Saves a lot time travelling to meetings if you put everything in the same building. Shall we?'

Dante nodded, and they headed for the entrance.

They entered a pleasantly chilled foyer that ran the width of the building. Marble flooring and an elegant mix of steel, glass and wooden fittings tastefully expressed the designer's message: *We are rich but not flashy. Welcome. Don't make a mess.*

A step behind his partner, Quinn strode up to the nearest reception desk. The young man on the desk looked up as they approached and flashed a dazzling smile. 'Welcome, gentlemen. My name is Ahmed. How may I assist you today?' He spoke in flawlessly unaccented Standard.

Dante glanced at Quinn, who waved him ahead, then turned back to the receptionist. 'It's an unusual request, but hopefully you can help us. We need to speak to whoever leads the congress here in Yej. I'm afraid I don't know the title—Speaker, perhaps?'

The young man's smile faded just an iota. 'I'm afraid the first minister is extremely busy with government business. If you would like to petition for an audience, you can fill in this'—he picked up a slim tablet from a pile on the desk and proffered it—'application form.' The smile returned with its original brilliance.

Dante smiled, shaking his head slightly. 'That won't do, I'm sorry.' He glanced around the foyer, as if checking that no one was listening—*Overdoing it a little,* Quinn thought, stifling a smile—then leaned in close to the receptionist. Pitching his voice low, he asked 'Can I trust you to be discreet?'

The man's eyes widened slightly, his smile disappearing. 'Of course, sir.'

'Excellent,' Dante replied. 'I need you to get a message to the first minister—tell only those who you absolutely have to. Can you do that?'

The young man nodded. His eyes shone, no doubt with excited anticipation of what secret message two foreigners could possibly have for the first minister.

Dante nodded. 'Wonderful. Tell him this, word for word: Less than six days from now, a Titan strike fleet is going to arrive in orbit around Karak and wipe the whole planet clean. After which there won't be any government business to do, or a first minister to do it. Unless he speaks to us right now. Got that?'

The receptionist froze for a few seconds, then nodded jerkily and jumped out of his seat as if stung. He disappeared through a door behind the desk, as Dante turned to Quinn with a grin.

Quinn shook his head. 'You didn't have to scare the lad.'

Dante shrugged, reaching for the bowl of complimentary wafermints on the desk. 'He should be scared. I am.'

* * *

'This is simply outrageous!' the first minister sputtered. 'How can they have the temerity—the sheer brutal *audacity*—to even consider such a thing?'

Dante and Quinn had been quickly called up to his office, once their message had been received. As Dante had laid out the situation and the inbound Titan response to it, the first minister's complexion had reddened until he looked set to explode with indignation. *I hope he doesn't give himself a heart attack. That would be... unfortunate, diplomatically speaking.* Dante adopted his most conciliatory and sympathetic expression. *And we'd need to find another minister.*

Quinn cut in. 'Indeed, First Minister. We completely agree with you. But the unfortunate reality is that the Titans answer to no one, and they never have. They may be under the rule of a new, more open-minded leader—'

'Open-minded!' the first minister interrupted. 'You call this open-minded? Wiping out millions of innocent people—peaceful people—just to kill one? It's madness. Madness!'

Dante held his hands up. 'Nevertheless, Minister. That is the situation.'

The minister—Tixri Bergistan was his name—slumped back in his plush seat on the other side of his broad and deep wooden desk. The first minister stared at the intricately painted ceiling and sighed. His colour returned to normal as his rage gave way to—Dante assumed—despair.

'Is there no appeal?' he asked plaintively.

Quinn shook his head. 'No one has had much luck appealing to the Titans in the past, Minister. An associate of mine even has a personal relationship with a member of Titan command, so I asked my superiors to attempt to... leverage that relationship, and slow the Titan fleet. They weren't successful.'

'Though the situation is not hopeless,' Dante offered. The minister's expression brightened a little. 'That is why we're here. We want to help you, and your people—but we need you to help us in turn.'

The minister's eyes narrowed. 'What is this hope?'

Quinn took up the baton. 'Simply: Venus.' The minister scowled at the name. 'If we can capture or kill her before the Titan fleet arrives, then... disaster averted.'

The minister threw up his hands. 'Oh, then all is well. How simple! All we need to do is bring down the witch who now rules half of Karak. The people said she was a witch long ago. I never believed it—I am a practical man. But then you come here and you tell me it is true, that she can change people's minds, and…' He sighed again and looked from Quinn to Dante and back. 'Do you have a plan, at least?'

Dante nodded. 'We do, minister. In a nutshell, we need to draw Venus out. She's gone into hiding with her second-in-command—'

'Who is, as it happens, a Titan himself,' Quinn offered.

How does that help? Dante frowned at his partner, then pressed on. 'So we need a lure. Something to bring her out into the open where we have a chance to take her down.'

'And that's where you come in,' Quinn finished.

'What? How do I come in? Me? I am your lure?' The minister paled. Dante sighed and cut in before the minister could dissolve into babbling protestations.

'Not you, personally. Your people—the Yalta. We believe you are going to be Venus's next target. And we want to bring her attack forward.'

Quinn nodded. 'She's been attacking tribes in order of how much bloodsalt they produce. And unfortunately, the Yalta are next on that list.'

The minister nodded slowly. 'We had realised this.'

Dante continued. 'That's why Quoma's Mouth is the key. It's the biggest bloodsalt deposit on the planet; Venus won't be able to stay away.'

The minister frowned. 'Stay away, when? From what?'

Quinn smiled—a little too enthusiastically, Dante thought. 'When she hears you're planning to blow it up just to spite her.'

'You want to blow up the mine?' the minister yelped.

Dante again held up his hands, placatory. 'No. We just need her to believe you're going to. First, we need you to start spreading the rumour that it's going to happen tomorrow at midday. Forcefully, you understand? There's no point to any of this if the information doesn't get to her.'

'Huh.' The minister rolled his eyes. 'Her spies are everywhere. Keeping it a secret would be a problem, not the opposite.'

'Fine. Second, you'll also need to clear out the workers from the mine tomorrow; just give them a day off.' Dante counted off the items on his fingers. 'Third, I'll need a small team to play the role of the destruction crew. We need to set the scene, make it look real. A few soldiers in bomb disposal gear should do the trick.'

The minister held his head in his hands. He peered out when he realised Dante had stopped speaking. 'That's all?'

'That's all.' Dante smiled—reassuringly, he hoped.

'And you promise you aren't actually going to blow up the mine?' the minister asked .

Quinn chuckled. 'Don't you worry, First Minister.'

The minister smiled weakly. Dante could sympathise. *Poor guy. He's not having a great day.*

Quinn continued, 'Not unless we absolutely have to.'

Dante closed his eyes. *I need a new partner.*

* * *

'I cannot allow them to destroy it. I won't.'

Hesch sighed. *There's no persuading her.* It was late, nearing midnight, and he and Venus were alone at the peak of the highest of the four torchlit watchtowers that marked the corners of their new base on the Droosi-Ghelt border. The fortress had been abandoned for decades, as attested to by the debris and windblown sand that the small Ruhim force they had retained were currently clearing out of the rooms below. But the pump from the spring below the main courtyard still ran clear, and three out of the five solar generators they'd found in the basements had come online happily enough. *I've certainly camped in worse surroundings.*

Venus paced, her footsteps marking an oval in the dust on the flagstone floor. The first call from one of their scouts in Yej had come through forty minutes ago, followed by two more, twenty and then thirty minutes later, all telling the same tale. *'The Yalta are going to blow up Quoma's Mouth tomorrow. Noon.'* Hesch had brought the news to her himself, and they'd been arguing since.

'Venus, this situation is an obvious ruse. It's a trap, intended to lure you in to an ambush. I've seen the like twenty times before. From both sides.' His tone was calm, measured, as always. Though his lack of emotion sometimes seemed to irritate his employer, for some reason he couldn't fathom.

Venus flashed an angry glare at him. 'Of course it's a trap. I'm not an idiot. But even if it is, we have no choice but to respond.'

'That's the part I don't quite follow, ma'am,' Hesch replied. 'Even if the Yalta were to go through with this, and collapse the mine. So what? It produces ten per cent of the planet's salt—the other ninety will still be yours to control.'

'Thank you for the arithmetic lesson, Caleb.' Venus shook her head. 'I need it all. For what we have planned—what *I* have planned—I need it all.'

I give up. 'Fine. At least, permit me to suggest the nature of our response?'

Venus stopped pacing at last and nodded. She even smiled slightly—that cold, beautiful smile. 'Proceed.'

Hesch nodded his thanks. 'I don't want you anywhere near that mine. It'll be the focus of their attention. Instead, I'll assault it with a small strike team, moving quickly and not offering them the target they want.'

'Which would be me,' Venus replied, again flashing that spectacular smile.

Hesch swallowed. *Sometimes I think she could get everything she wants just with that.* 'Indeed. But at the same time we can't allow the mine to be reinforced by troops coming from the capital—Yej is less than forty miles away from Quoma's Mouth. So we'll need to keep the city occupied.'

Venus narrowed her eyes. 'You want to bring the assault forward.'

'I do.' Hesch nodded. 'I know the troops are supposed to be resting after the mission against the Ghelt, but they'll follow orders. It'll be the toughest battle they've faced—the Yalta are very strong—but I have confidence in the troop commanders. And your presence should give us the edge once again.'

Venus stepped up close to Hesch and rested her hand on his arm. Her blue eyes glittered in the dim light. 'You have such faith in me, Caleb.'

Hesch gazed into those eyes, frowning as, for the hundredth time, he tried to understand what the woman really wanted. *And I still have no idea.* He took a deep breath, blew it out. 'I recognise your commitment. That's all. You want this badly enough to make it happen. Whatever it takes.'

Venus nodded slowly. Her hand dropped to her side, and her gaze shifted over his shoulder to the second moon rising behind him. She smiled again—a little sadly, it seemed.

'Indeed. Whatever it takes.'

12. Primed

Quinn sipped his coffee and watched the morning commuters stream through Patrician Square, the vast open space at the centre of Yej, where the highways from each of the four causeways met like spokes on a city-sized wheel. Hundreds of people passed through every minute, on their ways to work or to school. A few weary-looking souls trudged along with expressions of dull apathy. *Night shifters. Better you than me, folks.*

He had been dropping off to sleep late the previous night when a call came in on the personal terminal he'd picked up at a surprisingly well-stocked mall that afternoon. Given that only two people on the planet had his contact info — one of whom was in the hotel room across the hall — he'd been unsurprised to hear Tasha's excited voice at the other end. Tasha had refused to give him any details of what she'd been up to or discovered; she'd just said she had good news, and they had arranged to meet the next morning in Yej.

The sun had barely risen when Dante had banged on the door of Quinn's room to let him know he was leaving for Quoma's Mouth to put his part of the plan in motion. After that, Quinn had tried but failed for an hour or so to get back to sleep, then given it up as a lost cause and headed out for an early morning coffee.

He checked the time. Tasha would be arriving soon. He wondered idly how she would get past the gate guards.

Quinn had just ordered another coffee from the roaming waiter when a hand fell on his shoulder. He turned around to see Tasha's smiling face looking down at him. Behind her was parked a flashy but incredibly dirty sandspeeder. He nodded at it with a smile. 'Is that yours?'

Tasha grinned as she took the seat opposite him. 'For the moment. I'll take it back later.'

I like this girl. He remembered his earlier thought. 'How did you trick your way past the guards?'

She frowned. 'What do you mean?'

'The guards at the causeway gate,' Quinn replied. 'What did you tell them?'

Tasha shrugged. 'Nothing. I'm a native. They just let me in.'

Quinn stared at her for a few seconds, then shook his head. 'Unbelievable.'

'So.' Tasha waved at the waiter and pointed to Quinn's coffee, then looked at him. 'Why are we in Yej?'

'That... is not a simple story.' It took five minutes to explain the situation: the call from LeClerq; the inbound Titan fleet; the six-day—now four and a half day—deadline; and finally the plan for Quoma's Mouth that he and Dante had come up with.

Tasha's face fell as he told her the news, her cheerful demeanour evaporating. 'That's unbelievable. That the Titans would do that.' She shook her head, amazed.

'The first minister here had much the same reaction. But if you knew a little bit more about them, you wouldn't be surprised.' Quinn placed his now-empty coffee cup on the table. 'What about you? You were excited when we spoke last night—

good news?'

'It was good news, but it's… less exciting now.' She thanked the waiter as he arrived with her coffee, and took a sip. 'Basically, I know where Venus and Hesch are hiding. It's an old, abandoned fortress in the desert on the Ghelt-Droosi border.'

Quinn grinned. 'That's brilliant! How did you figure it out?'

He listened with growing admiration as Tasha recounted her overnight journey from Parkum to the Ghelt territory and how she had tracked down the information.

Tasha brightened a little bit at his enthusiasm. *Good. Titan megadeath on its way or not, she should be proud.* Quinn clapped his hands. 'That's grand. Now we have a fallback option if today doesn't go to plan.'

'What is the plan?' Tasha asked. 'The full plan, I mean. Why are we here, if Quoma's Mouth is where everything is happening?'

'Well, Dante and I reckoned that there's a good chance that Venus—or Hesch, rather, assuming he's the military brain in the operation—would realise that they have a much better chance of securing the mine if they just bring their entire assault on the Yalta forward to the same time. Otherwise they'd have the Yaltan…' Quinn frowned. 'Yaltese?'

Tasha smiled. 'Yaltan is fine.'

He grinned. 'Yeah, the whole Yaltan army on them immediately. But not if said army is fully occupied defending the gates of Yej.' He spread his arms expansively. 'So that's the plan. If Venus goes to the mine, Dante takes her out. If she comes here—'

'We do,' Tasha finished.

'Bingo.' Quinn pulled his terminal out from his trouser pocket. 'Now, let's call Dante and give him your good news.' He grinned. 'Nothing like a good backup plan to take the pressure off when you're trying to assassinate someone during a massed battle.'

* * *

Dante was as certain as he could be that the mine was deserted.

There were four ways in; the main entrance to the vast hangar that sat over the central shaft was ten metres wide and spanned two pairs of broad rail tracks. Three smaller satellite buildings covered minor shafts, Dante had been told by the first minister's nominated liaison. Each entrance was fitted with imposing steel doors, which were securely locked. Dante hadn't seen another soul since he'd arrived about an hour after sunrise.

He checked the time on his terminal. *Two hours until the 'destruction crew' arrives.* He'd made it clear to the army liaison that the men he sent for the job would be in danger—that one or more would likely lose their lives unless they got lucky. The liaison—a colonel, Dante had guessed, though he wasn't sure of the insignia—had shrugged dispassionately, and told him that all of the men were prepared. Dante had just nodded. *I've heard that before.*

With the mine itself reconnoitred, Dante's next task was to scope out a prime position in which to wait. He'd need high ground and a clear line of sight to the main entrance, where the crew would be setting up to pretend to blow the mine. He looked about, shading his eyes with one hand as the still-low sun slid out from behind the rapidly dissipating cloud cover. Happily, the Quoma's Mouth compound was bordered on three sides by low hills. *Should be plenty of choices. Let's try the north side first.* Dante picked up his duffel bag and moved out, his combat boots kicking up sand and bloodsalt dust as he walked.

Halfway to the nearest hill his terminal beeped. He pulled it from his pocket and glanced at the screen—it was Quinn. Dante tapped the micro-transceiver in his right ear as he slipped the terminal back into his pocket. 'Morning. How's it going? Did Tasha arrive?'

'She did indeed,' Quinn replied. 'Twenty minutes ago.' There was a lot of background noise, vehicles and chattering people.

'Are you in Patrician Square?' Dante asked.

'Good guess. How did you know?'

Dante snorted. 'Last night, you said, "I might get coffee in Patrician Square tomorrow morning." It wasn't the biggest intuitive leap I've ever made.'

'Haha! Hmm. Right. Anyway,' Quinn went on, 'the lovely Tasha had some marvellous news. She's only gone and tracked the chaos twins down to their desert hideaway.'

'Really? Great job.' Dante veered right to avoid a rust-coloured snake that basked on the sand.

'Great job is right. So we've got that to fall back to if everything goes to shit today.'

'Such faith,' Dante replied. 'Did you give her our news?'

'Uh-huh.'

'And how did she take that?' Dante asked.

Quinn took a breath and exhaled in a puff. 'You know. As well as could be expected.'

'Mmm. Bet it knocked the wind out of her sails a bit.'

'You could say that.' Quinn cleared his throat. 'How's your end, anyway? All looking good?'

'So far,' Dante answered. 'I'm just finding somewhere to set up.'

'Got your bag of toys?'

Dante smiled and hefted the duffel. 'Never leave home without it.'

'Give them hell. Talk to you later.'

'You, too. See you at home.' Dante tapped his earpiece again to end the call. The weight of the bag in his hand was solid, reassuring. He smiled again.

Give them hell, indeed.

* * *

In the courtyard of the fortress, in the shade from a first-floor balcony, Hesch stood motionless. Waiting. Before and around him his troops moved—briskly, efficiently— loading up vehicles, checking weapons. All the mundane necessities of preparation for conflict.

Hesch barely noticed them. His mind wandered to another time, another theatre of war.

It was fifteen years ago—Titan years, not Standard. He had just been promoted to unit commander, and his unit along with a full tenth of the cohort had been shipped out to some backwater province to put down an uprising on a different desert world that had got very bloody, very fast. It was one of the Commonwealth's periodic requests for assistance; the enemy was bedded in, using guerrilla tactics, street to street and door to door. *Not a Commonwealth strength.* Hesch frowned. *But why hadn't their senate sent in the Peacetroopers?* Those elite troops were extremely capable. Not Titan-capable, but good. *And why can't I remember the name of the world?*

The Titan strike fleet—just a pair of Rapier destroyers, hardly worthy of the name fleet—had unfolded from subspace in a close planetary orbit, one over each hemisphere. Crippling the world's satgrid and lancing the handful of spaceports had taken a few minutes, then the troops had deployed.

They could have taken the Rapiers in-atmo and just landed one outside each of the two continental capitals they were assaulting, but that was generally more trouble than it was worth. *Especially on sandy planets. Gets too much crap in the intakes.*

So instead, the cohort had dropped solo. Each soldier suited up in full vacuum-sealed heavy armour, pulse rifles folded up and strapped to their right thighs. Then into the airlock, wait for the bay doors to open... and drop.

Hesch could remember every detail of that freefall, as he could for the other twenty freefall drops he'd done in his time in the cohort. The world below had seemed to rise towards him, filling his vision, then the buffeting pressure had hit as he struck the atmosphere, the suit's micro-thrusters making fifty infinitesimal course corrections per second to keep him on target. He remembered looking to his right and seeing his second-in-command barely a hundred feet away. Beyond and behind him dropped half of the unit, armour glowing a dull red in the heat of atmospheric entry.

He remembered smiling at the sheer, joyous exultation of dropping from space onto a foreign rock, with his men at his back, to bring justice. Swift, brutal, unimpeachable justice.

And they had. The campaign lasted thirty hours. The

recently overthrown rulers were released from prison — those who hadn't already been executed — and the fleet had departed, as quickly as they had arrived.

Good memories. Hesch nodded to himself, then frowned again. *But I still can't remember the name of the world.*

'What's troubling you this time, Caleb?' Hesch looked up to see Venus standing ten feet away. She wore local garb — loose-fitting white trousers and a matching tunic, her head wrapped in a hood against the sun.

'Nothing. Just thinking. Other worlds. Other battles.' He shrugged.

Venus said nothing for a moment, her expression wistful. 'Will you ever go back, do you think? Go home?'

Hesch rolled his shoulders and stepped out of the shade. He glanced at Venus as he walked past her and bent over his gear. 'When the time comes.' He heard her turn to face him.

'You'll meet me at Yej afterwards, yes?'

Hesch nodded, rummaging through his pack as a final check. *Everything's here.* He straightened and turned to Venus. 'Once the mine is secured, I'll bring the remainder of my force and join you. The troop commanders will run the assault until then.'

'Well.' She smiled prettily. 'We'll see each other later, then. Good luck, Caleb.'

He nodded. 'Founder with you.'

She laughed. 'Oh, somehow I don't think your Founder would have approved of me.'

Hesch smirked. 'No. Perhaps not.'

Venus climbed into the light utility vehicle that would take her and her bodyguard to the rendezvous point where the bulk of the Ruhim army would be waiting. She turned back and gave Hesch a wave as the vehicle started forward towards the compound gate.

He waved back, watching until the LUV passed through the gate and turned out of sight, then turned to check on the preparation.

Always another world. Always another battle.

13. Spark

Come on. What are you waiting for?

Dante lay motionless on his stomach, on a patch of flat ground atop a low hill a kilometre and a half northwest of the main shaft of Quoma's Mouth. Six inches above him, propped up on four fold-out telescopic plasmetal legs, was his smart-camo shade. It was a simple piece of kit—set it up, switch it on, and the beige fabric would shift into a pattern that blended seamlessly with the surrounding terrain. From above, anything under the shade was invisible.

He had been lying in that position for over an hour. He'd watched the Yaltan team arrive: a group of six soldiers in full body armour, four toting serious-looking pulse rifles, the other wheeling all-terrain carts packed with explosives. It had looked believable. All that was needed was an audience to come and see it. It was only—he checked the time on his terminal, which was on the ground just in front of his face—eighty minutes until midday. If Venus, or Hesch—or both—didn't show up soon... *We'll have no choice but to assault a heavily defended fortress. And I'd rather avoid that.*

Movement caught Dante's eyes. He quickly brought his binoculars up to his eyes and focused in.

There you are.

Five light assault vehicles were barrelling in from the east at high speed, rapidly closing with the mine. Dante swung the binoculars right—yes, the Yaltan soldiers had seen the approaching vehicles and were taking up a defensive position behind their own vehicle. Dante didn't think much of their chances, but the plan was in motion; it was too late to change course.

He was about to go back to tracking the incoming troops when his peripheral vision picked up more movement, appearing from the west from behind the last in the line of low hills. Half as fast, but just as aggressively, two trucks were rumbling over the desert towards the mine. Dante groaned. 'What the hell...?' he muttered.

The trucks seemed to have the edge; it looked as though they would arrive just before the assault vehicles. A minute passed, with both groups seemingly racing to reach the mine first. The trucks squeaked home by ten seconds, veering around the Yaltan soldiers' transport and skidding to a halt directly outside the main mine shaft entrance.

Dante watched with growing horror as each truck disgorged a rabble of men, all dressed in orange and yellow overalls and gloves, unarmed but clearly furious.

Miners. Shit. This is going to complicate things.

He swung the binoculars to his left. The assault vehicles had come to a stop also, just inside the edge of the mine compound. Troops emerged, fifty or so in total, each heavily armed and wearing light combat armour. Dante frantically scanned the faces, looking for a woman amongst the group.

She wasn't there.

But the Titan was: a full head and a half taller than the men around him, and easily hefting a massive pulse rifle that Dante knew he himself would have struggled to even lift.

Hello, Mr. Hesch. I guess you'll have to do, then.

Keeping the binoculars to his eyes with his left hand, Dante reached to his right with the other. His hand came to rest on a slim metal object just a quarter of a metre long. Sliding his fingers over the surface, Dante felt for the recessed power button and pressed it.

He pulled his hand back, gaze still fixed on Hesch, as the microdrone rose off the ground with a low hum. It was barely smart technology—a tiny fusion engine in the rear, a short-range thermal warhead packed with irradiated metal shards in the nose, and guided by a tracking computer clever enough and single-minded enough to follow any target relentlessly until the its engine died. Which would take roughly three years.

The drone online, Dante flicked a switch on the side of the binoculars. A red dot appeared in the centre of his sight. He held it steady on Hesch's torso as the Titan began to walk towards the mine entrance, his troops close behind. Holding his breath, Dante paused for a second, then clicked the switch again. The binoculars beeped, the target successfully marked by the built-in laser rangefinder.

The drone was tethered to the rangefinder, and its hum rose in pitch to show it had armed the warhead. A third and final flick of the same switch would send the drone screaming towards its target. Dante's finger hovered over the switch.

Goodbye, Mr. Hesch. He brought his finger down.

And stopped it millimetres from the button. Hesch and the troops around him had, as one, brought up their weapons. The Titan yelled, as did his men. Dante jerked the binocs to the right to see the group of miners running towards the heavily armed troops. *Are they insane? They're going to get mowed down!*

But the Ruhim and their Titan commander were showing some reluctance to open fire on the group of civilians. There were barely a hundred metres between the two groups, and they still yelled warnings. The miners didn't slow.

Shit. Shit shit shit. Dante thought frantically. He knew the drone would take at least six seconds to cover the distance to its target. By that time, the quickest of the miners would be close to the blast range. But if he waited any longer, the entire group would surely be cut down by rifle fire. *Reluctant he may be, but I've never heard of a Titan letting civilian casualties stop him from completing a mission.*

Dante took a deep breath. 'Forgive me,' he muttered.

And pushed the button.

The drone shot forward with a tiny thunderclap. Dante watched it disappear into the distance, kicking up sand and dust in its wake as it flew in low, just a metre above the sand. He swung the binocs back to Hesch and his troops. The miners were closing fast, just fifteen metres away, and the Ruhim soldiers were bringing their rifles up to a firing position. The drone was three seconds away.

Hesch turned to face Dante—the confused frown on his face was clearly visible.

The first of the miners were ten metres away.

Two.

The Titan's eyes widened as he threw his rifle forward, at the same time twisting his body away, back towards his troops.

One.

'Not possible,' Dante breathed as he watched Hesch leap away from the path of the incoming drone just as the machine, an oversized bullet gleaming in the sunlight, slammed into the head of the Ruhim soldier behind the spot where the Titan had stood.

And erupted.

The scene vanished, replaced by a cloud of fiery gas, sand and red mist. The first wave of miners had been caught in the blast, and three at least were certainly dead. Dante fought back a wave of nausea and forced himself to scan the scene, desperately searching for an indication that the Titan had been killed.

The kicked-up sand was long in settling. Thirty seconds passed before Dante could make out any features. There was a small red crater where the drone had struck, the sand fused into glass by the heat. Limbs and viscera lay strewn around the blast area, and soldiers and miners alike staggered drunkenly away, shaking their heads and vomiting.

There was no sign of Hesch. Not whole, at least. *But I have no idea if I got him.*

Or if I just wasted the lives of three civilians.

Dante lay motionless, unable to move.

And stared at what he had done.

* * *

The general alarm had been sounded twenty minutes ago, informing the citizens of Yej that they should clear the streets and return to their homes or businesses. Tasha had translated for Quinn as they sat in her borrowed sandspeeder, parked a little way down an alley just off Patrician Square.

Quinn watched the movement on the square, mostly military now, trying to get a feel for the Yaltan army's disposition. *I'm almost certain, but it doesn't hurt to ask.* 'Which way does it look like most of the army is going, to you?'

Tasha, sitting in the driver's seat to his left, pointed. 'East causeway gate. More than half of the troops have been going in that direction.'

Marvellous. Not just me, then. 'Shall we?'

The young assassin nodded and gunned the speeder into life. They nosed out of the alleyway, and she pointed the vehicle east.

In the interest of inconspicuousness, they took back streets parallel to the main highway that would have taken them in a straight shot to the gate. When the city walls came into view just ahead of them, Tasha swung the speeder back towards the highway and brought it to a stop just before the junction. They climbed out and peered around the corner, at the gate a few hundred yards away.

'That didn't take long.' The Ruhim had already breached the gate. The Yaltan defenders were lined up behind makeshift barricades—groundcars, buses, and hastily erected quickset concrete walls that looked to Quinn as if they would only take one solid hit before crumbling. The defenders fired towards the breached gate, plasma bolts and old-style metal slugs slamming into the copper doors and dropping the Ruhim invaders as they threw themselves almost mindlessly through the gap.

But the rate of fire from the Yaltan force was slowing. There was a hesitation, an uncertainty, as if…

Venus.

And there she was. Crouched low on the back of a heavily armoured assault vehicle, protected from incoming fire by a thick steel barricade, but clearly visible to Quinn from his vantage point. She had one hand to her temple, eyes half closed, as though she were concentrating hard. As her transport rolled through the gates and into the city, the Yaltan forces rocked back as if by a wave, then resumed fire. But slowly—oh so slowly and lazily—as if they'd lost heart, or hope, or belief.

It's now or never. Quinn turned to Tasha, who stood beside him. 'Are you ready?'

She smiled as she slipped two long-bladed black knives from sheaths at her belt. 'Ready. I'll cover you. Just like we said.'

Quinn nodded. *And how often do things go just like we say?* 'Let's move.'

They slipped out of the alleyway and, hugging the front walls of the buildings lining the highway to their right, made their way towards Venus.

Every time they neared a Ruhim soldier—some who were on the verge of spinning towards them to open fire—he threw a burst of mental static into the man's mind. Every time they stopped, shook themselves, and frowned as if struck by a sudden headache—just long enough for Quinn and Tasha to slip past.

That journey was the hardest thing Quinn had ever done.

He and the young assassin covered a hundred yards in that fashion, bringing them almost level with the front of Venus's vehicle.

But between them and their quarry was a thick knot of Ruhim warriors.

Now for the even harder part. 'Let's go.' Sounding far more confident than he felt, Quinn struck out towards Venus, directly into the heart of her bodyguard.

He had never been more creative with his gifts. He and Tasha got halfway through the throng of soldiers purely on the back of Quinn's mental blocking—sowing confusion and disinterest, fear and blindness. They were a mere twenty yards from Venus. He could see the frown lines on her brow as she concentrated, building her own vision, he knew—her own truth—to set into the minds of the men who had set out to bring her down but in a moment wouldn't want to.

But so close, the bodyguard was too thick. *Too many.* Too many faces turned towards them in anger and confusion, mouths opening to shout the alarm. Quinn frantically shut those down, but he could feel himself flagging, struggling to keep up with the need. *Damn it. At this rate, I won't have anything left for Venus. I could do with some bloodsalt right about now, if it didn't make me black out.*

Right on cue, Tasha sprung into action. Her knives flew, gleaming silver blurs in the sunlight as she pirouetted around Quinn. Blades caressed arteries, pommels slammed into temples, crushing them as she danced around and away. The pressure on Quinn's mind eased as the crowd around them thinned, consciousnesses snuffed out by the horrifying competence of the young killer.

And then, just like that, Venus was in front of him. She frowned even harder for a moment, then opened her eyes. Her gaze locked with Quinn's, and he felt a wave of desperate emotion rush over him.

Battening down his mental hatches, barely aware of Tasha as she threw hands and feet and blades into the soldiers around them, Quinn locked his mind onto that of his former love and willed her, commanded her, demanded that she submit.

The vehicle she rode on seemed to slow as they held each other's gaze. The sound of the surrounding battle dropped to a dim, indistinct hum. Their gazes locked, fury in Venus's glare, and a searing pain rapidly built in the back of Quinn's skull. But he held on.

Submit.

Stop.

End this.

He saw her expression quiver, shift. A thin trickle of blood appeared below her left nostril, bright against her cocoa skin. Her brow relaxed, and Quinn thought—just for a moment—that he'd done it. That he'd—

Venus's gaze shot to his right and locked onto Tasha as she dropped her leg after slamming her foot into a soldier's windpipe. Quinn felt more than saw the young assassin turn towards Venus. His mouth opened in a noiseless protest as he threw every ounce of power he had at his opponent.

But it wasn't enough. Venus winced but didn't waver, and Quinn could only turn in horror to see Tasha's limbs relax, her expression clear into a dull neutrality.

But only for a second.

Shit.

Then Tasha turned on him.

He barely had time to shift his focus from Venus to the girl at his side before she was on him, a high kick speeding toward his temple as the knife in her opposite hand angled towards his heart.

With an anguished cry, Quinn let his power erupt forward in a brutal mental burst that struck Tasha like a hammer. Her limbs spasmed, her knives dropped to the floor, and she hit the ground as if her skeleton had been yanked out.

Quinn staggered, struggling to stay upright, boots slipping on ground that was slick with blood from Tasha's vanquished opponents. The pain in his head was like nothing he'd ever felt—that last burst felt as if it had ruptured something. He'd never expended so much power in such a short time. Just barely, he was aware of Venus's vehicle skidding to a halt, then slamming into reverse to pull back through the ruptured causeway gate.

Shall I go after her? Should I... His gaze dropped to the body on the ground before him. Tasha looked dead, but he could sense sluggish brain activity. She had cleared a wide area around them — corpses lay scattered around in horrifying numbers — but there were still a hundred Ruhim soldiers nearby, and doubtless thousands more just beyond the gates.

Quinn couldn't go after Venus. Couldn't leave Tasha there. Shaking his head violently, trying to clear his frazzled mind, he bent down and picked the girl up. *She's so light. So strong, but so light.* He threw her over his shoulder and, turning away from the gate, headed for the nearest alleyway.

Leaving his quarry behind. His nemesis. *For another day.* He stepped over a Ruhim soldier, who gasped as he clutched at his crushed throat.

Another day, Venus. I'll get you for this.

* * *

Quinn. Venus felt a dampness on her upper lip, and she wiped it away with her sleeve. The white cotton came away red. She dabbed again at her nose. *It makes sense. Who else would they send?*

At her urging, the driver kept the assault vehicle barrelling down the causeway and away from Yej. Her own Ruhim soldiers, the bulk of the force yet to breach the city walls, jumped or dived out of their path as the armoured car rumbled back towards the open desert. One of her troop commanders hailed her, his words lost on the wind, but the question clear. Venus nodded, waving him on towards the city.

A few minutes' drive brought them beyond the last of the ranks of Ruhim troops, and to the end of the causeway. Her driver brought the vehicle to a halt as they cleared the causeway gate, the thick-treaded tires squealing as he braked. Venus closed her eyes and leaned heavily on the defensive barricade. Her head screamed with pain.

How long, since I was last tested like that? She smiled grimly, spat away the sweat and blood that had dripped onto her lips. *Too long, maybe.*

She turned back to look towards Yej. Her men should still

take the city—they were brilliantly trained, and their passion was fierce. But they would need to do it the old-fashioned way, and it would be much harder than if she were with them. Hundreds would die. *Thousands.* Venus shook her head, exhausted. *I make them give so much. Is it worth it?*

The rumble of an approaching vehicle made her turn. She smiled as she recognised Caleb's LUV and wearily swung herself down onto the ground, her boots crunching on the layer of gravel and windblown sand that lined the highway. Caleb brought his vehicle to a stop just before her and climbed out.

Venus gasped. *How is he even alive?* The Titan's left side was… shredded. His armour hung off him, the flesh beneath looking like nothing more than tenderised meat. Slivers of metal embedded in his skin, and muscle glinted as he walked towards her. His face was horrifically burnt, his left eye a cracked, seeping ball, and his left ear mangled into a shapeless mass. Yet he strode towards her with his usual strong gait.

A thought flashed unbidden through Venus's mind. *If these Titans had ever found us, I don't think we would have survived.*

'What happened?' she asked as Caleb stopped in front of her.

He winced, then spat out a gob of bloody mucus, along with two of the metal shards and a tooth. He raised his eyebrows— the right one, at least, as the left had been burnt off. 'What happened is that it was a trap. As expected. I'll give them credit, I didn't think it would play out like that.'

Venus frowned. 'Give who credit? The Yalta?' *Surely not.*

Caleb shook his head. 'No. They were just the bait. Whoever pulled the trigger was from the Commonwealth—I've seen the type of explosive drone that hit us before. But only from the other side, until today.'

Venus's mind whirled. *The Commonwealth? And the Agency? Together?* 'You're sure.'

The Titan grimaced, his cheek splitting and bleeding freshly as a result. 'I'd bet on it.'

She nodded. 'We have other enemies, too—I'll fill you in on the way back to the fortress. I don't completely understand their motives yet, but we need to strike back. Hard.'

'My thoughts exactly, ma'am.'

Venus smiled, and reached out for his face, then pulled back and placed her hand on his shoulder. 'Are you going to be all right?'

'It's just a scratch.' He looked down at the wreckage of his left side. 'I'll dose up on proteins and drop into a regenerative coma overnight. Eight hours, and I'll be as good as new.' He looked up at her and snorted. 'Well, almost. A little tender, but I'll be whole.'

'Good.' Venus turned to climb back into her assault vehicle. 'Because we've got lots to do.'

14. Reprisal

Hesch opened his eyes. The familiar cracked plaster on the ceiling of his quarters on the second floor of the hideout filled his vision. *Same place as when I went under, then. Good start.* He rolled his head to the left and looked at the room's single window. By the angle of the light hitting the blinds it was just past the seventh hour of the morning. *Right on time.*

It wasn't completely clear, though. He experimented, opening one eye and closing the other, then switching sides. He sighed. His left eye hadn't perfectly regenerated overnight; his sight was still blurred. *It'll take a day for that to sort itself out. Pain in the arse.*

Throwing back the light blanket from his body, Hesch sat up. He looked down at himself. The flesh along his left side had healed cleanly; it was pink. Raw and sore as hell, but it had healed. *The flesh is solid, at least.* He brushed away the scattering of metal shards, which lay on the mattress of his cot after his body had rejected them, and swung himself off the bed.

Standing, he grimaced. His left arm and leg were stiff, as if he hadn't used them for days. Gingerly, he stretched. 'Can't be helped,' he muttered to himself, shaking his head, then slowly began to dress. *Better see what Venus is up to.*

One of the sentries on Hesch's floor directed him to the courtyard. As he spoke, the man's eyes shone with the fervour that Venus inspired, which Hesch had started to find quite irritating. He well understood its strategic value, but to see it over and over in the faces of his men…

He snorted as he started down the winding spiral staircase to the ground floor. *His* men. That was a joke. *They're hers, and they'd tear me to pieces in a heartbeat if she gave the order.*

He stepped through a gate into the courtyard and stopped — brought up short by the bizarre scene before him.

Venus stood to his right, once again dressed in her plain white robes, either newly laundered or another identical set. Her hair was tied back in a simple ponytail. She stood motionless, head bowed, hands clasped in front of her.

Facing her knelt fifty Ruhim soldiers in complete silence, their heads bowed.

Hesch watched for a minute, then another. No one moved.

Then, without sound or signal, Venus's head snapped up. As one, the heads of the fifty came up. With chilling uniformity — and still with that unnerving silence—the men stood, turned, and left the courtyard through the open main gate.

That was… odd. Hesch turned to look at Venus to find his employer watching him, a faint smile playing on her lips. She waved him over, and he approached.

'As you see, I've sent out my eyes and ears. Each of them has in their mind the face of the Seryn, Quinn, and his assassin colleague. They'll scatter across Karak, reaching every town and city, and seed those images in the minds of our friends.' Venus smiled. 'We'll know where our enemies hide before the day is out.'

Hesch swallowed hard and nodded. He couldn't think of

anything to say.

'I must say, you're looking much better, Caleb. To be honest, I wasn't convinced that your coma would be sufficient in healing you; I half-expected to wake up and discover that you'd died of your wounds overnight.'

Yet somehow, I think you would have managed to get over your grief. Hesch coughed. 'As you can see, I'm fine, ma'am. Ready for our next step.'

Venus laughed prettily. 'Oh, that step's an easy one, Caleb.' She turned away and started towards the door that led to the fortress kitchens. 'We just wait.'

She looked back over her shoulder and nodded towards the kitchen. 'Now come and have breakfast.'

With a numbness that wasn't entirely due to the stiffness in his limbs, Hesch followed.

* * *

Midday was just a few minutes away as Dante waited on the roof of the safe house, an utterly nondescript residence in a suburb on the edge of Thrace's foundry district. He closed his eyes and pinched the bridge of his nose. After a ten-hour sandspeeder journey overnight from Quoma's Mouth, the blinding sunshine, constant background noise from the nearby foundries, and growing humidity were giving him a killer headache. *I need to sleep for about a day.*

Quinn had called in a few minutes earlier to say he and Tasha were about to arrive. He had sounded pretty rough himself, and hadn't gone into any details. Headache or no, Dante was eager to hear what had unfolded at Yej. *Although something tells me it didn't go well.*

A flash in the sky to his right brought Dante's head around. There was a craft incoming, flying low over the rooftops. He squinted, shielding his eyes with one hand. As the vehicle neared, he saw that it was a two-man vert-lift microcopter. Dante peered closer at the markings on the nose... then grinned. *Military. Cheeky bastard's stolen a military copter.* He shook his head as he turned and headed for the stairs. *They're never going to let us into Yej again.*

By the time Dante reached the house's rear courtyard, the copter had landed. He covered his mouth and nose against the dust and sand the thrusters had kicked up, then walked up as the craft finally settled down. Quinn stepped out as the engine shut off with a whine.

'Afternoon. Good flight?' Dante held out his hand, and they shook. 'Who lent you the microcopter?'

Quinn half nodded, half shook his head. 'Flight was all right, yeah. The bird was an... unofficial loan. I'm sure they would have donated it to us, if we'd asked. Good cause, and all.'

He looks as tired as I feel. Dante turned to view Tasha as she climbed out of the other side of the cockpit. *And she looks worse.*

'What happened to you?' Dante asked. 'Not to be hurtful, but you look terrible.'

She winced as she shakily walked over. 'Thank you. So kind of you to notice. We had an... encounter. It was going well, until it wasn't.' She cocked her head at Quinn. 'He had to... do his thing that he does.'

Dante looked at his partner. 'You knocked her out, too?'

Quinn had the decency to look a little sheepish. 'Didn't have much of a choice. She was about two seconds away from slipping a knife between my ribs. And I'm quite attached to the idea of my organs remaining puncture-free, so I had to, uh—you know.'

'Knock her out.'

'Knock her out, yeah.' Quinn nodded, then sighed deeply. 'Venus got to her, turned Tasha against me.' He shook his head wearily and wandered towards the house. 'Stupid. I should have seen it coming.'

Tasha stepped up beside Dante, and they followed Quinn into the house.

She spoke quietly. 'I've told him I don't blame him; he had no choice. It is Venus who is to blame. But nonetheless...'

Dante grunted. *I think he feels responsible for a lot of this.*

They found Quinn in the kitchen, with his head stuck under

a torrent of cold water from the faucet. He stood, gasping, and turned off the tap, then dried himself with a threadbare but clean-looking towel.

Tasha slumped down into a chair next to the chunky wooden table in the corner of the room and closed her eyes.

Dante looked from her to Quinn and back, then winced as the movement set off a stabbing pain in his temple. *We're in great shape. What a team. I need a morphine tab.*

He sighed, then with an effort, clapped his hands. 'So. What now?'

Two weary faces turned to him.

Quinn smiled weakly. 'Time to assault a fortress, I guess.'

Tasha snorted. 'Yippee,' she muttered.

Great shape.

* * *

In his quarters, eyes closed, breathing deeply, Hesch moved. He'd been practising Kapp-Marr every day for forty years, ever since discovering the martial art while part of a Titan force liberating… somewhere. *Too many worlds. The names are slipping away. I still remember the faces, though.* Kapp-Marr was great for loosening up the body, and his still ached from the healing overnight.

Knees slightly bent, he slowly swung his right arm across his body. As it touched his left shoulder, he stepped forward with his right leg and swung the arm back, bringing his left along after it. Palms open, he flexed his fingers as his right foot touched down on the cool tile floor. Shifting his weight onto his right foot, he turned to his left, leaning back as he lifted his left leg up in a high, arcing crescent, his foot rising above his head before he slowly let it drop back to the floor.

As his foot touched the ground, he exploded into action. His weight shifted forward onto his left foot as he snapped a kick forward with his right, his loose canvas trousers cracking like a whip in the small room. Throwing his torso forward in the wake of the kick he threw a lightning-quick rabbit punch with his right hand. With a sharp exhalation he planted his foot after the kick and instantly moved his weight again, tucking his head and arms down low as he brought his left leg around his body in a reverse kick that blew the blanket half-off his cot.

For the final move in the sequence, Hesch brought his swinging leg back into his body, planted both feet together and immediately pushed up and into the air. He twisted his body, bringing himself into the correct position, before dropping like a stone—right palm, left foot, and right knee struck the ground simultaneously with a loud crunch.

Three floor tiles cracked.

Hesch looked down at the damage. *Damn it.*

A knock sounded at the door, three quick taps, then the thick wooden door swung open. Hesch smirked at the impropriety and, without looking up, welcomed his visitor. 'Venus. What can I do for you?'

He looked up to see her smiling, eyes gleaming in the afternoon light shafting through the blinds over the window. 'We've found them.'

There was a light breeze blowing as they crossed the courtyard to the main barracks building, the wind taking some of the edge off the sweltering afternoon heat. Even with the innate Titan ability to control his temperature by recycling or expelling body heat, Hesch found he was getting pretty tired of the relentless Karaki sunshine. *I'm going to forget what cold feels like, if this job lasts much longer.*

'So where are they?' he asked, nodding in response to a crisp salute from a soldier servicing an LUV.

'Thrace. The Hereb capital. We'd thought the Hereb had been keeping their distance, perhaps hoping to avoid a conflict, but it looks like that was a façade.' Venus shrugged slightly and flashed Hesch a contented smile. 'Oh, well. Now we know.'

Hesch nodded. 'Is it just the two of them? The Seryn you recognised, and the girl?'

'Interestingly, no,' Venus replied, pushing a lock of hair back behind her ear. 'Our spies report that there's a third resident of the building. Another foreigner. Why don't you guess where they think this foreigner is from, Caleb?'

He grunted. 'The Commonwealth.'

'Exactly. So it looks like we'll be able to take out our three birds with one stone.' They reached the barracks door and Venus waved him forward. 'Shall we?'

They strode through the main room of the barracks. A handful of troops were present, each man scrambling to stand to attention and salute as their commander and leader passed. Hesch tossed them a casual salute back as he walked briskly past, Venus a step behind.

Ahead of them was a swinging pair of double doors. Hesch shoved them open without slowing.

Two men and a woman sat around a cheap folding table, playing a game that Hesch didn't recognise with cards, plasmetal dice, and small steel discs. Another man sat on a stool in the corner, sharpening a long bladed knife with an atomic whetstone, while the fifth occupant of the room stood near the window. All were dressed in nondescript dark clothing. All exuded the bored tension of professional soldiers with nothing to do but wait.

The waiting's over.

Five faces turned towards Hesch. None of the five saluted. The four who were sitting stayed sitting. Hesch repressed a smile. *I like this lot.*

Venus stepped up beside him and surveyed the unit. 'We have a location.'

At that, the game players laid down their cards, stood, and silently left the room. The man on the stool went back to sharpening his blade.

The man at the window—the oldest, sporting a beard flecked with grey hairs—nodded slowly and asked the only question that mattered:

'Where?'

* * *

Quinn's eyes flicked open. He'd barely been asleep, just lightly dozing, but something had prodded him into wakefulness.

Sitting up in bed and swinging his legs onto the floor, he cast about with his senses.

Ah. That's what woke me up.

He stood and walked quickly but quietly out of the bedroom. He crossed the hallway of the safe house's upper storey to Dante's room. Quinn tapped on the wooden door, then nudged it open.

The barrel of a gun appeared in the gap at eye-level, the metal gleaming in the moonlight.

Quinn said, 'Evening, Dante. We've got company. Five bodies converging on the house.'

The door opened fully. Dante looked as though he hadn't been sleeping. He shook his head as he stepped past Quinn and headed for the stairs. 'Some safe house, this.'

Quinn snorted and followed. They reached the downstairs hallway without incident.

Dante turned to Quinn. 'Where exact—'

'I heard a noise.'

Both men spun, Dante raising his sidearm, to see Tasha. She'd appeared like a ghost a few feet behind them, her hands held behind her. Quinn glanced down, took in the young Karaki's nightwear—*small vest, very small shorts, perfectly reasonable, it's a hot night*—then looked away with a small cough. *I wonder what Odette's wearing right now. I should call her when this is over. If any of us is alive, that is.*

Dante lowered his weapon. 'I was just asking—'

'Yeah,' Quinn cut in. 'Five in total. Two at the front, two at the rear, one on the roof. Moving slowly and deliberately. My guess is they're not friendlies.'

Tasha nodded and brought her hands around from her back to reveal she once more held twin long knives, identical to the ones they had been forced to leave behind in Yej. Their black blades were almost invisible in the near darkness. 'I'll take the roof.' Without waiting, she slipped past them and noiselessly padded up the stairs. Quinn tried not to watch her go.

Dante let out a low chuckle. 'I guess Tasha's taking the roof, then.' He reached into the back pocket of his baggy trous and retrieved a slim silencer, which he then screwed into the barrel of his weapon. 'You want the front or the back?'

Quinn shrugged. 'All the same, isn't it? I'll take the front.'

Dante nodded and headed for the kitchen. 'See you in a few minutes. Hopefully.'

Quinn padded, barefoot, along the hallway to the long salon that ran across the front of the house. He stepped carefully around a tall, thin glass vase filled with dried flowers, onto a long patterned rug that would dampen the noise of his quiet steps even more. Stepping lightly, he headed past a dining table towards the wall between the front door and the bay window next to it. He closed his eyes. *Two bodies, just the other side of the door. Crouched, waiting for something —*

He misjudged the layout of the room in the dark, and his foot nudged one of the dining table chairs. Something hissed under the table, and Quinn opened his eyes to see a white cat bolt out from its hiding place and speed towards the hallway.

Oh crap. Please don't hit the —

The animal's swinging tail whipped into the vase, which wobbled drunkenly for a few seconds…

Then toppled.

The crash was cacophonous in the quiet. It was followed a moment later by a second, as the window shattered. Quinn dived for cover behind the dining table as a small dark object — *grenade, surely* — sailed into the room.

One.

Quinn clamped his hands over his ears.

Two.

The explosion was still louder than anything he'd ever heard, accompanied by a flash that lit up the world outside his eyelids with a fierce white glow. But the absence of heat — and the lack of shrapnel thudding into the furniture and walls around him — told Quinn it was a stun grenade. *Generous of them.*

Gingerly he took his hands off his ears — which were ringing slightly — and opened his eyes. Spots danced in his vision.

Closing his eyes again, he stayed motionless and cast out with his mind.

The front door slowly swung open. There was no accompanying klaxon sound, so the intruders had handily disabled the alarm system. *Professionals.*

Keeping low, the two bodies entered the room. By their bulk, they were probably men.

Quinn would find out soon enough. He waited until they were even with the dining table, just six or seven feet away. *Close enough.*

He focused, opening the first of the mental doors on his power, letting it rush into the reservoir behind the second, building in pressure as it condensed and folded in on itself into a tight, throbbing ball.

Quinn smiled. *Here's my stun grenade.*

He opened the second mental door.

The pressure in the room dropped, then snapped back as the energy exploded from his mind and slammed into the two hostiles. They dropped like... *Like Tasha did,* Quinn thought with a twinge of regret as he pushed himself to his feet. He wobbled a little—the shockwave from that grenade had done a number on his balance.

At that instant, a staccato of gunfire sounded from the back of the house—one shot, followed by a burst. *Shit.* Shakily, Quinn headed for the kitchen.

As he entered the hallway, stepping carefully around the broken glass on the floor—*damned cat*—he saw Tasha coming back downstairs. Blood was spattered across her white vest, but she moved freely. He pointed at it and frowned.

She stepped close and whispered, 'Not mine.'

He nodded, then gestured at the kitchen. Tasha raised her knives in a ready stance, and they crept down the hallway.

Quinn stopped outside the kitchen door and concentrated. Three bodies were present, but all were down on the ground, and two were cooling fast. Heart in his mouth, he held up one finger to Tasha, whose lips tightened. He pushed open the door.

Dante sat propped against the island counter in the middle of the kitchen. A body lay half through the open back door, and a bullet hole scarred the kitchen window.

The operative looked up at them and smiled. 'Are we all good, then?'

Tasha dropped her hands, and Quinn let out a sigh. 'We're all good.'

'Excellent. Glad to hear it. Now that we have a minute,' —he pushed himself up into a kneeling position and pointed at the bloody puncture wound in his left shoulder—'could one of you take this bullet out for me?'

15. Manoeuvres

Mid-morning, Hesch entered the wide war room at the top of the fortress's main building and found Venus staring up at the world map. It was a thin, parchment-like screen, stretched ten feet by thirty across the length of one of the room's long walls, and hooked up to an ancient-looking terminal. The screen displayed a map of the whole of Karak: the single continent that encircled the globe like a ring, carved up into territories of different colours.

He inspected it himself as he walked up beside his employer. *Red, Hereb. Yellow, Loman. Purple, Droosi. Green, Yalta.* Those covered around fifty per cent of the land. The rest... *Blue: Ruhim, Bobun, Mani, Ghelt.*

Venus either heard or sensed his approach. 'Has the strike team called in yet, Caleb?'

'No, ma'am.' He coughed. 'At this point, we can reasonably assume that the squad has been terminated. There's no strategic or tactical reason for them to stay dark for this long.'

He had expected an angry outburst, a frustrated curse, or at least an icy stare. But Venus just nodded thoughtfully, gaze still fixed on the map. *That's a strange reaction.*

'Thank you, Caleb. Is there anything else?'

Anything else? He turned to look at Venus. 'If you don't mind me asking, ma'am... Why aren't you bothered by the squad failing to complete their mission?'

Venus glanced at him, then back to the map. 'Because, dear Caleb, we have reached the tipping point. Observe.' She reached out and tapped a few commands into the old terminal that stood beneath the map screen.

Hesch looked back at the map and watched as the large green block shifted to blue. 'We have control of the Yalta territory?'

Venus nodded. 'The troop commanders called it in half an hour ago. The last of the resistance in Yej broke this morning, and the final two border towns surrendered. Marvellous news, isn't it?'

News that I should have received before you. If the commanders are no longer reporting to me... That doesn't bode well. Hesch cleared his throat. 'Excellent.'

Venus continued, 'With the Yalta out of the way, we control more than half of the landmass of Karak, and seventy per cent of the bloodsalt. Hence—the tipping point.' She turned, went over to a counter in the corner of the room, and poured two glasses of iced sparkling water. 'Assaulting the safe house will have distracted our irritating antagonists, which was reason enough to do it. Hopefully one or two of them were killed in the process, but it doesn't matter. Either way, we've come too far.' She came back and handed Hesch one of the drinks. 'In two days, it'll be too late for them to stop me.'

Hesch frowned. 'Two days? Do you plan to attack another tribe so soon? Venus, we really must discuss—'

She held up her hand to cut him off. 'No more assaults. No, the last act of our campaign will be a little more... subtle.' Venus smiled like a child with a secret, then—no doubt seeing the confusion on his face—pouted sweetly. 'Poor Caleb. I shouldn't toy with you. But you ought to know your Karaki calendar better.'

Hesch barely noticed the chill of the water glass numbing his fingers as his mind raced. *The calendar? Why? What happens in two—*

Oh.

He understood.

* * *

In the Hereb territory, the midday sun was blessedly hidden behind a bank of fluffy white clouds, providing a few moments' respite from the blazing heat, as Tasha, Dante, and Quinn climbed out of the utility vehicle they had borrowed from the safe house garage and stepped onto Commencement Square.

Tasha looked across the street at the Meklis. *Has it only been six days since I was here? It seems like a lifetime.* Dante locked their vehicle with a solid click, and the trio set out towards the council building.

'So what does the council do, exactly?' Quinn asked, as they stopped to wait for a slow-moving truck to pass. A row of goats peered down at them from the rear bed.

'They govern, by committee,' Tasha answered. 'Each councillor is elected by one of our districts. I think it is not dissimilar to your senate, Dante—yes?'

He nodded, smiling slightly. 'A little smaller scale, but the principle's the same, sure.'

The goat truck passed, and they started across the road again.

'You don't elect a first minister or president, then—there's no supreme leader of the Hereb?' Quinn asked with a grin.

'No.' Tasha shook her head. 'We never have. Everything is done by committee, by majority vote. But the spokesman has the casting vote if a decision is tied. He's chosen by the other councillors.'

Dante's eyebrows rose. 'He? Never a woman, then?'

Tasha sighed. 'No. Not yet.'

Quinn clapped her on the shoulder. 'Don't worry. It's only been eight hundred years. You'll get there.'

They entered the Meklis. The foyer was cool and quiet, with none of the midday loiterers Tasha had been expecting.

They crossed quickly to the council chamber door, and Dante let out a low whistle. 'That's some door. You wouldn't get that in the Commonwealth Senate, that's for sure.

Quinn chuckled. 'Score one for the Hereb.'

Shaking her head wearily, Tasha pushed open the thick copper door and stepped into the chamber.

She had expected the same ring of thirteen faces that had greeted her on her last visit, but only four looked down at her from behind the council bench: Alu-Jak, the spokesman, of course; Pharc, her friend, smiling at her again; Halim, her father's old sparring partner; and Bej, the career politician.

'Greetings, councillors.' She bowed, then gestured at her comrades. 'These gentlemen are Dante Zo, of the Commonwealth,'—Dante nodded—'and Quinn, of the…' Tasha glanced at him.

'Corinth,' Quinn finished.

Alu-Jak frowned. 'Corinth is also in the Commonwealth.'

Quinn grinned. 'That's right. Commendable knowledge, Councillor. Kudos.'

Tasha stifled a smile and waited for the spokesman to begin.

Stroking his beard, Alu-Jak said, 'Only the four of us are here tonight, for one reason: we do not wish to spread a panic. The intelligence that you have provided us this morning, Tasha, regarding the incoming Titan fleet, is so shocking—'

'Outrageous!' Halim squawked. He did indeed look outraged: his cheeks were a fiery red.

'Yes, so outrageous and shocking,' Alu-Jak continued, 'that the general populace must not find out. There would be rioting, looting, all manner of incidents.'

Tasha fumed in silence. *The people shouldn't have the dignity of knowing their possible fate, apparently. How democratic.* She thought of all of her friends, her family—like Duru's parents with their restaurant, like her aunt and uncle and cousins on the farm outside the city. Everyone struggling to make something of their lives, struggling just to make ends meet, blithely unaware that at that moment, none of it mattered. They were doomed. *We're all doomed.*

Alu-Jak went on. 'So. We have a deadline—with which there is no negotiating, it seems. Against that deadline, we have but one opportunity: to bring down the foreign witch Venus. Have I summarised this situation correctly?'

Pharc chuckled. 'I think we've all grasped the gist, Jak. Let's move on to the details, before we find a Titan walking through that door.'

Alu-Jak's gaze narrowed on his colleague. 'Of course.' He looked back down at Tasha. 'Your proposed plan is to attack the suspected location of Venus and her associates, with the Demir Yumruk providing the bulk of the force for a large-scale but primarily diversionary, assault. Correct?'

If I followed all of that verbosity, then... 'Correct, Councillor.'

Alu-Jak nodded sharply. 'Meanwhile, you and your... associates, here, will enter the Ruhim hideout—some kind of fortress, you said?'

'Yes, Councillor,' Tasha replied. 'Deserted for years, until now.'

'Hmm. So, you'll enter by some other more covert route and attempt to eliminate or capture the target. Correct again?'

Before Tasha could speak, Quinn chimed in, 'Three out of three, councillor. You've got a knack for this. You should run for office.'

Tasha bit her lip and heard Dante stifle a laugh, turning it into a coughing fit.

'Excuse me,' he apologised, glancing at Tasha with a smirk.

Halim had been silent too long, apparently. 'Someone needs to point out that these Ruhim, since the arrival of the witch and her Titan colleague, are seemingly unbeatable! How many engagements have the Ruhim lost since they began tearing up

Karak? None!' Halim threw his hands in the air in exasperation. 'What makes you think the Yumruk will fare any better?'

Tasha bit back a venomous retort and took a breath. 'Your concerns are justified, Councillor. But it seems to me and my colleagues—and, I hope, to you—that we simply do not have a choice. The Titan fleet arrives in two and a half days. My friend Quinn knows the Titan character well; when they say will do something, they do it.'

Quinn nodded, his smile gone. 'One hundred per cent of the time. It's the Titan guarantee.'

Pharc spoke up, directing his words at his fellow councillors. 'My friends, we have deliberated this decision from every angle in the hours since Tasha's communiqué. As unwelcome as it is to have to send our forces into combat, knowing that some of them will not return...' He shook his head. 'The greatest test of history is when leaders are faced with a choice between a bad decision and a worse one. We must not lose our nerve.'

Silence fell for a little while after Pharc's words.

With a deep sigh, Alu-Jak nodded. 'It is right.'

Halim too, acquiesced. 'It is right.'

Bej just nodded. *No sermons from him today. Perhaps I misjudged him. Or maybe he only performs for the cameras.*

Pharc looked down at Tasha, then shifted his gaze to Quinn, then Dante. 'You will have your diversion, my friends.' He smiled, so sadly that it made Tasha's heart break. 'I pray you make it count.'

* * *

'That went well,' Quinn said as they walked back through the foyer of the Meklis. *A job well done.*

Dante snorted. 'Yeah, I think they really liked you.' Tasha snickered.

Quinn spotted a man in the doorway that led onto the street. He pointed. 'Who's that?'

Rather than answer, Tasha broke into a run and wrapped the newcomer in a huge hug.

'Do you think they know each other?' Dante asked.

Quinn grinned. *He's picking up my sense of humour.*

They followed more slowly, and Tasha disentangled herself just as they arrived. 'This is my brother, Ruben. He's a commander in the Demir Yumruk. Rube, this is Dante and Quinn. We've been working together.'

The young man—*tanned, crew-cut, muscled; I bet he has a lot of trouble with women*—offered his hand and shook with Quinn, then Dante. 'It's a pleasure to meet you. And I want to thank you for doing so much to help our world. Not many offworlders come to Karak, and few of them would do what Tasha tells me you have done to help us.'

'No need to thank us,' Dante replied. 'Venus needs to be stopped. The whole galaxy is at risk. We're just...' He shrugged. 'Doing our jobs.'

'Well, you have my thanks anyway. Our world still needs protecting, and you've put your lives on the line. I won't forget that. Nor will Tasha.' His arm around her shoulder, he gave her a squeeze.

Quinn smiled. *Odd how she looks so much younger, standing next to her older brother.*

'So.' Ruben turned to Tasha. 'What did the council say? Did we get the go-ahead?'

Tasha nodded, much less excited and happy than a moment before. 'We did. We move on them tomorrow—there's no more time to prepare.'

Ruben shrugged easily. 'Then, we'll work with the time we have. When there's a Titan fleet speeding towards you, there's no time to complain, right?'

'Right,' Quinn replied with a smile.

'Well, I'd better get going. I need to brief my men and get ready for the mission.' He looked down at Tasha. 'Look after yourself, okay? In case I don't see you before we move tomorrow.'

Tasha nodded and wrapped her brother in another big hug. 'You, too. Don't do anything stupid. I'll see you soon.'

After a few seconds, Ruben pulled away and, with a wave to

Quinn and Dante, turned and left. Quinn watched Tasha watch him go.

'He looks like he can look after himself. I'm sure he'll be fine, Tasha,' he offered, with a smile.

The young assassin turned and gave him a look that spoke of experience far beyond her years. 'Do you have any family who serve in the military, Quinn? Do your people even *have* a military?'

Quinn's smile faded. 'No. And no, we don't.'

Tasha looked away again. 'I didn't think so. If you did, you would never be so sure. However strong, however skilled or experienced they are…' She shook her head. 'You can never be sure that they will come home. That's the price we pay for doing our duty.' With that, she stepped through the open double doors, out into the street.

Quinn watched her as she walked towards their vehicle. He felt Dante's hand fall onto his shoulder.

'She's right, you know. When you're going into combat… You just never know when it's going to be your day.' Dante squeezed. 'Come on. Let's get back to Tasha's barracks. And hope it's a bit safer than that safe house.'

Quinn smiled weakly and followed Dante out into the sunlight.

* * *

It was late. A glass of whisky in his hand, Dante sat at the desk in the private room the Bichak masters had generously provided for him. Quinn was just across the hall. *They probably feel guilty about their safe house being not as safe as advertised.* Dante gingerly touched the bandage over the wound in his left shoulder, and winced. He'd got lucky; the slug had missed both artery and bone. *Just a flesh wound. A painful, aching flesh wound. But I've had worse.*

A bell had rung half an hour ago, signalling the evening curfew for the Sessiz Bichak initiates—or so Tasha, laughing, had explained to Dante when he'd gone to find her and asked if the compound was on fire. Feeling a little sheepish, he'd returned to his room.

He knew he should get as much rest as possible, but if he went to bed, he wouldn't sleep. Sipping his drink, Dante realised with a stab of guilt that he'd yet to call Phoebe.

Shit. It's been nearly ten days. With a groan, he placed his glass on the table and pulled out his personal terminal. 'Time check: Nexus Prime, Central, Midtown Four.'

The answer came back in the terminal's androgynous voice. 'Current time is twenty-two hundred hours and seventeen minutes.'

Late, but not too late. The terminal was still patched through to his subspace wave communicator, which was powered on at the bottom of the cupboard in the corner of the small room. Dante flicked through the contact list. *E, F, G… Home.* He tapped the call icon and waited.

One ring. Two rings. Three.

Come on.

Click. Phoebe's face appeared on the terminal's small screen. Dante held it up in front of his face and smiled. 'Hey.'

'Hi.' She was a little bleary-eyed, and her long brown hair was rumpled. 'What time is it?'

'With me or with you?' he joked.

Phoebe smiled slightly. 'You. I know what the time is here.' She yawned massively. 'I must have dozed off after dinner.'

'It's about the same time here, coincidentally. I was just thinking about going to bed. How's Violet?'

'Asleep. Not great.' Phoebe rubbed her eye. She looked exhausted. 'She's caught a bug again. That pre-school could double as a bio-disease research centre, the number of viruses they've got going around.'

'Give her a kiss for me.'

Phoebe nodded. 'You could come home and give her one yourself. When might that be?' Her tone had tightened a little.

'A few days. The job will be over then, whatever happens.'

She frowned. 'That sounds ominous.'

'No, it's just… Either we pull it off, or we don't. Regardless,

I'll be home in a few days.' Dante gave her what he hoped was a reassuring smile.

'Unless something happens.'

His smile faded. 'I'll come home, Phee.'

A sudden wave of tiredness hit him, and he closed his eyes. A vision of people dying in a cloud of hot red mist flashed unbidden through his mind. It had been happening every time he'd let his mind wander or tried to sleep for the last two days.

Dante snapped his eyes open.

Phoebe frowned at him. 'What is it?'

'It's nothing,' he replied, trotting out the same old answer he'd been giving for years. Dante saw her expression close up and realized, *I think… maybe it's time to let her in.* 'Actually, yeah. There is something.'

Phoebe raised her eyebrows.

'Phee, I think… I think I need some time off. When I get back.'

She smirked. 'You? Take time off?'

'Hear me out,' he replied. 'I've got some leave saved up—well, you know I have. A couple of months' worth. I was thinking… maybe we could go somewhere. You, me, Violet. Get her out of that germ-farm of a pre-school—maybe take her to the lake. See your parents.'

Phoebe looked stunned. 'You're suggesting we visit my parents? You. Dante.' She pinched her cheek, winced. 'Nope, I am awake.'

Dante laughed. 'I'm serious. It'll be good—for Violet to see her grandparents, for us to get out of the city, and… to see you. And maybe when my leave's over…'

He took a deep breath. Thoughts had been swirling through his mind in the last few days, since the incident at the mine. He'd been doing what he did for too long. Almost five years, month after month, doing the things he had to do and seeing the things he had to see… it had been enough.

Dante loved the service, cared deeply about his job and believed, wholeheartedly, that it was worthwhile, but… he'd served. Perhaps it was time for the next generation to pick up the load. And as a veteran quartermaster back in the Corps had said to a much-younger Dante Zo: *'However good a tool is, however perfect it is for the job, you work that tool for too long, and it'll break.'* With a wink, he'd added, *'Or go crazy.'*

These thoughts coalesced all at once and became a decision. *Yes. It's taken me too long to realise it, but…* 'Maybe it'll be time for me to do something else. Something where I'm not away so much.'

She looked wary, but something shone in her expression that Dante hadn't seen in some time: hope. 'You've said things like this before, Tay.'

He smiled. It had been a while since she'd called him that, too. 'I know. But I mean it, this time. I think… I think I might be done.'

Phoebe's eyes shone. She looked near tears, but she was smiling. 'Okay. I'll see you when you get home, then.'

Dante took another breath, more relaxed than he'd felt in a long time. 'A few days. Phee?'

'Yeah?'

'I love you.'

She nodded, and wiped her eyes. 'Love you too, Tay. Come home safe.' She reached towards the screen and vanished. His terminal beeped with the call end tone, and Dante slumped back in his seat.

A tap came at the door.

'It's open,' he called, turning.

It was Tasha.

'Hi. I just wanted to let you know; I just spoke to Ruben. Everything is ready for tomorrow.' Tasha frowned, looking a little confused.

Dante realised he still had a big dumb smile on his face. He coughed. 'Great. Good. Thank you.'

Tasha nodded. 'Okay. Good night, Dante.'

'Night, Tasha.'

She closed the door quietly.

Dante yawned and reached for his whisky. Tossing it back, he stood and walked to the bed. *I think I might sleep well tonight.*

16. Attack

It was late morning the next day when the Demir Yumruk assault force—a massed formation of heavy armoured vehicles with a smattering of LUVs bringing up the rear, including the one carrying Dante, Tasha, and Quinn—entered Droosi territory. The onboard computer in the dash of their vehicle pinged an alert, announcing that they'd crossed the border.

Dante tapped the screen to acknowledge it, then half-turned to Tasha in the passenger seat. 'Right, we're on Droosi land. It's the narrowest point of their territory, so we're only fifteen kilometres out from the fortress.'

When there was no response, he glanced over at the young assassin, to see her looking at him blankly. She turned to Quinn in the back seat.

'About ten miles,' he offered.

'Ah. Good.' Tasha frowned slightly at Dante. 'Why didn't you say that?'

Dante shook his head. *Damn independent worlds with their non-standard units.*

The vehicle's radio crackled, and Ruben's voice emerged. 'Hidden Fist, this is Red Leader. Do you copy? Over.'

Tasha grabbed the radio handset and answered, 'Red Leader, Hidden Fist. We copy. Over.'

'Awesome,' Quinn murmured to Dante in a low voice. 'Hidden Fist's a great codename.' Dante ignored him.

Ruben continued. 'Just calling to say good luck, and we'll see you on the other side. Over.'

'You too, Red Leader,' Tasha replied. 'See you in a while. Over.'

Out of the corner of his eye, Dante saw her swallow hard as she replaced the handset. He thought for a moment about saying something, but he didn't. *What is there to say? She knows the risks as well as I do.*

A minute passed in silence before the computer pinged again to announce they were five kilometres out from their destination.

'That's our cue,' said Dante, and swung the steering wheel to the left. Their LUV pulled out of the speeding convoy and headed west. While the rest of the force continued on their northwest route direct to the Ruhim hideout, they would approach more indirectly in a long looping course that would bring them to a point just a klick southwest of the fortress, where—hopefully—they would find their way in.

'How confident are we about the intel you got from that nomad, Tasha?' Dante asked.

'Very. Everyone seems to agree that Shadaman knows pretty much everything,' she replied. 'He seemed very sure of himself.'

Dante rolled his eyes. *Because no one's ever been sure of themselves* and *wrong before.*

Quinn chirped up from the back. 'Well, we'll soon find out, won't we?'

The desert was quiet without the thundering rumble of the passage of a hundred other vehicles. Just theirs, rolling over the sand with a quiet rasp. It would have been relaxing if Dante wasn't so wired.

'So we're looking for a rock that's shaped like an eagle. Right?' Quinn asked.

'That's what Shadaman said,' Tasha answered.

Dante scanned the horizon. There were a few indistinct shapes visible through the heat haze, but nothing that looked eagle-shaped. They rumbled onward.

The computer announced that they were one kilometre southwest of their destination, and Dante brought the vehicle to a halt. There were four large stones within a short walking distance.

He examined them one by one, then turned to Tasha. 'Okay, I have no idea which one of these is supposed to be an eagle.'

Tasha frowned. 'Maybe we're looking at it from the wrong angle. Take us a little bit further.'

Dante obliged, and they rolled forward another hundred metres.

'There!' Tasha cried, startling Dante, who jammed down on the brakes. Quinn thumped into the back of his seat with a muffled curse.

Dante looked where the young assassin pointed and squinted. 'Uh... Okay. I can kind of see it.'

Quinn had recovered and leaned forward to peer at it himself. 'Looks more like a penguin than an eagle, but it's definitely got a beak.'

'What's a penguin?' Tasha asked.

Dante grinned. 'Cold-weather bird. They're swimmers, not fliers. They probably wouldn't like Karak.' He pushed open his door, and the midday heat rushed into the car in a hot gust. 'Ooof. Nor do I, sometimes. All right, let's get going.'

Gear retrieved from the vehicle's rear bed, they set off on foot. Tasha led the way to the foot of the eagle rock. 'Shadaman said to start from the rock, then go north two hundred paces, and we should find a ravine.'

'Lead on,' said Dante, and they struck out.

'Keep your eyes open, though, in case it turns out to be less than two hundred paces,' Quinn said.

Sure enough, two hundred paces later they came to a steep, narrow valley, seven or eight metres deep.

'Huh.' Quinn raised his eyebrows. 'I expected something a little bigger.'

'Don't complain. The smaller it is, the easier to climb down.' Dante crouched and reached into his pack, pulling out a length of slim black rope with a shiny metallic claw at one end. Tasha and Quinn watched as he tossed the non-claw end of the rope down into the ravine, then grinned. 'Watch this.'

Tasha shouted something as he dropped the claw onto the rocks at his feet, no doubt expecting it to bounce off and tumble into the ravine—then gasped as the little claw sprung into life. It scuttled over the rocks until it found a suitable spot, then let out a high-pitched whine as it drilled an anchor into a tight crevice between two large boulders before clamping tight to the surrounding rock.

Dante looked up, pleased.

Tasha looked horrified. 'Is it… alive?'

Quinn choked down a laugh. 'I don't think so, Tasha. Just smart enough to do that one thing. Neat, though.' He pulled a pair of gloves from his own pack and slipped them on.

Dante and Tasha did likewise, and one by one, they climbed down into the ravine. It was blessedly cool at the bottom, shaded from the worst of the sun. Tasha came last, landing lightly, then pointing. 'This way—northeast, back towards the fortress.'

Quinn waved her on, and he and Dante followed. They had covered a few hundred metres in near-silence, the only sound the scrape of their footsteps on the sandy rock, when the ravine abruptly ended. Dante pulled up with a frown. 'I expected some kind of… entrance.'

Tasha tutted at him and began feeling around behind and between the rocks at the base of the wall. 'You have no faith, and so little patience. I just need to find the lever—'

Clunk.

The wall—or rather, the door, false rock cleverly built onto a steel plate—swung towards them with a creak, forcing Dante and Quinn to jump back to avoid it. Behind it was revealed a dark tunnel.

Tasha rose with a smile. 'This will take us into the cellars of the fortress.'

Quinn turned to Dante. 'That was pretty neat, too. Maybe even better than your rope spider gadget.'

Dante shook his head tiredly. 'Let's just go in, shall we? Oh, and before I forget—' He unclipped his trusty sidearm and handed it to his partner. 'In case you need something a little more conventional.'

Quinn took the weapon. 'Not a bad idea. I really should have brought something myself, so—thanks.'

'Do you know how to—'

Quinn ejected, checked, and reinserted the magazine, then flicked off the safety and chambered a round.

'Use one of those, I was going to ask.'

Quinn smiled wryly. 'This isn't my first time, sadly.'

Waving them to follow her, Tasha led the way into the tunnel as she pulled a torch from her belt and flicked it on. Her voice echoed when she called back from a few metres inside. 'Let's hope the Ruhim didn't find the door at the other end.'

Reaching down to check his rifle, Dante followed her in. *What could go wrong?*

* * *

The torch—at its dimmest setting to minimise the risk of attention—only illuminated the door at the end of the tunnel a second before Tasha's foot struck it. 'Ow,' she muttered.

'Okay?' came Dante's whisper from behind her.

'Fine. We're here.' Tasha powered down the torch and reattached it to her belt, then began patting the walls around the barrier in front of them. Her right hand found a lever similar to the one in the rocks at the tunnel entrance.

'Ready?' she whispered. The answering whine from Dante's pulse rifle seemed awfully loud in the confines of the dark tunnel.

Dante had moved up to her side. 'Quinn, any hostiles?'

'None that I can sense. Seems clear.'

'Let's play it safe, regardless,' Dante said. 'Tasha, open it, then drop back. We'll clear the room. Okay?'

'Understood,' she replied.

'Now.'

Tasha yanked the lever, and the door swung outwards. Light flooded into the tunnel as her two comrades stepped past and out into the room beyond, weapons swinging left and right.

After a second, both relaxed.

Quinn called, 'No one's home. Maybe they're busy doing something else.'

She stepped out into the cellar. Barrels and crates were stacked all around, an eclectic mix of foodstuffs, drinks, fuel, and weapons. *They're not very organised. How do they ever find anything?*

A loud thump startled her a bit. Dante cocked his head. 'Sounds like artillery hitting the walls. Not that close, though. The other side of the fortress. Gunfire, too.'

Quinn had found the stairs up to the next floor. He gestured at them. 'Up we go, then. As high as possible, you said?' he asked Dante.

He nodded. 'Seems as good a place to start as any. It's where I'd position myself to coordinate a defence—high up, with a view over the battlefield.'

Tasha slipped her other knife from its sheath, and twirled the pair in her hands. The weight was reassuring, somehow. She realised she was nervous, almost trembling slightly. A few deep breaths calmed her.

Dante looked at her, faint concern in his expression.

She smiled reassuringly. 'Let's go.'

The journey to the top of the fortress was nerve-wracking. Five times, Quinn's sensory ability saved them from encountering soldiers scurrying around the lower floors, before they reached a tower with a spiral metal staircase. It looked ancient, the metal rusted badly in places, but it held their weight as they made a swift ascent to the top floor.

Quinn spoke in a low voice as they emerged from the tower. 'I can't sense anyone nearby. Everyone's down near the ground.'

'Hopefully at least *someone* is up here,' Dante replied.

They moved more quickly, jogging past room after room as Quinn muttered 'empty' at each door.

They came to another tower, and turned right into the adjacent wing of the fortress. Four more rooms were passed without stopping before Quinn held up his hand and slowed. Ahead and to their left was a short flight of a few steps, leading up to a pair of double doors.

Tasha looked at Quinn, who was frowning. 'What is it?' she asked.

'There's someone there. Just one. But the image is...' He winced. 'Distorted, somehow. It's odd.'

Dante flicked his rifle into fire mode. 'Odd or not, that someone is our first candidate. Ready?'

Tasha twirled her blades and nodded. Quinn grimaced, but gave a quick nod also.

Moving in a silent crouching walk, Dante approached the doors. Hunkered down next to them, he pulled a device from one of the many pockets in his combat fatigues.

Tasha shook her head in amazement. *Another one? How many gadgets does he have?*

Dante extended a stiff cable from the small box and slipped it through the gap beneath the doors. Tasha peered over his shoulder to look at the machine; a small screen showed the view from the end of the cable. *Oh, it's just a camera.*

They could see the occupant of the room, a man, standing several yards away with his back to them. The perspective from the camera was fish-eyed and not completely clear, but he looked...

'Big,' Tasha whispered.

Dante pulled the cable back and slid it into the device with a nod. 'Could be Hesch.'

He slipped the machine back into his pocket and prepped his rifle. 'Get ready. Quinn, let's do this quietly if we can—see if you can drop him.' With one hand, he gripped the handle of the nearest door and slowly eased it open.

Tasha peered through the gap. The man was huge and stood staring up at a wide screen of some kind, which itself displayed—she counted—twelve different screens, showing views from around the fortress. Three were showing static, presumably knocked out in the firefight.

Hesch—it had to be him, the man was seven feet tall—wore crimson body armour of a kind Tasha hadn't seen before, including a helmet. He was protected, from head to toe. Wrapped around the top of the helmet was a silvery band of some kind. It didn't look like armour. *A communicator, maybe?* As she wondered that, he barked out a command to someone.

Quietly Dante slipped into the room, angled left. Tasha followed, heading right, with Quinn bringing up the rear and taking centre. She kept her knives cocked and ready to throw as she watched Quinn out of the corner of her eye. He raised his hand to his temple, then frowned. Deeper. Sweat broke out on his forehead and a vein throbbed in his neck.

It's not working—

Hesch moved. With amazing speed he spun, bringing up a slim rifle and firing even as he began sprinting towards a large table at the end of the room.

The plasma pellet struck Quinn in the right shoulder, knocking him to the floor. He let out a yell of pain as he hit the ground, clutching his arm. The wound sizzled and the nauseating smell of charred flesh struck Tasha's nostrils even as she began to move, low and quickly towards the Titan.

Hesch had flung himself forwards in a dive for cover when Dante fired a burst from his pulse rifle. One plasma slug struck the wall behind the Titan, the second slammed into his rifle, knocking it from his hands, but the third took Hesch in the thigh, throwing him off course—

And keeping him out of cover. Tasha drew her arm back to

throw, then paused. *Where do I throw? There are no gaps in his armour! Maybe—*

'Neural scrambler!' The shout came from Quinn, half ragged gasp, half yell.

Neural what— The band. It wasn't a big target. A couple of inches from top to bottom, and wrapped around the head of a man twenty feet away who had already started to move again. Without thinking, Tasha threw the knife.

It whirred briefly as it spun. The weight of the pommel shifted, then carried it forward in a blur—

To hammer into the silver band. A small burst of blue and white sparks flew up as the device shorted out. Frantically, Hesch yanked off his helmet and tossed it away, rolling behind the table as he did so.

'I don't have a shot!' yelled Dante as he scurried further into the room.

It started quietly. Tasha thought Quinn was moaning in pain, to begin with. But the sound got louder, and then louder again. She blinked and winced in discomfort as the pressure in the room shifted, dropping and then rising sharply as if a storm was coming. Quinn's moan became a scream, and the pressure became unbearable.

She turned to see him still on the ground, leaning on his good left arm. His mouth was wide, his eyes bloodshot. Tasha opened her mouth to ask him, beg him to stop, when all of a sudden—

He did. The pressure burst, a wave of... something, rushing past Tasha and Dante, buffeting them.

Then silence.

No one moved. Quinn had collapsed onto his back, and Tasha rushed to his side, conscious of Dante edging around the table to check on Hesch.

Quinn was unconscious but breathing. She turned to Dante, who had straightened and lowered his rifle. He looked over at her and nodded. 'The Titan's dead.'

A gasp spun Tasha around to see Quinn's eyes shoot open.

He blinked up at her, disoriented and breathing hard. After a moment he focused on her face, then winced and reached for his injured shoulder.

'Arse. This hurts like buggery.' He closed his eyes again and rested his head back on the ground. 'Given that I can only sense the three of us in the room, I assume we got the bastard?'

Dante stepped close and knelt down. 'We did. Nice job. You too, Tasha. Hell of a throw, that.'

Quinn grunted. 'Good. I never liked Titans.' He opened one eye. 'Now which one of you has got the medkit?'

* * *

It took a few minutes for Quinn to be patched up. He gritted his teeth as Dante sprayed medigel onto his wound; the initial stinging agony as it touched the burnt skin quickly faded into an irritating tingle. Tasha applied a dressing while he dry-swallowed a morphine tab, and he was back in action.

Stiff as hell, and I'm glad I'm left-handed, but back in action. Leaning mostly on his left hand, he pushed himself to his feet, wobbled, but stood.

Dante smiled. 'Like a newborn lamb. Feel all right?'

'How did you feel a few minutes after you were shot?' Quinn retorted.

Tasha clapped. 'Ha! I just realised. Now you have matching injuries.' Her smile vanished under two glares.

Dante checked his rifle. 'We got one of the two, but not the one we wanted. When that Titan fleet gets here tomorrow, they won't care that we took down Hesch,'—he jerked his head in the direction of the Titan's body—'so we still need Venus. Let's go get her.'

An ear-piercing siren wail split the air. Quinn groaned. 'Shit. I'm going to guess that's the "Our commander stopped talking to us and all we heard was gunfire" alarm.'

Dante cursed, while Tasha walked over to retrieve her knife.

She slipped it into its sheath as she returned. 'I think we need to split up, yes? Venus is surely going to flee as soon as the battle turns in our favour—we need to cover more ground than we can if we stay together.'

'Agreed,' Dante replied. 'Will you manage?' he asked Quinn. *I'll have to, won't I?* 'Sure. Never been better.' He cocked his — Dante's — sidearm, grimacing as pain lanced through his shoulder. He gave Dante a tight smile. 'Let's do it.'

Five minutes later, Quinn peered down from the middle level of the fortress, surveying the carnage below. The defending soldiers swarmed over the battlements and through the courtyard. The main gate was battered and bent, but somehow still holding, while huge chunks of masonry had been blasted off the upper part of the fortress's thick walls.

Bodies lay crushed and broken all around. He felt a little sick. A few of the corpses had no obvious injuries, and Quinn wondered how they had died.

While Tasha covered the floor above and Dante the ground level, he was to cover the middle floor. So far, so little: twice he had sensed approaching bodies and quickly knocked them out once they were in range. Both times he'd emerged from hiding and been disappointed to find they were just soldiers; even though it was unrealistic to think that he'd be able to take Venus down that easily. *That's me: perennial optimist.*

He had neared one of the fortress's corner towers, when he sensed someone moving at a run along the corridor adjacent to his own. He looked quickly about. *Nowhere to hide within range. Looks like I'll have to do this the less than subtle way.* Dropping into a crouch, Quinn levelled his weapon at the junction, and waited. And counted.

Three. Two. One.

A shape flashed past the junction. All-white clothing. A glimpse of flowing black hair. *Venus.*

But she was past. Quinn hissed a curse and jumped to his feet, wincing as pain broke through the morphine and shot through his shoulder at the sudden movement. Running as quickly as his injury would allow, he gave chase.

He reached the junction just in time to see her disappear around a corner. Feet pounding on the flagstone floor, he pushed himself after her. His shoulder complained more and more forcefully at his rough treatment; the painkillers had almost worn off. Quinn reached the next turn and took it... again just in time to see Venus duck through a doorway.

'Shit!' He bit his lip against the pain, tucked his right arm tightly into his side, and ran as fast as he could.

There was only one doorway in the wall near where he had last seen her. Pausing at the threshold, Quinn took a deep breath and raised his weapon, then kicked open the door.

To be faced with a sandspeeder. *What the—where is she going to go?*

Venus's head was just visible in the cockpit of the single-person speeder. Quinn trained his weapon on her and slipped his finger over the trigger—

Then closed his eyes, dazzled by sudden sunlight, as the opposite wall simply... fell away. With sudden horrified realisation—*She's not trapped at all!*—Quinn brought his gun up and fired five quick shots as the speeder engine fired into life.

None of his slugs struck—all were deflected away by the cockpit shield, and the speeder shot through the gap towards the desert beyond. Quinn ran to the hole and looked down to see the vehicle bounce, hard, as it landed on a strategically placed hill of sand piled up against the fortress wall, then bolt forward as the thrusters kicked in. He dropped his weapon to his side and watched as the speeder headed for the open desert.

Shit. Again.

A thought struck him. *At least I don't need to worry about bringing myself to kill her.*

* * *

Dante had swept the ground floor of the fortress twice, and found no sign of Venus. Four times, lone Ruhim soldiers had crossed his path, and he'd had to bring them down with his pulse rifle. It was unpleasant—in a way, the Ruhim were as much Venus's victims as anyone.

He waited in the cellar near the entrance to the desert tunnel, sitting hidden behind a barrel of either fuel or cooking oil; the labelling was in Karaki and he couldn't be bothered to get his terminal out to find out which. Rifle propped up against one knee, Dante closed his eyes. *I'm tired. So tired. I can't wait to get off this rock. I just hope either Quinn or Tasha had more luck than I did.*

A scuffed footstep at the cellar stairs snapped his eyes open. He waited, and heard the low double whistle that they'd agreed on. Dante stood and turned to see a joyless expression on Quinn's face.

'What happened?'

'She got away.' Quinn slumped down onto the floor and put his head back against the rough stone cellar wall. 'Drove a speeder through a wall and off a twenty-foot drop. Gone. Into the desert.' He shook his head.

Dante turned away. *I can't believe it. After everything, after all this... We've failed.* 'We're not going to get another chance. There's barely more than a day before that fleet arrives.'

Quinn shook his head again. 'I don't see how. She could hide anywhere, lie low for a day, thinking she's got plenty of time to come out and retake control.'

Damn it. 'Damn it!' Furious, Dante swept a crate off the top of a stack next to him. Vegetables flew through the air and hit the wall, the tomatoes bursting on impact. He stopped still for a few seconds, struck by the ridiculousness of the gesture.

Quinn started laughing. After a moment, so did Dante. Huge, body-shaking belly laughs that brought tears to his eyes. It took them half a minute to calm down.

'You're not being very stealthy,' Tasha said from the bottom stair. She looked at them as if they'd gone mad. 'What's going on?'

'It's... nothing. We just went a bit crazy for a second.' Dante shook himself. The fit had passed. 'Venus got away. And... I don't have another plan. I don't know what we're going to do.'

Tasha stayed quiet. Dante glanced at her and saw her expression had closed up.

She sat down heavily on the stair. 'Hesch has gone, too.'

'What?' Quinn yelped, jerking around to look at the young

Karaki.

Tasha nodded. 'I came back through the big room on my second sweep of the floor. His body was gone. I don't know why someone would have moved him, so…' She shrugged.

That's impossible. 'He was dead,' said Dante. 'Completely, stone-cold dead. Quinn, you said yourself—there were only the three of us alive in that room, when we left it.'

Quinn smiled grimly. 'Son of a bitch. Those bloody Titans. They've got more lives than a bloody alley cat.' He stood and strode towards the tunnel entrance. 'Let's get out of here. I've had enough of this damned fortress.'

With that, he disappeared into the tunnel.

Tasha rose and followed him.

Dante brought up the rear. As he swung the door closed behind him, the light in the tunnel dimmed, dimmed again, then was gone.

* * *

The battle was going badly. Hesch scanned the courtyard from the top of the watchtower at the furthest corner from the fortress's main gate. Judging by the pounding that gate had taken, it was a matter of a few minutes before the Hereb would break through.

I'm amazed it's lasted this long. Shaking his head with a weary sigh, Hesch reached down to a small cubbyhole in the parapet wall and extracted a coil of cable and a rappel device. Gripping one end of the cable, he tossed the coil over the wall, then secured the end to a sturdy pillar. The rappel device he clipped to a grenade loop on the armour at his waist, and then to the cable.

He was ready. As he climbed over the parapet and began rappelling the eighty feet to the desert below, Hesch thought back to those frenetic moments in the war room.

He'd known his chances were bad as soon as that crafty little bitch had put a knife in his neural scrambler. That, and the damage to his pulse rifle—he glanced down at it, strapped to his thigh; he didn't know why he'd bothered to pick it up—had put him in a bad spot. *If I'd hit the Seryn in the head instead of the arm, it might have all gone differently.* But he hadn't, and the bastard had told the girl about the scrambler, and that was that.

Hesch had felt the wave coming, of course. He'd been on the wrong end of a Seryn power surge before, and it wasn't pleasant. Add in the fact that Venus had told him this one, Quinn, could actually *kill* just by thinking about someone the wrong way...

It hadn't looked good. Which had left him one option:
Killswitch.

It was a Titan legend, almost. They taught final-year neophytes at the Academy how to use it: how to release just the right hormones and fire just the right neurons to flip that switch in your brain. Stop the heart, shut down all mental activity. Flatline everything for ten minutes until it wore off and your body started up again.

Except sometimes, it didn't. Only three men in history had survived attempting it. Eleven more had died. *Though two of those were burned to death, and one was evacuated into space without a suit.* Regardless, the odd weren't great. But he hadn't had a choice, so in that second up in the war room before the Seryn had fried his circuits for good, he'd done it. Thrown the switch.

And been pleasantly surprised to wake up what seemed like a few seconds later, to find his opponents had buggered off.

Hesch's feet touched down on the sand with a crunch. He unclipped the rappel device and tossed it, then turned to face the desert.

Time to get off this rock. Because the interesting thing, about those few seconds that were actually ten minutes, was that despite being totally, clinically, mind and body dead to the world... he'd heard something. Something bad.

'When that Titan fleet gets here tomorrow...'

Very bad. *I'm not sticking around for that.*

He'd stashed his ship a short ten-mile hike north of the fortress in a handily placed cave, for just such an unforeseen eventuality. Detaching his rifle from the thigh holster, he set off.

Venus… Venus will have to deal with my compatriots on her own. Hesch felt a twinge of guilty regret about not completing the job he'd signed on to do, but he wouldn't delude himself: He was a mercenary. There was no honour, there. *And that's all I am. For now, at least.*

He looked down again at the rifle. It was scarred and blistered from where the Commonwealth agent's plasma slug had hit it. Hesch reached for the power switch to give it a test charge, then thought better of it. People had lost hands, firing up busted pulse rifles. *Screw it.*

He tossed the rifle down on the sand and strode on.

I'll get another one.

17. Endgame

Dante brought the LUV to a stop behind the last rank of Hereb vehicles, a few hundred metres from the fortress walls.

'Look, the gate is down,' said Quinn, pointing. The Yumruk had finally broken through, and the gate hung in mangled strands. Troops were streaming through the gap to the sound of gunfire. Dante pushed open his door and climbed out.

'I'm going to go find Ruben,' Tasha said. 'Do you want to come?'

Quinn shrugged. 'Sure. Dante?'

'No.' He shook his head. 'I'm going to call LeClerq and fill her in.'

'Okay. See you later.' Quinn waved, and he and Tasha headed for the command tent pitched a short distance away.

Dante slumped down onto the ground on the shady side of the LUV and pulled out his personal terminal. The sand was hot on his legs, and the background noise of the ongoing battle was an indistinct clamour. He could feel a headache coming on.

LeClerq answered the call after one buzz. Her voice was a little crackly, but he could understand her. *The satgrid coverage isn't so great in the middle of the desert, then.*

'Zo. I've been expecting a call from you for days. What's going on?' She sounded stressed.

Dante was silent for a moment, trying to find a way to phrase it—

He gave up. 'We lost her, Director. Twice we had a shot; twice she got away.' He let his head fall back and hit the side of the LUV with a thud. 'There's only a day left, and we have no idea where Venus is.'

It was LeClerq's turn to be silent. Her voice, when it came through, was weary and sad. 'Damn it.'

'Pretty much.' Dante watched a dark blue beetle crawl onto the toe of his left boot.

'Is there anything you can do? Any way to draw her out?'

'We did that once already,' he replied. 'She isn't going to fall for it again. Venus has no reason to show herself for a while— she can just hide out, regroup, and go back to what she was doing. Well,'—he snorted—'at least as far as she knows. No, I can't think of a way out of this.' Dante tracked the beetle as it investigated his laces for a few seconds, then returned to the shiny toe.

LeClerq's voice crackled badly for a second. She said something, but all he heard was 'Zo?'

'Yes, boss?' The beetle had stopped moving. It seemed to be sunning itself.

'Did you do your best?'

'Pardon?' *What is she asking?*

LeClerq's voice was firmer. 'I said: Did you do your best?'

Dante sighed. 'Yes.' *I did. At least I can say that.* 'But it wasn't enough.'

'It's all you could do,' LeClerq replied. 'Remember: What's about to happen, this… travesty. It's on the head of Corralin and his damned Titans. Not you. Do you hear me?'

'I hear you.' The beetle climbed down from his boot and scuttled away across the sand. Dante watched it go. *It doesn't make it any better, but I hear you.*

LeClerq's voice seemed quieter, further away. Maybe the local sat had drifted out of range. 'It's time to come home, Zo. Okay? Come home, Dante.'

He nodded, then felt stupid. It wasn't like she could see him, he had video disabled. 'I'll see you soon.' The connection ended with a click, and Dante dropped the terminal into his lap. Ahead of him, soldiers were moving, yelling to each other, restocking, and changing gear. A bustle of purposeful movement. Dante closed his eyes.

In a day, they would all be dead.

* * *

Tasha strode towards the khaki command tent, Quinn trailing just behind. She wasn't looking forward to telling Ruben that all of their efforts had been in vain. *I wonder how many men he lost today.*

She spotted Azir, one of Ruben's lieutenants and his old mentor since he joined the Yumruk. He stood outside the tent briefing a small group of soldiers. The men saluted and left as Tasha and Quinn reached the grizzled veteran troop commander.

'How is the battle going, Azir?' she asked.

The commander turned and looked down at her. He'd lost his right eye in a firefight twenty years previously and defied convention by choosing to have an old-fashioned mechanical prosthetic installed, instead of having a new eye grown. The mechanical eye watched her, glinting and unblinking, while the living eye frowned, gaze softening.

Azir's lips turned down. 'Oh, Tasha. I've been waiting for your return.' He shook his head and let out a deep sigh. 'I'm so sorry...'

Tasha's stomach heaved, and her chest tightened as if a cold hand had gripped her heart. *Oh no. Don't tell me that. No, please don't tell me —*

'Ruben was killed. Just half an hour ago. It was a freak accident. He was behind cover, coordinating the attack, but... a bullet fired from the walls, it took an unlucky ricochet off a transport and...' Azir shook his head again. 'I'm so sorry.'

The sounds of the battle had faded to a dull murmur. Tasha's vision seemed to narrow to a tight tunnel focused on the mournful face of the man in front of her. She barely felt a hand come to rest on her shoulder. She barely felt anything.

But she knew she should... say something. Ask something. 'Was it quick? Was he in a lot of pain?'

Azir spread his arms and half-nodded. 'Yes. And no. The bullet took him in the throat. It was quick, but... not painless, no.' He glanced over her shoulder, presumably at Quinn, his expression imploring as if to ask: *What can I say?*

'I want to see him.'

'Tasha, I think—'

'Take me to see my brother, please. Now.' She kept her gaze fixed on the gleaming gold medal in the shape of an eagle that he wore at his left breast.

Tasha heard him sigh, then he waved her forward. 'As you wish. This way.'

He led her—and Quinn, whose hand still rested lightly on her shoulder—past the command tent, around a pile of artillery ammunition, and to a long, narrow tent of pale-grey canvas that was clearly set up as a field hospital. Men with minor injuries sat outside, resting or wincing in pain or just complaining to each other. The soldiers fell silent at their approach, several saluting Azir and nodding to Tasha. She was well known.

She ignored them all and followed the old soldier into the tent.

The dead were at the far end: six cots with the occupants covered by faded white sheets. Azir stopped next to the nearest cot on the left and turned back. 'You don't need to do this, Tasha. You—'

'Show me.'

Slowly and with great care Azir lifted the hem of the sheet

and folded it back, tucking it just below Ruben's jaw. *So I don't see the damage. As if I've never seen an opened throat before.*

He was pale. So, so pale. *Almost as pale as Quinn.* The thought shot through her mind, a bizarre and macabre joke. Tasha felt as though she might fall down. Or float away.

She knelt at her brother's side and reached out to gently touch his brow. It was cold, icy, even in the warm afternoon air. Tasha leaned in and placed a kiss on Ruben's forehead, then pulled the sheet back up to cover him.

Then she just knelt there. In silence, waiting. Waiting to feel something.

Anything.

* * *

Night had fallen, and Karak's two moons bathed the desert in a pale blue glow. Quinn stared into the heart of the campfire he and Dante had built to keep away the chill. They had offered to help the Yumruk with the retrieval and wrapping of the dead, or the watch on the Ruhim prisoners who had been corralled in a makeshift stockade. But the troop commander they had spoken to had just waved them away.

I don't blame him. We've not been much help up to this point, so why would we be now?

Dante had pulled a fresh bottle of whisky from a bag stowed in their LUV. Quinn had wondered where the man got them from. *Did he bring a case from Nexus P? Impressive dedication, that.*

Half an hour and a quarter of the bottle later, Tasha had arrived and slumped down on a rock next to the fire. Quinn had surreptitiously glanced at the girl—she looked... Well, he didn't know what she looked like. *Not quite stunned, but something like that.*

No one spoke. Quinn watched ten or fifteen moths fluttering in the air above the fire, dancing on the warm updrafts. Every so often, a buzzing insect or flying lizard would zip through the crowd, snatching a moth away and disappearing into the night, while those left danced on, regardless. *Mindless.*

He was about to toss the bottle back to Dante when Tasha

stuck her hand out for it. Without a word Quinn passed the whisky to her. Tasha unstoppered the bottle and took a large swig, grimacing slightly at the burn, then recapped it. She lobbed it to Dante, who caught it with one hand.

Tongue seemingly loosened by the booze, Tasha asked, 'Have either of you lost someone?' She pushed up her sleeve and unclasped a delicate bracelet of silver or pale gold from about her wrist, and turned it over in her hands. Tiny blue gems, studded along the bracelet's length, sparkled in the firelight. 'Someone close.'

Quinn shared a glance with Dante, then answered first. 'My father. He caught Trex before we knew how to cure it.'

Dante chimed in. 'Both my parents. It was an accident, years ago.'

Tasha nodded thoughtfully. 'So you understand.' She was silent for a moment, still staring into the flames, then looked up with eyes that were completely dry. 'Can one of you tell me why, when my brother is lying dead a hundred yards away, I... I can't cry?'

Damn. Quinn looked away, swallowed.

Dante replied. 'It takes time, Tasha. You're in shock—it's to be expected. Just give it ti—'

Tasha snorted a laugh. 'How much time do I have, Dante? How much time to learn how to grieve for my brother, who I loved? A day? Less?' Her voice was bitter.

Quinn had been rolling the question around his mind for hours, unsure whether he would ask it. 'You could come with us.' Tasha's gaze had gone back to the fire and didn't budge. 'One of us, I mean. If you wanted,' he finished lamely.

After a few seconds of silence Tasha shook her head. 'No. You two should leave. There's no reason for you to die here. But this is where I belong. I have one day left to spend with my family, and that's what I'll do.' A grim smile curled one side of her mouth. 'And it's Hal-Ap-Khet tomorrow, so perhaps the gods will smile on us and save Karak. I doubt it, somehow.'

Dante frowned. 'What's Hal-Ap-Khet?'

Tasha sighed. 'It's a religious festival. The most important one, for all of the eight tribes. It comes around every fifteen months, marking the last day of the year in the old calendar from our Home-That-Was.' She picked up a stick and tossed it into the fire. 'All Karaki come together and ask the gods for forgiveness and blessings for the coming year. As I said, I doubt it will help.'

Quinn looked at Dante, who seemed interested. *What's got him so excited?*

'Exactly what does that mean, "come together"?' Dante asked.

Tasha frowned. 'Just that. All of the tribes put aside their differences for one day and gather together across the planet. The biggest gathering is always in the Karkas Basin, where the old statues of the Elu-het stand. Four hundred thousand people come, fifty thousand from each tribe. The leaders speak, and we pray, and…' She tailed off.

Quinn realised at the exact same moment. He looked back at Dante, who smiled. *Son of a bitch.* 'That's it, isn't it? That's where she's going to be. Fifty thousand people, from every tribe…'

The operative nodded. Tasha leaned forward. 'You really think—'

Dante cut her off. 'Do we have any other ideas?'

'But you're supposed to leave, get off the planet. If we attempt this and we're wrong—'

Quinn interrupted, 'We want to see this through. To the end, whatever that might be.'

Dante nodded. 'There are eleven million people on Karak. We have to try.'

We have to give them a chance. A log snapped in the heart of the campfire, and sparks shot up into the night. The moths rose and fell, dancing with death. *Because the fire that's on its way is a million times worse.*

* * *

A coyote howled somewhere nearby. Venus looked up from the pot in her hands and stopped stirring the mixture for a moment.

With the glare from the small fire she knelt in front of, it was almost impossible to see anything beyond the speeder she'd parked across the entrance to the cave. She was near the centre of the Domu hill range, hundreds of miles from the nearest town.

The coyote stopped howling. Venus went back to stirring.

The mixture gradually turned into a thick paste the colour of clay. She'd taken a pint and a half of water and added to it seven heaped measures of bloodsalt. The gritty mineral resisted dissolution, but half an hour of persistence had done the job.

The fire was ready, the flames low, and the wood glowing white-hot. The mixture was ready, too. Careful to keep the iron pot steady, Venus placed it in the centre of the fire. The first bubble popped on the surface of the brew soon after.

She crossed her arms in her lap and waited. And, idly, wondered, *How many times… How many silent, solitary vigils? Waiting for someone, or something.* She smiled slightly. *Though rarely for something so mundane as a pot to boil.*

A few minutes later, before the mixture had fully come to the boil, a wind sprung up and whistled past the speeder and into the cave. The fire flared indignantly, and Venus shivered against the sudden chill. She leaned closer in to the fire, her gaze fixed on the bubbling liquid.

There. The colour of the brew shifted in an instant from a dark orange to a deep crimson. Venus quickly slipped on a pair of heat-resistant gloves and rose to a kneeling position. She gripped the handles of the iron pot and lifted it clear from the fire, then stood. Feeling the heat even through the heavily insulated gloves, she walked to the cave entrance and squeezed past the speeder. The nose was dented and badly scratched, looking worse for wear after its heavy landing earlier.

The water bucket sat on the ground ten feet beyond the speeder, exposed to the cold night air and the harsh winds. Wasting no time, Venus sunk the pot into the bucket as she turned away and closed her eyes. Steam shot upwards, hissing violently and bathing her face and neck with a sheen of sweaty condensation.

She held it there for a full minute, until all noise had ceased and the bloodsalt mixture had ceased bubbling.

It's time.

Venus returned to the campfire inside the cave, her body relaxing in the warmth, already chilled after just a minute's exposure to the desert night. She gently placed the pot on the ground—*careful, don't want to spill it and have to do this all over again*—then reached into the trunk at her back, which she had stowed there weeks earlier. After a moment's rummaging, her hand closed on the ceramic goblet.

For the... hundredth time? Two hundredth? I've lost track. Venus poured half of the thick bloodsalt brew into the goblet. The water bucket had done its job; the drink was merely warm.

As Venus raised the goblet to her lips, a memory popped into her mind, unbidden: Quinn's face. She felt a little... nostalgic, all of a sudden. *Poor boy. Dear, sweet Quinn. I wonder if he'll ever forgive me.*

'*Salut,*' she whispered, then downed the draught.

Quickly, before the bloodsalt overcame her, she poured the remainder of the mixture into the cup. With barely a breath between drinks, she gulped down the second draught.

And now it comes.

She slumped back against the trunk, her vision blurring. *It's so strong... So much, never so much before...* The goblet rolled from her fingers and landed on the sandy granite floor. Venus closed her eyes and let the power course through her.

She felt it coming, the geas rushing up from her belly, hammering her heart like a drum, blazing into her mind—

And she was out. Her viewpoint was high, high above the hills, looking down upon a dim spot of light that she knew was the entrance to the cave where her body lay. Swaying on the wind, dipping and rising, Venus danced and spun, revelling in the freedom.

Her consciousness vibrated, pinged by some presence nearby. *The coyote, maybe? I'll give him a scare.* She turned, in all directions at once, casting out to find the source of the—

Oh, many sources. Many, many... Fifteen miles away—twenty, perhaps. Not a town, not a village, a... camp? *Nomads.* Living off the land. *Part of the land, they say.* Feeling mischievous, Venus threw her mind-self forward.

She sped over the intervening distance in seconds, and looked down upon the camp half a minute later. There were almost a thousand in the camp, ranged around a large oasis in its centre. Most were asleep; Venus could see, or... feel, the threads of their consciousnesses, swaying gently as they dreamed. A few vibrated more strongly, and moved steadily—no doubt sentries patrolling the borders of the settlement.

Venus let her mind float down, dropping towards the largest tent near the centre of the camp on the edge of the oasis. The canvas roof rose to meet her, then vanished as she slipped through.

An old—no, ancient—man slept on a comfortable-looking bed. The thrum of his mind was strong, deep and steady. Had she a mouth in her current form, Venus would have smiled as she reached out and gripped the thread of the elder's mind.

And squeezed.

He whimpered in his sleep, limbs quivering and shaking as his dreams were thrown into a tumult. Venus wondered what he had been thinking of and what catastrophe had befallen his dreamscape.

Enough playing. I'm ready.

Releasing the old man's mind, she drifted upwards, up and out of the tent, up and away from the camp. Back, swiftly, speeding over the desert towards the hills and down towards a tiny spot of dim light in the dark—

Venus opened her eyes.

Tomorrow. She breathed deeply, her speeding heart slowing. *Tomorrow it all ends.*

18. Incarnate

Dante stood on the rim of Karkas Basin and stared out at the largest gathering of people he had ever seen.

How the hell are we supposed to find her in this?

The basin was a natural depression, a circle four hundred metres in diameter and almost fifty deep. Circling the edge at regular intervals were twenty or thirty statues of enormous proportions, each as tall as the basin was deep and five metres thick at their base. Dante had studied them when they arrived three hours earlier, and the nearest was just a few metres to his left. Some of them looked roughly human; others seemed to depict hybrid creatures from myth and legend.

The Pillars of the Elu-het, Tasha said. Or the Elu, as we'd call them back home. Looks like they made it to Karak, too. Dante had never gotten familiar with the confusing mixture of history and fable that surrounded the ancient civilisation that pre-dated humanity by tens of millennia. *But they knew how to make statues, I'll give them that.*

The bowl of the basin was lined with deep stone steps in concentric circles around a wide open space at the centre, in which a stone platform had been built. He only knew the steps were there because when he arrived, only two hundred thousand people or thereabouts had been present, and some of the basin floor had still been visible.

It wasn't now.

Looks like the full complement. Fifty thousand from each tribe — four hundred thousand in all. And it's almost time to begin. Dante raised his binocs to his eyes and focused in on the central stage. Eight men, all older than middle age, sat in a half-circle in the centre of the stage. Around its edges stood twenty or so guards, dressed in ceremonial robes and armed with long, curved swords that looked anything but ceremonial.

Above them stood a scaffold topped with four enormous screens; as Dante watched, they flickered to life, displaying a close-up of one of the tribal elders sitting below the scaffold. A ragged cheer rose from some parts of the amphitheatre. Louder boos followed, from other areas.

This could kick off without any help from us.

His terminal buzzed. Keeping his eyes glued to the binocs, Dante raised it to his ear.

'It's Quinn.'

'Have you got her?' Dante asked.

'I think… almost.' The chatter in the background made Quinn's words difficult to make out. 'I've criss-crossed about three-quarters of the basin trying to get a sense of her, and I thought I just did, but… I can't see her. I should be able to see her, if I can sense her, unless…'

'Quinn?'

A few seconds of silence followed, then Quinn's voice came through, his tone thoughtful. 'Unless she's stronger than she was last time. I'd feel it from farther away. Maybe… I'm going to head towards the source. Stay on the line.'

What else am I going to do? Dante waited impatiently, his heart drumming.

After half a minute, Quinn came back on the line. 'It's her. I think. I mean, I'm pretty sure, but... I can't believe it.'

'Believe what?' Dante asked.

'The power signature she's giving off; it's Venus, definitely, but amplified beyond anything I would've imagined. If she *is* the woman I'm following, then she's still two hundred feet away — but it feels like she's sitting on my shoulder.' He groaned faintly. 'It's giving me a headache.'

'Where are you? And how is she disguised?' Dante's hand itched from his eagerness to get sight of the target.

'Between the statue that looks like a bearded man with breasts, and the one of a... I don't know, jackal-turtle? Turtle body, but with a dog head,' Quinn answered.

'Got it.' Dante swung the binocs to the right sector.

'I'm halfway between the edge and the centre, moving towards the stage. Venus — or the woman I'm following, rather — is dressed as one of the attendants. She's carrying a basket of those bloodsalt wafers.'

Dante snorted. 'I'm sure she's enjoying the irony.'

'Ha. Quite. Look, I need to get closer. Get in touch with Tasha and tell her to meet me?' Quinn asked. 'She's in the crowd too. I can barely hear you, and if I call her, neither of us will be able to make each other out.'

'On it. Keep me posted.' Dante tapped the connection closed with his thumb and, with his other hand, zoomed the binoculars in further. In his sights, a woman walked slowly and solemnly, dressed all in black, with only her mouth and jaw visible below a broad hood. Every few steps, she reached into her woven leather basket, also black, and retrieved a small circular wafer the colour of rust, which she passed to a nearby worshipper.

Dante watched her for a few seconds more. *Is that you, Venus?* With a sigh, he lowered the binoculars and looked to his terminal.

Tasha, you're up.

* * *

Venus smiled down at the elderly woman kneeling to her left as she handed her a bloodsalt wafer. The lady, dressed in the shapeless black dress-cum-toga that seemed to be the uniform amongst Karaki females once they passed a certain age, nodded her thanks.

Gently, Venus slipped into her mind, checking for a seed of belief.

There. The old woman already carried the notion, but not strongly. *She must have picked it up second- or third-hand from a neighbour, a friend, or perhaps just a stranger in the street.* However it had been implanted, the lady was already primed with the idea—a simple idea, of a more specific kind of worship rather than the directionless wailing that would normally be about to start.

Normally.

No, the woman was ready for a more focused faith, one with no need for belief in a pantheon of deities and heroes that had been absent for millennia. One based around a single figure. A living figure.

A saviour.

Venus touched the seed in the woman's mind—reinforcing it, amplifying it—making it a repeater and a beacon. She watched with delight as the expression on the lady's face changed from plodding, solemn devotion to a vibrant, fierce joy. Her eyes shone, and her lips trembled.

Turning away from the old woman and closing her eyes, Venus reached out and touched the threads, those tightly packed tendrils that connected her to almost every person inside the basin. She had been there for hours, walking the aisles, up and down and back and forth. More than three hundred thousand people were on the edge of religious exultation. All primed. All ready.

Ready to meet their new god.

A few hundred yards ahead of her, Venus saw the Ruhim representative to the religious quorum rise and approach the lectern that would carry his voice to the furthest edges of the amphitheatre. Venus glanced up—the man's face was crisp and clear on the fifty-foot high screen, with every weathered wrinkle captured. No one in the basin would miss a thing.

Perfect.

Venus resumed her slow walk. A young man on her right looked up at her, eyes shining. Smiling, she handed him a wafer.

* * *

The earpiece linked to the terminal in Quinn's pocket made his ear itch and sweat horribly. He found it hard to resist the urge to tear it out and throw it away. *Damn cheap plastic.*

His headache had gotten worse, too, which didn't help his mood. Gaze fixed on the woman ahead of him, he pushed his way through the crowd of standing Karakis and stepped carefully between the kneeling worshippers, trying not to tread on anything. *Don't want to start a brawl right now.*

Making his way through the crowd was like wading through treacle, but Quinn was only a hundred feet away from the attendant. *It has to be her.* The power Venus gave off was almost impossible to credit, and yet... Quinn shook his head, wincing, and wiped sweat from his face and neck. And came to a realisation.

I'm not going to be able to do this the usual way. Without taking his eyes off of Venus's back, he reached into his pocket and tapped the redial button.

'Hey,' Dante said. 'Tasha knows where you are. She says she's a minute away.' Quinn could barely hear the words over the cacophony of chanting, singing, and prayer.

'Good, thanks. But that's not why I called. Look...' Quinn sighed. 'Venus is too strong for me to be able to shut her down the way I normally do. She's amped up her power something massive since the assault on Yej.'

'So what's the plan?' asked Dante.

'I think I can still do it, but I'll need to get close. Really close. Touching distance.' Quinn almost tripped over an old man who stretched a leg out in his path, but recovered his balance.

Dante was silent for a moment. 'You need a distraction.'

Quinn snorted. 'That's what I like about working with you, Dante. We're on the same page. Do you have anything in mind? Anything left in your bag of tricks?'

The operative's low chuckle was almost malevolent. 'Oh, there's always something left in the bag. Let me think.'

Quinn shouldered his way past a portly middle-aged man, then stopped abruptly to avoid knocking over a girl of six or so who appeared in front of him out of nowhere. *Come on, Dante. We really don't have—*

'Ha. Yes, that'll do it. It'll take... three minutes or so, before I'm ready. Okay?'

'Not a problem,' Quinn replied. 'It's going to take me that long to catch up to her. I'll ping your terminal when I'm in position.'

'Understood. Out.' Dante dropped the call.

Quinn kept moving. He was seventy or eighty feet away now; Venus kept disappearing for an instant, as worshipers crossed his path. Every time she reappeared, he was a little bit closer.

Three minutes, at least. Quinn pushed on.

* * *

Tasha couldn't see Quinn. She stood near the stage in the centre of the basin, and she was definitely in the right section of the amphitheatre. Dante's description of the statues would have been downright offensive to anyone from the more devout elder Karaki generation, who treated the Pillars almost as idols, but Tasha had understood which he'd meant. *Bask, half man–half woman. Hep, the turtle-dog. I'm here, but where are you, Quinn?*

The first speaker had begun his sermon a few moments ago. Tasha let the words wash over, gaze fixed on the crowd, scanning for any sign of Venus or that familiar mop of red hair. But gradually the speaker's words wormed their way into her consciousness. And she realised why. *This sermon is... odd.*

Normally the speeches at Hal-Ap-Khet were the same every year. Tolerance, forgiveness for past slights, unity, faithfulness— all worthy notions, but not particularly exciting. But that day...

The speaker—Tasha glanced up at the screen, and recognised him as Ruhim; *What a coincidence*—recounted a story from the old world. A legend, almost: a fable of old heroes, and ancient gods, of a golden age when times were better and all the people of the world were united. *Where is he going with this?*

Most of those in the crowd in front of Tasha were nodding and swaying, some shouting agreement at the speaker's words. Tasha felt herself nodding along with them, caught up in the rhythm and cadence of the sermon. She shook herself and frowned, trying to concentrate on the mass of people in front of her and the speech at the same time.

The tone had changed, the tale complete. Instead the Ruhim elder spoke of prophecy, of old gods and ancient heroes returning—coming to Karak to find their lost followers, to walk amongst the believers and bring blessings to the faithful and divine retribution to the faithless.

Tasha's pulse raced, her skin hot under her clothes. *What's happening to me? Why is this affecting me like—*

It struck her. It was so obvious, once she realised: *Venus. Why did I think I would be immune? I wasn't, last time.*

But knowing what was happening didn't help. Her limbs trembled, frozen, attention caught by the words of the Ruhim speaker. His voice rose to a crescendo, exhorting the crowd who roared their approval and their belief in return. Tasha opened her mouth to shout with them.

One of the ceremony attendants stepped past her, dropping an almost-empty basket of bloodsalt wafers as she passed. Tasha's mind felt sluggish, drugged, as she turned to watch the woman climb the steps onto the stage and approach the lectern.

The speaker turned to her with an exultant cry and fell to his knees.

The woman raised her hands, unbuttoned her robe, and threw it back.

Venus.

She was dressed all in white, perfect and pristine. The giant screens above the stage were zoomed in close, fixed on her face, her eyes... Eyes that blazed red with a fire that was not human.

Tasha exhaled in a gasp, releasing a breath she didn't know she'd been holding. *My lady my leader my saviour no wait my—* She couldn't breathe. The air seemed to have been sucked out of the basin as the whole crowd fell silent.

Then two things happened at once.

The first was a man rushing past her, ramming an elbow hard into her ribs and hissing 'Now!' as he headed for the stage steps. The sharp pain jerked Tasha into life—her head seemed to clear, at least a little. She spun to track him. Red hair, pale skin.

Quinn.

The second was an explosion.

Against the hushed reverence of the crowd the blast was like a clap of thunder brought down to the ground. Tasha spun again in the direction of the noise and watched, disbelieving, as a cloud of grey and brown dust burst out from the base of one of the Pillars. *Kolp, the eternal child.* Thousands screamed at once as the ancient statue began to lean, mercifully away from the basin, further and further until the tipping point was reached.

Then toppled. The impact sent shock waves throughout the amphitheatre, shaking Tasha where she stood. For a moment, she just stared. *Oh, Dante. What did—*

Quinn. Cursing her lethargy, Tasha turned and ran for the stage.

* * *

Quinn took the steps up to the stage two at a time. To his left, Venus raised her arms to the crowd. Four hundred thousand people fell to their knees as one, the earlier cacophony of the basin replaced by a church-like hush.

To his right the nearest guard, elaborately dressed in gold and red robes and strapped with a gleaming sabre, stepped forward, barking something in Karaki. *Sorry, fella.* Not wanting to attract attention, Quinn flicked out just enough power to stun the man; he slumped to the ground as Quinn headed for Venus.

He was only thirty feet away, his path clear. *Dante, any time now would be—*

A distraction, he'd asked for. Quinn had been expecting something, but even he was briefly stunned at the explosion that erupted from the bottom of the statue near Dante's position. He could only stare in awe as the pillar began to fall. The entire crowd in front of him turned away from the stage and watched, finding their voices again to scream and shout in disbelief and outrage.

Thanks, partner.

Quinn was only ten paces away. Venus's arms were slowly dropping to her sides as she, too, watched the massive statue slam into the ground with a thunderous impact.

Five paces away. Quinn took a breath.

Three. He reached out.

One.

Quinn stepped up close behind Venus and gripped her head in both of his hands. She gasped and grabbed at his wrists as he pressed his forehead to the back of her head, closed his eyes — and poured himself into her mind.

It was like flying through a lightning storm. Solid tendrils of energy hung all around him, hundreds, thousands in all directions, emerging from the maelstrom ahead of him and stretching back past him into the real world.

Bursts of electricity, changing in colour through blue and purple and green a hundred times a second, flew across his path as he seemed to both fall and rise all at once. Quinn felt the intent behind them as they shifted, directed towards him with purpose and outraged malice.

Hastily erected mental barriers appeared in front of him, shimmering multicolour translucent walls stretched across the infinite space of Venus's mind in every direction. Quinn hammered through them one by one, blasting them aside with every ounce of his power.

His initial attack had come too quickly, had gotten him in too close, for Venus to recover.

He hoped.

Dodging arcs of power that would cripple his mind if they

struck, slamming into and through walls like a flooding river, Quinn raced for the centre of Venus's mind, and the core of her power.

Some residual surface consciousness shouted for his attention somewhere behind or above him. Flashes of vision came through, scattered images. *Tasha. Dancing around him once again, blades flashing, parrying and slashing as sabre-wielding guards rush in towards him.*

Still he fell—or rose. There was no direction in that place, only motion, momentum, danger, and a pure energy that went beyond any adrenaline rush.

He could sense the core ahead of him—the knot at the centre of Venus's mind where all of those tendrils, those flickering threads of pure energy, were tethered.

More images from the real world: *The crowd turning back to face the stage, realising what was happening. The first rows surging to their feet and rushing for the stage, pushing each other aside in a desperate bid to be the one to destroy the man who had dared put his hands on their god. Tasha, blades gleaming red, bodies at her feet, face and clothes spattered with blood, stepping between him and the mob.*

He didn't have much time. There was one wall left between him and the core—one last barrier, thicker than any other. With a soundless war cry, Quinn threw all of his power at the wall, crashing into it at the speed of thought.

It cracked.

Fractured.

Burst.

Only seconds remain before the first of the mob will reach Tasha and tear her apart.

Quinn wrapped his consciousness around the core of Venus's mind—that dazzling, fulgent storm of furious, violated indignation—enveloping it in a mental fist.

The mob is a few paces away.

He felt every thread, every link between Venus and one of her followers, millions reaching out mile after mile across the world.

And cut them loose.

19. Recovery

Dante watched in horror as the crowd, their attention no longer pulled away by the falling statue, surged towards Tasha and Quinn. The assassin stood with her blades bared, facing down a mob of thousands, while Quinn stood close behind Venus, his hands clamped to her head.

'Come on. Come on,' Dante muttered. The crowd had reached the stage and the first of them were climbing onto it. They were only moments away. *They're going to be torn apart.*

He held his breath, and forced himself to watch.

Tasha raised her knives.

Come on.

Venus slumped to the ground.

Dante, his eyes on the charging mob, saw a wave seem to pass through them. The worshipers reeled back drunkenly, the wave rippling out in all directions across the entire basin. Those who had a moment earlier been in a violent rage merely stood, looking about themselves with confused expressions.

He exhaled. 'Talk to them, Tasha. It's not over yet,' he murmured, then watched as she slipped her bloodied blades back into their sheaths and stepped towards the nearest of the former mob. Hands empty and help up placatingly, she began to speak.

In the background, a few of the religious leaders who had fled the stage during the excitement were warily returning.

Dante shifted the binocs slightly to find Quinn. He stood with his eyes fixed on the body at his feet. Dante couldn't tell if Venus was alive or dead. Either way, it hardly mattered.

Dropping the binocs to hang at his chest, Dante pulled out his terminal. Two taps patched him through his subspace wave communicator to LeClerq.

She answered on the first buzz. 'Zo! Where the hell are you? I expected—'

He cut her off. 'Karak, ma'am.'

'What?' LeClerq barked. 'I told you to—'

'We've got her, boss. We have Venus. I won't know which for a few minutes, but she's either dead or in custody.' Dante waited for a response. 'Ma'am?'

'I'm here, Zo, I'm just… That's excellent news. Don't go anywhere—I need to call the Titan liaison and get that fleet to stand down.' She cut the connection with a click.

Dante slipped the terminal into his pocket and headed down into the basin towards the stage. On all sides, people were holding their heads or crying or having anxious-sounding conversations with their neighbours. No one paid any attention to him. *No one noticed it was me who rigged the pillar with explosives.*

His terminal chimed when he was only halfway to the centre of the basin. 'Yes, ma'am?'

'The Titan fleet is holding in orbit.'

Dante sighed with relief. 'That's tremendous.'

LeClerq continued. 'For now, at least—they're waiting for confirmation from us that, quote, "the memetic has been contained or killed," end quote.' She sighed with what sounded to Dante like a huge amount of relief. 'It was a job very well done, Zo. Bring this last part home.'

'Thank you, ma'am.' Dante frowned. 'There's one thing we haven't discussed, though. Who exactly has jurisdiction here? Of all the parties involved, we've probably got the weakest claim. The Karakis would be perfectly justified in wanting her brought to trial here for war crimes, and the Seryn have been after her for years, from what Quinn's told me.'

LeClerq hemmed. 'That question is still up for debate. I hope to have an answer for you shortly, but I'm not finding it easy to get in touch with the relevant Seryn authorities. No one seems to want to admit they even exist, for a start.' The director snorted. 'And we think we keep a low profile. I'll get back to you, Zo.'

'Understood, ma'am.' Dante ended the call. On the stage, some form of order seemed to have been restored. There was no fighting underway, at least, although a medical team scurried in from somewhere to treat the ten or so guards who Tasha had brought down during the madness.

Time to make sure Venus is dead or contained.

* * *

'Do you all understand?' Tasha looked between the faces of the eight tribal leaders.

The men, all elderly or close to it, looked at each other with expressions of sheer bafflement on their faces. But one by one they nodded. *Good.*

Gyr, the Hereb leader, spoke. 'Your story would be impossible to believe, Tasha, if we hadn't each felt ourselves under that foreign influence. And now, blessedly, we are ourselves again.' He nodded again. 'We will do as you ask, and ask the people to keep the peace until we can come to terms with what has happened these past months.'

Tasha bowed her thanks, and the leaders turned away.

'Hey.' She spun to see Dante approaching. 'Everything okay here?' He looked down at Venus, still slumped on the floor. Quinn hadn't said anything since she dropped, but he looked up as Dante's spoke.

Gods, he looks terrible. He seemed to have aged five years in that one minute; his eyes were sunken and ringed with dark circles, and there was an unhealthy pallor to his skin.

But his lip curled in that familiar half-smile. 'That was your idea of a distraction? Blowing up a two hundred foot tall monument that's been here—how long?' Quinn looked at Tasha.

She shrugged. 'Before we were here. At least a thousand years.'

Quinn shook his head in mock outrage. 'Shocking behaviour. What kind of way is that for a tourist to act?'

Dante laughed. 'Did the job, though, didn't it?'

'Aye,' Quinn nodded. 'It did.' He closed his eyes and rocked back on his heels as a wave of tiredness seemed to pass through him. 'Good lord, do I need a holiday. Somewhere... cold.'

Tasha smiled. 'So what now?'

Dante answered. 'The Titan fleet is holding off for the moment. They won't be completely satisfied until they've seen Venus for themselves, though.' He stepped over to the fallen Seryn and knelt, pressing his fingers to her neck. 'She's still alive, but just barely. I don't know what you did to her, Quinn, but she's in bad shape.'

Tasha called over to Gyr, who stood nearby, quietly conversing with one of his counterparts. '*Baba*—I think we should move the witch out of the basin. The crowd is calm enough now, but they may just be in shock. Once they come to their senses, there's going to be a lot of anger, and most of it directed at this woman.'

The elder nodded his acquiescence. 'A sensible notion. You four,' he called to a group of guards nearby who had avoided conflict with Tasha, 'provide an escort out of the basin for our... guests.'

Dante pulled Venus over his shoulder and straightened, lifting her easily as the guards closed in and formed a square. 'Good thing this isn't that Titan, Hesch. I would have had trouble carrying him.'

It was a nerve-wracking journey up and out of the basin.

Tasha kept her hands near her knives at all times, but the worst they faced were a few angry shouts and one thrown water bottle, which one of the guards batted away.

Everyone's too stunned to know what's going on, thankfully.

As they reached the lip of the basin and stepped out onto the flat of the desert plain, a burbling chime ran out. Tasha looked around to see Quinn frown and stare back at her as Dante carried Venus still further from the soon-to-be hostile crowd.

'Eh? You and Dante are here, so who...' Quinn pulled out the local terminal he had picked up and stared at the screen. 'Contact unknown.'

Tasha shrugged. 'Worth answering, I would think.'

Quinn tapped the screen and held the terminal to his ear. 'Hello?'

* * *

'Good afternoon, Quinn.' The clipped, crisp tone was instantly familiar and yet struck Quinn as strangely surreal.

'Sebastien. I would ask how you got my contact information, but I feel like you're about to surprise me even more.'

That familiar low chuckle rang out of the terminal. 'Possibly, possibly. I just called to congratulate you on a job well done.'

How the hell— 'The job I just finished doing two minutes ago, you mean.'

'Quite.' The senior agent cleared his throat. 'And also to give you new orders—simple ones, I assure you. Merely hold your position and wait. A retrieval team will be with you imminently. Understood?'

'Just about, but Seb—' A click told him the call was over.

Quinn slipped the terminal back into his pocket and briefly closed his eyes. *Feels like someone's shaken my head back and forth for about an hour. I can barely think straight.* He opened his eyes; a short way in the distance, Dante had lain Venus down in the shade of one of the pillars as Tasha waved away the Karaki escort. Quinn walked over to join them.

'That was my boss.' Tasha and Dante turned to look at him. 'There's an Agency retrieval team on their way.'

Tasha's face clouded. 'You cannot simply remove the woman. There is a decision to be made first, over what to do with her. She needs to stand trial, here on Karak, and face justice.'

Dante pointed at the sky to his left. 'Then you'd better hurry and find someone to enforce that claim, Tasha, because I'm pretty sure that team's going to be here in a minute.'

A small dot in the sky above the western horizon grew quickly as it approached. Tasha turned, spitting a curse in Karaki, and sprinted back down into the basin. Quinn and Dante watched the shuttle approach—for a shuttle it was, small, sleek and black—then covered their faces as the vehicle cruised into land, the landing thrusters kicking up a cloud of sandy dust in all directions.

After a few moments the dust had settled, and the shuttle door swung open.

'There are no markings anywhere on that ship,' Dante noted.

'No,' Quinn replied. 'We don't have a logo.'

He watched as four men emerged from the craft and fanned out. None spoke.

Quinn sighed and stepped forward. 'Afternoon, fellas. I don't mean to be a pain, but I don't know who the hell any of you are, so until I see some identification—'

'You know me, don't you, Quinn?' The voice came from just inside the shuttle and was soon followed by its owner: a young, slim woman. Bright blue eyes sparkled beneath cropped auburn hair. Freckles dotted her cheeks.

'We've not had the pleasure, but yes.' Quinn licked his lips and swallowed, feeling nervous. 'It's nice to meet you, Ariadne. I'd heard you might be doing some work for us, but no one seemed to know for sure.'

She walked towards him, smiling. 'They keep me busy. No time to meet your co-workers in this job, is there?'

Quinn weakly returned the smile. *This isn't helping my headache.*

'Anyway,' she went on. 'You've done a wonderful job. Truly

marvellous. Super impressive. We can take it from here.'

Quinn frowned. 'And where exactly will you be taking it from here? Where is Venus going?'

Ariadne shook her head apologetically. 'Sorry, but I've been told you don't need to know that.'

You're kidding me. 'Look, I know who you are, and I know a bit about what you've done, but it's not clear you've got the authority to—'

'Did Sebastien not call you?' Ariadne interrupted.

'Yes, he did, but—'

'Well, there you go, then.' Ariadne smiled sweetly and turned to the man on her left. 'You can put her in the ship now, please.' Quinn watched impotently as two of the nameless men retrieved Venus and carried her into the shuttle. He felt as if the ground beneath his feet was, all of a sudden... uncertain.

Ariadne turned back to Quinn and smiled—sincerely, he thought. 'You can go home now. You've earned it.'

'What happens now?' he asked.

Ariadne shrugged slightly. 'Not for me to say. I'm sure we'll want to work closely with the Karakis, to stop something like this ever happening again. The salt's too dangerous—we need to make sure it's controlled.'

Huh. Why doesn't that answer surprise me in the least? Quinn just nodded. There didn't seem to be anything worth saying.

Dante chimed in as Ariadne turned and started back to the shuttle. 'Out of interest, just how are you planning to get past the Titan fleet? And how did you get past them on the way in, for that matter?'

Ariadne looked back from the entrance hatch. 'Oh, that was no problem.' She flashed that sweet smile and gave them a wink. 'I'm friends with their boss.'

The hatch slid closed with a whoosh and the shuttle's thrusters roared to life. Quinn stepped back and shielded his face once more as the ship powered up off the ground and spun to face back the way it had come.

With an extra burst of power, it jumped forward and headed

up, up, and away into the afternoon sky.

* * *

Dante watched the shuttle shrink into a dark speck against the afternoon sky, then vanish altogether. *There she goes.* Bon voyage, *Venus. I hope they put you somewhere dark and forget about you.*

'Tasha's going to be pissed,' said Quinn.

'She's not the only one,' Dante replied. 'There are going to be some awkward conversations when your bloodsalt security teams arrive.'

Quinn snorted. 'I doubt it. My lot can be extremely persuasive when they need to be.'

Dante glanced at his partner. '*We*, you mean.'

'Hmmm?'

'You said *they*,' Dante pointed out. 'You meant "when *we* need to be."'

'Oh. Sure, yeah.' Quinn still gazed up at the empty sky.

The scrape of footsteps on sand turned Dante around. Tasha, red-faced and panting, skidded to a halt. 'They took her?'

Dante nodded. Quinn turned. 'Sorry. I don't like it any more than you do. Honestly.'

The young assassin clenched her jaw. 'I'm not sure you appreciate how much I don't like it, Quinn,' she spat out the name with some venom. Dante looked away. *I'm glad we didn't send in a Peacetrooper team to pick her up.*

Quinn still looked exhausted, far too tired to argue. He just shrugged. 'I'm sorry, Tasha. I am. If it's any consolation, some of our… representatives will be coming back to Karak soon.'

'For what?' she shot back.

Quinn opened his mouth to answer, then shut it and turned away. 'Yeah, you're not going to like that, either.'

Dante stifled a smile. It was time to say goodbye. 'Time for me to get going.' He stepped towards Tasha and offered his hand. They shook. 'It was a pleasure working with you. You've got a bright future. If you ever want a change of scenery — or a change of career — get in touch.' She just nodded.

He turned to Quinn. 'You, too. We worked pretty well

together, I thought.'

'I've had worse partners,' Quinn replied with a smile. 'Oh, I almost forgot.' He unclipped Dante's sidearm from his belt and held it out.

Dante reached out to take it, but at the last moment, he pulled back. 'Actually, you keep it. Call it a souvenir.' *Because I'm damn sure not going to need it anymore.*

Quinn cocked his head. 'Really? Well, thanks. Hopefully I'll never need to use it again.' He turned to Tasha. 'And thanks to you. For helping me clean up our mess. For everything.'

She shrugged. 'I was just doing my job.'

'Yeah,' Quinn sighed. 'We all were.'

No one spoke for a moment. *There doesn't seem to be anything left to say.*

But Tasha broke the silence. 'Things are going to change now, aren't they?'

Quinn nodded. 'I'm afraid so.'

'Oh, Karak,' Tasha murmured. She turned to face the east, where the sun had begun to set. The light cast her face with a reddish tint, and Dante thought he saw a tear in the corner of her eye. 'My world. But for how long?'

No one answered.

Postlude

Hesch sat on the narrow cot and looked around him at the cell. No window, just a floor, ceiling, and three walls of bare steel, the other wall a pale blue stun field emitting a faint hum. The sound was quite relaxing, but he knew touching the field wouldn't be.

His wrists and ankles chafed slightly beneath the repressor bracelets, but he knew better than to touch them. Any tampering, and the collar around his neck would stun him into unconsciousness. The same if he just moved his limbs faster than a certain speed. *Makes for peaceful prisoners.* It wasn't the first time he'd worn them.

Leaning back against the cell wall, Hesch closed his eyes.

He'd arrived in orbit around Mission four days earlier, and brazenly requested a landing at the primary military spaceport in Rift Seven. His name had piqued enough interest that the defence fleet had allowed him to land rather than blast his ship into dust. They'd also passed that name along, as by the time

Hesch landed, a team of four cohort were there waiting, there to escort him to the short-stay prison a couple of miles upriver from the city of Rift at the centre of the octants.

Short-stay prison. Makes it sound like a hotel. Inmates typically only spent a few days there before being shipped out to somewhere like Gulgalta, the prison asteroid that had been Hesch's home for six years. He opened his eyes and glanced around the cell again. *Now that I think about it, compared to that hellhole, this almost is a hotel.*

Footsteps sounded in the corridor beyond the stun field. Hesch listened to them approach, his gaze fixed on the floor, until they stopped outside the cell.

He looked up. 'Corralin.'

The young man looked tired. The sandy blond hair and gold eyes were the same, but there were lines that hadn't been there a year and a bit earlier, when they last met. *Leadership's weighing on him. No surprise.*

'Hesch.' Corralin stood, arms crossed, a foot beyond the field. He wore light armour and a purple Praetor's cloak trimmed in gold. *So that's what the Primarch wears.* 'You came back.'

'Well spotted,' Hesch replied with a slight smile. 'I said I would, once you'd cleaned house. I heard that all of the old guard on the Council and in the cohort were either dead or… elsewhere. So here I am.'

Corralin nodded slowly, eyes narrowed.

'I heard some other rumours, too,' Hesch continued, stretching out his legs slowly so as to not trip the repressors. 'Namely, rebellion. A fifth of the fleet gone AWOL, seed planets claiming independence. I was confident it was bullshit, but looking at your face now, I'm not sure.'

That drew a sigh from the Primarch. Corralin closed his eyes and pinched the bridge of his nose. 'It's all true.' He shook his head wearily. 'We've tried diplomacy, but without any success.'

Hesch snorted. 'Never been one of our strengths.'

'Quite. But those who oppose what we've done…' Corralin

shook his head again. 'Their ideology is too deeply entrenched. They don't want to live in a universe where we aren't battling the Collective and hunting the Seryn.'

Hesch nodded, then frowned. 'I have to ask. Why are you here, Corralin? Why are you telling me this?'

'Because…' Corralin answered, 'because my father always said you were a pragmatist. And I'm betting you don't give a damn that we're not at war with the Collective or the Seryn.'

Hesch shrugged. 'There's always another war to fight. Founder knows we've had plenty over the years.'

Corralin nodded. 'Indeed. So there's that. And also, before my father died, and you were put away, you were a damn good commander. One of the best the cohort had. Frankly—I need you.'

Nice to be wanted. Hesch barked a short laugh. 'I'm not much of a diplomat, so I assume the situation has evolved beyond the point of diplomacy.'

'It's about to,' Corralin replied. 'We'll open hostilities and strike the first target in ten days. It's the Morrigan shipyard. It's under rebel control. And it's also the only one they have, so once we take it, they'll be stuck with the ships they've got.'

Morrigan. That brought back memories. Visions of the shipyard filled Hesch's mind—attack vectors, choke points, defensive positions…

'The alternative is returning to Gulgalta,' Corralin went on. 'It's your choice. But given the opportunity—will you join us?'

Perhaps there's another orbital freefall for me yet. Hesch smiled. 'As you command, Primarch.'

* * *

Dante stared out at the lake. The top of the water was ruffled by the stiff breeze coming through the gap in the hills to the west. It had rained hard that morning, and Violet had sulked that she wouldn't be able to go outside and play, but happily the skies had cleared around midday, and a tantrum had been averted.

Phoebe sat beside him, leaning into his chest. His arm was loosely draped around her waist. She dangled one foot over the edge of the wooden dock on which they sat, the tip of her boot kicking up sprays of water.

An excited squeal to his left drew Dante's attention. Violet stood in the stream with her grandfather Mort, ostensibly searching for the tiny crabs that lived amongst the rocks but mainly just splashing noisily about in the new pink Wellington boots they'd bought for the trip.

He caught a whiff of something on the wind, and his stomach rumbled. *Must be lunchtime soon.* Back at the house, Phoebe's mother Bella was fixing up a meal that would doubtless be big enough to feed fifteen. *This… I could get used to this.* Dante sighed contentedly.

'Hmm?' Phoebe murmured.

'Nothing. Just… having a nice time.'

She patted his leg. 'Good. Me, too. And so is Violet—she loves it up here.'

Dante looked over at his daughter again. 'She looks well, doesn't she? The fresh air's working its magic. That, and your mother's cooking.'

Phoebe chuckled. 'Cures all known ills. I don't think I ever got sick when we lived up here. Vi will probably pick something else up when she goes to school, but we'll deal with it.'

'Pre-school,' Dante corrected her.

'No, Tay—school. She's starting proper school in a month. Remember?'

Dante groaned. 'Shit. Sorry, forgot.' *At least she sounded amused by my idiocy, rather than exasperated.*

'Anyway,' Phoebe continued, 'let's just make the most of the time we've got here.'

'Agreed. We should come back more often, though. I like how… peaceful everything is.' Dante took a deep breath and let it out slowly. 'I needed this.'

He looked down at his wife as she turned to peer up at him with that slightly concerned half-frown that he had grown used to seeing whenever she was thinking about what he did when he went away. The things he saw. She'd never asked him about it—

about any mission—in all their years together. *And I've had some bad ones. Karak was… bad, but not the worst.*

'So, have you thought any more about what you want to do?' Phoebe asked.

He nodded. 'There are a few options. Maybe some strategic consultancy for private security firms. And there are some engineering jobs that look interesting. I might see if I can do a bit of both. Variety, you know.'

Phoebe hemmed. 'Strategic consultancy isn't a euphemism for exactly what you do already, is it?'

Dante squeezed her waist. 'No, honey. Just listening to their problems, giving them advice and the benefit of my many years of experience. Lots of former DSO and Peacetroopers do it when they leave the service.' He had a thought. 'Shit.'

'What?' asked Phoebe.

'I just realised I'll need to break the news to LeClerq at some point. I hadn't thought about it. She's not going to be thrilled.' *Yep, I am not looking forward to that conversation.*

'She's a big girl. She'll get over it.'

'Yeah.' He nodded. Behind them, Bella called out that the food was ready. Violet squealed again and ran for the house, followed more slowly by Mort. Dante bent and kissed Phoebe on the forehead. 'Yeah, she'll have to.'

* * *

Quinn returned to Corinth to find that it had stopped snowing, the picturesque coating of flakes replaced with biting winds, black ice, and freezing fog. He stepped through the door of the Agency building once again, shocked to find himself almost wishing he were back on Karak.

Darla sat at her usual post. She smiled brightly when she saw him. 'Quinn! Welcome back. How was your business trip?'

'Hot and stressful, but ultimately a success,' he replied. 'How have things been here?'

The receptionist shrugged. 'Same as ever. Nothing happens. Not to me, at least.'

Quinn nodded. 'Don't knock it. I could do with a couple of

weeks of nothing happening.' He headed for the stairs. 'Sebastien in his office?'

'No, he's not in.'

That stopped Quinn in his tracks. He turned back. 'Really? I expected a debrief. Do you know when he's going to be in?'

Darla shook her head. 'Sorry. But he did leave a note to tell you that you should... Give me a second.' She tapped away at her desk terminal for a few seconds. 'Ah. You should "Take some well-earned leave, and we'll call you in when we need you."'

'Huh.' Quinn just stood there for a moment, at a loss. *Well, that's my day cleared, I suppose.*

'Leave is good, remember?' Darla smiled. 'Take a break. Sounds like you deserve one.'

'Yeah, thanks.' Quinn started back for the exit. 'I'll see you soon, Darla.'

She waved goodbye, and Quinn stepped out into the bitter winter air. He looked about, wondering what he should do. *Odette's got lectures today, so not much point going home. Maybe I'll grab a drink.*

Quinn walked the few miles to Max's bar, enjoying being out in the cold. His sunburn had already faded to almost nothing in just the day since he'd arrived back on Corinth, but he could feel the chill bringing a different kind of pink to his cheeks.

Max's road was empty of traffic. It was—again—too early for the place to be open, so Quinn hammered on the door and waited. Half a minute passed before his friend swung it open.

'How did I know it would be you?' He seemed to be wearing exactly the same clothes as when Quinn last saw him. Max waved him in and swung the door shut behind him with a slam. 'Well, it's eleven now, so you're an hour closer to a respectable drinking time than you were on your last visit.'

Quinn shrugged. 'Yeah. I would have got here sooner, but I walked.'

Max guffawed as he pulled two beers from the chest behind the bar. 'So.' He opened them both and handed one to Quinn.

'Cheers.'

'Cheers.' Quinn took a large swig.

Max leaned back against the bar. 'Did you catch up to her, then?'

'I did.' Quinn nodded thoughtfully. 'It was touch and go, right up until the end, but yeah. We got her.'

'We?' asked Max.

'Had some help. Local and… not quite so local.'

Max held his hands up. 'All right, say no more. Regardless, I'm glad to see you still standing. I half hoped you wouldn't get near her. Far too dangerous.'

Quinn half-smiled. 'Someone had to bring her in. Might as well be me—that is what they pay me for, after all. And seeing as you take about a third of my pay every month, you shouldn't complain.'

'Far from it, brother. I'm always happy to see you.' Max took a huge gulp of his beer. 'You and your credit chip.'

They drank in silence for a minute. Quinn looked up after a while to see his friend peering at him. 'What?'

'So all's well with the world, then? Job done, *et cetera*.'

Quinn nodded. 'Yep.'

'Hmm. Except it's not, is it?' Max asked. 'Because you're here before noon on a weekday with a big black cloud hanging over you worse than the real ones outside that are keeping my customers away and at home. So what's up?'

That's the question. Quinn took another slow swig of his beer and let the fizzy, bitter brew roll slowly down his throat as he turned things over in his mind. After a moment, he sighed. 'I don't know. Truly, I've no idea. I've just got this… hunch, that something's going on in the background, and I'm only seeing half of it.' He shook his head wearily.

Max blew a raspberry. 'Par for the course for you secretive types, I'd have thought. Need to know, classified whatever, plausibly deny every bloody thing.' He threw his empty beer bottle into the plasmetal bin, where it broke with a smash. 'Who gives a toss? No point getting worked up about something you can't do anything about.'

Quinn chuckled. 'Sound advice—as ever, Max.'

'Always. That's what I'm here for. That, and helping folks drink away the pain.' He scratched his broad belly. 'Want a sandwich?'

'Sure.'

Max nodded and wandered off into the back of the bar.

What's up, indeed. Quinn frowned. *I wish I knew.*

* * *

Tasha sat at the ancient wrought-iron table on the roof of Pharc's house and watched the old historian pour two cups of chamomile tea. It was early evening, still warm but no longer swelteringly hot, and the crickets and other insects had emerged to buzz and chirrup amongst the plants that lined the edge of the roof.

'Doesn't it make you furious, though?' she asked. 'The way they just snatched her away from under our noses?'

Pharc smiled slightly. 'As I get older, I find it more and more difficult to summon the energy required for fury, my dear.' He put down the teapot and pushed one of the cups towards Tasha. 'I'm irritated, of course. It's simple to argue how they have impinged upon our sovereign right as in independent world. But I'm not sure what practical recourse we have.' He sipped his own tea. 'I have little faith in the ability of our own council, and its counterparts amongst the other tribes, to present the kind of unified political effort that might force an extradition. And from whom would we extradite? These people, these Seryn, have no world. No central government. No,' he shook his head, 'I fear we have lost our chance to hand down justice.'

Tasha scowled. 'There must be something we can do.'

Pharc raised his eyebrows. 'That's another thing that comes with age, I'm afraid; the knowledge that sometimes there is *not* something one can do.'

I don't accept that. Tasha fumed in silence for a minute. 'It's completely unfair. And they compound their offence by having the gall to come to Karak in droves! Have you seen them?

Studying the bloodsalt, they say.'

The historian nodded. 'Indeed I have. I was at a meeting of leaders of commerce and industry a few days ago. Many of the mining corporations were represented, from the Hereb and other tribes, and several of these companies brought along their new Seryn liaisons.' He frowned. 'They spoke very little, but when they did it was in fluent Karaki. That surprised me. Surprised everyone, I'd wager.'

Tasha still scowled. 'I've seen them out in the desert too. Whenever I go past one of the mines, there they are. Encamped, watching everything. I don't like it, *baba*.'

Pharc sighed. 'I like it no more than you do, Tasha. It seems the world is changing before our eyes, and sometimes...' He shook his head. 'Sometimes I feel as though our days of independence are coming to an end.'

Tasha gazed out over Thrace, wondering what she could do. *I've already taken my world back once. I can do it again if I have to.* She set her jaw.

I've had enough of foreigners.

* * *

Venus opened her eyes.

She lay in a comfortable bed, in the corner of a large, tastefully furnished room. A sleek, low table stood in the opposite corner, ringed by elegant couches. An ultra-thin screen hung from the wall. Recessed lighting bloomed to life as she sat up, swung her legs over the side of the bed, and stood. The floor was bare wood, but warm. She padded barefoot over to the window screen on the wall next to the bed and palmed the pad next to it.

The field cleared, and she looked out onto a vista of mid-sized tower blocks. Contemporary transpods zipped between them, cornering sharply and avoiding each other by scant metres. *Could be anywhere in the Core. Definitely not Karak, though. That's for sure.* Venus smiled to herself.

A faint chime behind her made her turn. The door of the room—which she hadn't spotted, so neatly was it seamed to the wall—slid open. Venus crossed her arms, realising that she wore just a thin silk shift.

'Hello, Sebastien.'

'Good morning, Venus,' he replied in his clipped, precise tone. Sebastien was as pale as ever, and dressed in his usual black. He walked slowly into the room, stopping near the couches. 'It's good to see you awake.'

She nodded, gaze fixed on Sebastien's pale blue eyes. 'How long was I out?'

'Nine days,' he replied. 'You went into a deep coma whilst your mind repaired itself. I'm afraid the damage done by Quinn's… intervention was not insignificant.'

A flicker of anxiety ran through her. 'Permanent damage?'

Sebastien shook his head briskly. 'We don't think so. The passive monitor in the bed reports a clean bill of health. That is what brought me here.' With a small smile, he pointed to a recessed cupboard in the corner of the room. 'There is clothing, if you'd like to dress.' He turned away to examine an abstract print on the wall beside the door.

'Ah.' A minute later, she had dressed in a blue skirt and white blouse. 'Thank you, Sebastien.'

He turned and gave her a nod. 'Of course.'

'So.' Venus leaned back against the wall and raised her eyebrows. 'Was it worth it?'

Sebastien nodded. 'Early signs are good. The Karakis have accepted our request to land several small teams to work with the mining companies and study the effects of the bloodsalt. It is the first step towards a more permanent presence.'

Venus found her gaze sliding away from Sebastien to the print behind him. The slashes of gold, red, and ochre were… evocative. *Of something.*

'Is something troubling you, Venus?' Sebastien asked, the concern in his tone entirely professional.

Venus looked back at her handler's expressionless face. 'Was it necessary?'

He was silent for a few moments before answering, his voice

low and quiet. 'Is it important to know that?'

She shrugged. 'Not entirely. But it would help my... peace of mind.'

Sebastien walked slowly over to one of the couches and sat, draping one leg over the other. He gestured at the couch opposite. 'Please.'

Venus joined him, and he went on.

'We considered other approaches, of course. We could have just acquired the entire supply of bloodsalt by purchasing all production through a network of dummy corporations, but it simply wasn't secure enough. We needed to gain control at the source.'

Venus frowned. 'I still don't see the need for such... extreme measures. Why is controlling the salt so important? It's powerful, I know that better than anyone, but—'

Sebastien cut her off. 'It's not just powerful, Venus.' He steepled his fingers together. 'It's a weapon.'

She stared at him blankly, her mind racing. *A weapon?*

'Or rather, a potential weapon. Our scientists confirmed what we suspected shortly before you arrived on Karak. For ninety-nine percent of our people, bloodsalt has the effect you experienced. A powerful enhancer of mental activity. But to approximately one per cent of our people, its consumption is instantly fatal.'

Venus snorted. 'Thank you for warning me.'

Sebastien spread his arms. 'It was a risk we had to take. The wider problem is this: that fatal element, that specific enzyme within the salt, can be extracted. Concentrated. Weaponised.'

Oh. 'I see.'

'I'm sure you do,' her handler replied. 'Any reasonably modern laboratory in the galaxy could use it to produce a water- or aerosol-borne toxin with a fatality rate of one hundred per cent—but only to Seryn. And regardless of our current state of *détente* with our former enemies, I trust none of them. Not the Titans, not the Commonwealth. Not even the Collective, however benign they have been. We couldn't take that risk.'

Venus took a deep breath and blew it out. After a moment, she frowned. 'Quinn had help.'

'Pardon?'

'He had help,' she repeated. 'From a Commonwealth operative and a ferociously talented local girl. You can't have taken that into account.'

Sebastien shook his head. 'We didn't. It almost went badly for us; if it hadn't been Quinn who eventually brought you down, our bargaining position would have been significantly weaker. But as it is...' He shrugged. 'We need luck, sometimes.'

Luck. Thousands dead, and in the end, it came down to luck. She stood and returned to the window, staring out at the cityscape. 'What now?'

She heard Sebastien rise and walk over to join her.

'We have another assignment for you,' Sebastien answered. 'Within the Commonwealth. It will go some way to compensating a senator for the unfortunate death of her brother—not that she is to know that, of course.'

Of course. 'What is the assignment?' At the base of the tower directly opposite, a cleaning bot rose into the air and began washing the first of several thousand windows.

'A simple one, this time. The Commonwealth has an internal security problem, which directly affects our people. The integration process has faced strong resistance in some quarters. Violent resistance, in a few cases. We need to influence public opinion. In a more direct way than the Commonwealth Senate is capable of themselves.' Sebastien chuckled dryly. 'After all, we pose no threat to Commonwealth society. The people should understand that. They will be happier for it.'

Venus nodded. The cleaning bot was on its fifth window, seemingly undaunted by the massiveness of the task awaiting it. She smiled faintly at the coincidence as she turned to Sebastien. 'Where do I start?'

Her handler smiled, somewhat coldly. 'Why, in the heart of the republic, of course.' He nodded at the vista outside the window. 'Right here on Nexus Prime.'

Afterword

Thanks for reading! I hope you enjoyed the book.

If you have a spare minute or two, I'd really appreciate a customer review! Also, if you would like to be the first to hear about my future releases, you can subscribe to my mailing list here: http://eepurl.com/msrZn.

You can also connect with me online:
Website: http://dan-harris.net/
Twitter: https://twitter.com/#!/sailingthevoid
Facebook: https://www.facebook.com/dan.harris.writer

Acknowledgements

Sincere thanks to Amisha, Ken and Melanie, for reading the first draft and kindly telling me what didn't make sense; to Stephanie, for a bleakly beautiful cover that perfectly captures Karak; and to my editor Misti, for helping make all of the words the right ones.

Printed in Great Britain
by Amazon.co.uk, Ltd.,
Marston Gate.